The Strength of the Sun

ALSO BY CATHERINE CHIDGEY

In a fishbone church

The
Strength
of the Sun

a novel

CATHERINE CHIDGEY

HENRY HOLT AND COMPANY

NEW YORK

Henry Holt and Company, LLC
Publishers since 1866
115 West 18th Street
New York, New York 10011

Henry Holt® is a registered trademark of
Henry Holt and Company, LLC.

Originally published in New Zealand in 2000 under the title
Golden Deeds by Victoria University Press, Wellington.

Library of Congress Cataloging-in-Publication Data
Chidgey, Catherine, 1970–
[Golden deeds]
The strength of the sun : a novel / Catherine Chidgey.
p. cm.
Originally published in New Zealand in 2000 under the title:
Golden deeds, by Victoria University Press, Wellington.
ISBN: 0-8050-6931-3
1. Traffic accident victims—Fiction. 2. Missing children—Fiction.
3. Medievalists—Fiction. 4. New Zealand—Fiction. I. Title.
PR9639.3.C535 G65 2002   2001046356

First American Edition 2002

Printed in the United States of America

1 3 5 7 9 10 8 6 4 2

For my mother, Pat Chidgey

18 October 1999
Dear Colette,

As you will have heard, Patrick is still in a serious condition in Saint Luke's Hospital. While we're able to visit him every day, we're aware that many of his friends don't live locally, so to keep you all up to date on his progress, we've decided to start this newsletter.

We're happy to report that his leg and his ribs are healing, and the bruising on his chest is much improved. The grafts on his arm are taking longer, but thanks to the wonderful surgeons here there shouldn't be much scarring. At this stage, of course, Patrick is still unconscious, so one of our main objectives is to talk to him as much as possible. We're asking all of his friends to send letters which can be read out to him, or tapes. If you do happen to be in the area, naturally you're most welcome to visit him at Saint Luke's.

When he returns home, Patrick will be facing a number of costs. To help meet these, we've established a bank account in his name, and any donations would be gratefully received.

So that we can provide you with regular updates on Patrick's progress, please be sure to let us know if your contact details change. In the meantime, we hope you will help in any way you can.

With best wishes,
The Friends of Patrick Mercer

One Sunday morning in 1988, a bite was taken from the sun. Temperatures fell, the sky turned a deep, deep blue, bands of shadow raced across buildings and car-parks and fields, and the earth appeared to tremble. Under trees, tiny crescent suns sprinkled the ground like leaves. Birds fell silent, flowers closed and stars and planets appeared. On the horizon, the shadow of the moon approached like a storm. Then, for three minutes, there was total darkness.

Some people were afraid. They stayed inside, told their children not to look, warned of damage to the eyes, possible blindness. Others carefully turned their backs on the sun, pushed it through pinholes and caught it on pieces of card. Many, many more, however, watched the entire spectacle. They saw crumbs of light shining through the valleys of the moon and agreed that they resembled a string of pearls, and also, for just three seconds, a diamond ring. They witnessed plumes of orange and pink; wisps and streamers dancing from the dark disc of the moon. Some saw a small comet. This was something, they told one another, they would remember forever.

The eclipse had been selling newspapers for weeks. Experts had charted the heavens, calculated optimum viewing times and locations. International airlines offered package deals to the southern hemisphere, to Australia or New Zealand, where motels and hotels were filling fast. Anxious ophthalmologists had cautioned against watching through binoculars, sunglasses, smoked glass or exposed film. They had provided the press with photographs of damaged retinas which, unfortunately, resembled the moon, and only fuelled enthusiasm. Street vendors sold eclipse T-shirts; lunch-hour prophets distributed warnings; school pupils drew crayon eclipses, visited the planetarium, fashioned hollow suns from wire and wet newspaper.

On the Sunday morning in question, in suitably positioned countries, the streets were full of people clutching maps of the sky and looking up, as if searching for something they had lost. Some met their neighbours for the first time. There was even interest from those who usually ignored the movement of clouds, the moon's changing profile. After all, they remarked to family members whom they also usually ignored, there wouldn't be another chance for seventy-two years.

In the northern hemisphere, half a world away, Patrick Mercer went to his sitting room late at night and turned on the television. The screen was filled with people looking at the sky, waiting for something to happen. Flashes from inadequate cameras dappled the crowds like lightning. Some groups were chanting rugby songs, urging the moon to advance. An announcer identified First Contact, Second Contact, Baily's Beads, the Diamond Ring.

Patrick watched the eclipse with Rosemary, to whom he was still married, and wished he was somewhere else. For weeks he had been trying to interest his wife in it, bringing home books and articles for her, telling her how ancient Norse tribes had believed a wolf was devouring the sun, how Siberians blamed vampires for its disappearance, how the Aztecs made sacrifices to Xolotl, the sun's assistant, how the Chippewa Indians fired flaming arrows to rekindle the light. He had explained to her the derivation of the word eclipse; that it came from the Greek for abandonment. Against museum rules, he had even brought home a tenth-century manuscript containing an illustration of an eclipse, its inky dimensions filling the parchment sky. The drawing held no fascination for Rosemary, though, and Patrick had to admit that she was right, it could have been anything: a spiky flower, an eyeball, a virus. He didn't raise his voice. He was patient with her; she was going through the change and was not, she said, herself. Perhaps, he suggested in a quiet voice, they should take a holiday, fly to New Zealand to see the eclipse. But Rosemary said don't be silly, we can't travel halfway round the world just for that, and besides, they both knew what happened when Patrick went to New Zealand. And so they watched it on television, and Rosemary kept butting in with questions and comments even though Patrick had asked her to be quiet, just for a few minutes, please.

'Would you call that black or blue?' she said as they sat on their narrow sofa, 'the colour of the sky?' For fifteen years she'd made a point of asking irrelevant questions: do you think I'm fat, why won't you talk to me, do you love me. 'It's like my blazer, isn't it?' she went on. 'My Hedley's blazer. It looked black in the shop, but when I got it home it was navy blue. I could only tell when I held it against something black, but I wanted to wear it with my black trousers and it just looked wrong, do you remember, and they wouldn't give me a refund.'

'In the Middle Ages,' Patrick said without shifting his eyes from the screen, 'eclipses were portents of doom.'

'I never wear that blazer now,' said Rosemary. 'It was a complete waste of money.'

The following morning, Patrick left her. He packed a few things together while she was at church, left a note anchored to the hall table with one of her ikebana arrangements. It was Rosemary's new hobby, and the house was littered with austere branches poked into green florist's foam.

'Less is more,' she had told him, arranging two willow twigs so they curled like the fingers of a crone. Ikebana, she said, ramming a stem of orchids, was influenced by Zen Buddhism. It saw beauty in imperfection, impermanence. Flawless blooms were contrasted with rough stones, say, or pieces of decaying matter that served as reminders of the briefness and harshness of life. Rosemary's last hobby had been patchwork; she'd made a quilt out of old dresses and cushion covers and scraps of curtain. She said it was a way of stitching her memories together. A kind of album. Before that it had been découpage: shreds of paper all over the sitting room like confetti. And before that, bonsai. She had given Patrick a tree to keep on his desk at the museum; a tiny, stunted maple that made him feel monstrous. He never watered it.

His bag was so light he could hardly feel it on his shoulder; it flapped like a perished balloon. He would collect the rest of his things when he'd found a place of his own. Or, maybe, he would leave them for Rosemary to give away, as if he had died. He unlocked the glass cabinet in the sitting room and took out the manuscript. It was the only thing of any real value that he owned. The only thing of any weight. The instructions it contained were eight hundred years old, and to Patrick they were as resonant as any of his wife's nightly prayers. He loved the detail, the advice on making ink, on grinding gold for the illumination of letters and figures, on tempering pigments with all manner of strange ingredients. He opened the clasp, found one of his favourite entries. *To acquire command of hand in using the stylus, begin to draw with it from a copy as freely as you can, and so lightly that you can scarcely see what you have begun to do, deepening your strokes little by little, and going over them repeatedly to make the shadows. Where you would make it darkest go over it many times; and, on the contrary, make but few touches on the lights. And you must be guided by the light of the sun, and the light of your eye, and your hand; and without these three things you can do nothing properly.*

Patrick shut the cabinet door, felt the lock click into place. His fingers left prints on the glass. It was as if there had been a burglary. He thought of the legend of Saint Columba, who had gained access to Saint Finnian's book of psalms and copied them without permission. He imagined Columba going to the church and beginning at the beginning, transcribing the manuscript letter by letter in his own hand, slowly filling vellum pages with the word of God. Perhaps his neck had ached, perhaps his back had grown stiff, but he had not stopped writing. Columba was untroubled by his conscience; Finnian could keep the original, and besides, the Word belonged to everybody. As night gathered, the church had grown darker and darker. God tolerates certain crimes if the intention is good, Columba may have told himself, squinting in the fading light, leaning in close to the pages. Maybe his nose wrinkled at the scent of calfskin, the sharp tug of the ink. He continued to write, and when he could no longer see, his fingers began to shine like candles, and the church filled with light.

Patrick decided to go to the museum while he thought about where to stay. He would sit at his desk, contemplate the dwarf maple in its shallow dish. If he had been on the other side of the world a few hours ago, if he had been standing under a tree—perhaps a maple, perhaps not—the ground would have been covered with thousands of hooked suns, the shadowy letter C repeated over and over at his feet. Yesterday's newspaper was still open on the table, the entertainment page dominated by promises of eclipse broadcasts. Coverage, they assured him, would be complete. They didn't mention how disappointing it would be on a television screen. They didn't say how little of the magic could be caught in a twenty-inch horizon. He should have ignored Rosemary, he thought, and gone to New Zealand on his own. He could have made it a holiday. He had contacts there.

Patrick slipped the eight hundred-year-old manuscript inside a soft pillowcase and zipped it into his bag. The obvious solution, of course, was to stay with his mother. That was what people did when they left their spouses. They went home to gravy still made the same way, towels folded four times, not three, hot-water bottles in knitted covers, tea brewed in the pot. They slept in single beds and heard noises they had all but forgotten: familiar clocks ticking, familiar trees knocking on the window, certain taps gushing, certain pipes groaning with pressure. There were antimacassars, doilies, telephones that rang rather than trilled. There were pieces of sultana cake, soft-boiled eggs, toast cut into soldiers. And years were erased.

Perhaps, he thought as he climbed into his car, he would stay at the museum for a night or two. Nobody would know. He could wash in any number of bathrooms, creep along the corridors in bare feet, his toes silent on cool wood. He could read by torchlight, eat peaches straight from the tin. And, when it was late, he could curl up in the sweet-smelling manuscripts room, a book for his pillow.

In the north of New Zealand was a hill overlooking the sea. Tourists called it a mountain, but to the locals, who didn't like to boast, it was a hill. The lower slopes were covered with bush, and children were discouraged from exploring it alone even though, as far as anyone knew, nothing dreadful had ever happened there. On top of the hill was a wind turbine. Erected as an experiment, there was a plaque at its base—the kind seen beneath trees planted for the dead— announcing that it provided enough electricity for seventy average households. On the morning of the 1988 eclipse, the hill was covered with mountain-bikers and secretaries and tourists and teachers and management consultants and children and lovers who sat and gazed up and up, and listened to the blades of the turbine churning the sky, demanding *look, look, look.*

Laura Pearse was there. Her parents were too busy to take her, but she had her own car and no brothers or sisters. She was used to doing things alone.

'I'm driving up to the wind turbine,' she told her mother at breakfast.

Ruth glanced up from the newspaper. 'You'll never get a park,' she said. 'I'd catch the bus, if I were you.'

Laura sighed. 'Why did you buy me the Mini if I'm never allowed to use it?'

'You're allowed to use it, love, of course you are. All I'm saying is there won't be anywhere to park today.'

Laura blew on her tea, glanced at her watch.

'Who else is going?' said Ruth.

Laura sighed again. 'Joshua has to work, but I'm meeting him afterwards for tennis, and then we're going for lunch, okay?'

'Remember not to look directly at it.'

'My lunch?'

'You know what I mean.'

Laura spread her toast with jam, right out to the edges. 'I can't believe you and Dad aren't going. You won't see another one, you know, not a total one. You'll be dead by then.'

'Well,' said Ruth, 'I'm sure you can tell us all about it.' She went back to her newspaper. She knew better than to push her daughter to converse; Laura never offered details of her life if she was prodded and questioned.

'Why do you have to know everything about me?' she'd sometimes demand. Other times she'd pretend she was being interrogated by the police when Ruth asked her about school, or tennis, or Joshua, or her weekend. 'There were around twenty youths present at the party, officer,' she'd answer. 'Some were behaving in a disorderly fashion. It is my belief that several were enjoying themselves.'

'She's just being fifteen,' said Malcolm. 'Fifteen-year-olds are meant to loathe their parents.'

The thing was, Ruth thought, Laura wasn't like that with him. 'It'll be cold up there,' she said now. 'Have you got a jacket?'

Laura rolled her eyes, bit into her blackberry toast. The jam dripped all over the tablecloth, but Ruth kept reading her paper. And soon, before she was past the front page, Laura had finished her breakfast and was swinging her satchel over her shoulder and grabbing the keys for her rusting Mini, and then she was gone.

Things could change in a flash, Ruth knew. Fortunes, reputations could be lost in the space of a breath. Lives could change or end. A car could skid on a black spot, a child could be drawn to a lonely place, names could be signed, buttons pressed, switches thrown. And only then did details become important.

'Three days have passed,' she said. 'Anything could have happened by now.'

'Teenagers run away all the time,' said the policeman. 'You'd be amazed how many do.'

Ruth described to him what Laura had been wearing that Sunday morning. 'The jersey was similar to her school one,' she said, staring out the window, 'although she hates the Westlake uniform. She's taken the skirt up as much as she can get away with, all the girls do, well most of them do. The blazers you can't alter so much. Red's never been her colour, she can't wait to get to seventh form. They get to wear what they want in seventh form.' As she talked she was aware of the speed of her voice, the way the words tumbled out of her, the useless, cheerful detail she was releasing. And although she spoke to the window, expecting to see Laura pull up the drive at any moment, out of the corner of her eye she could see the policeman writing things in his notebook while his partner, a young policewoman, stood in front of the fireplace and scanned the lounge. The policeman listened and nodded and wrote, so Ruth kept going, but the whole time she was addressing the window, Malcolm sat silent on the couch, his face blurry, as colourless as water.

No, Ruth said in her airy new voice, Laura was not the sort of girl who would take off without telling anyone. She had a game of tennis organised, and she'd never skip that. She'd certainly never pick up hitch-hikers, she had no unsavoury friends and no problems at school.

'Do you have a recent photograph of your daughter, Mrs Pearse?' the policeman asked. And so Ruth rummaged through the boxes of photos that were yet to make it into an album, flicking through piles of Malcolm's landscapes, pictures of Laura's labrador, pictures of their cat at four weeks, six weeks, pictures of Malcolm drinking beer with Phil, his colleague, whom Ruth had never liked, pictures of their antique sideboard taken for insurance purposes, and when she found a good one of Laura and showed it to the officers it was as if they were just having a chat, as if they were interested in hearing what Laura liked and didn't like to eat, about how she'd once won a prize for a drawing of their house, how she'd just started baby-sitting for the neighbours. She held the photograph by the edges so she wouldn't damage it.

'Malcolm took this one,' she said. 'We were on a bush walk. We had to turn back early, though. It started to pour. He's quite a good photographer, he does a lot of landscapes.'

'Everything is usually fine in these cases, Mrs Pearse,' they said, again refusing a cup of coffee. They told her they'd ring if they had any information at all, and asked Ruth and Malcolm to contact them if Laura arrived home. In her airy voice Ruth assured them they would, and that she too was sure everything would be fine.

'We'll need to take this with us,' the policeman said as they were leaving, and it was then, as the photograph of Laura was slipped into a notebook and the notebook into the pocket of a blue jacket, that Ruth realised nothing was fine.

It was after dark again by the time Malcolm returned from searching. Ruth heard two sets of footsteps coming up the stairs, but when she rushed to the door it was only Phil who accompanied her husband.

'Well?' she said, and Malcolm shook his head.

'Me either.'

'Is there anything else I can help you with?' said Phil. 'Anywhere else you want to look?'

'Thanks,' said Malcolm, 'I think we'll leave it for today.'

'Ruth? Anything I can do for you?'

'No thank you.'

'Just give us a shout, won't you?'

Malcolm cleared his throat. 'I don't think I'll make it to the office again tomorrow—'

'I'll let them know,' said Phil.

It wasn't until later that Malcolm said it, not until after they'd tried to eat some dinner and had fed Laura's labrador and watched the news and answered the phone over and over again. 'You didn't tell them the truth,' he said. 'She did pick up a hitch-hiker. You lied.'

Ruth looked at him. He'd hardly spoken for three days.

'Right after she got the Mini. The Danish boy. He rang here that time, and left a message to contact him at the youth hostel.'

'Yes, but he was only in the country for two weeks,' said Ruth, 'and we told her—you told her—how silly she'd been. Besides, he was perfectly nice. You drove him to the airport, for God's sake.'

'You still should have mentioned it,' said Malcolm. 'They asked you, and you said no.'

Ruth knew that this small piece of information, this detail from summer, was of no use at all. It would only give a false impression of their daughter, and already she was wondering what sort of picture of Laura had been constructed from the jottings in the policeman's notebook. Later, in bed, it occurred to her that Malcolm hadn't offered the information either. She nestled into her husband's back. He was awake, she knew, but neither of them spoke. Through a crack in the curtains the moon slipped a long white arm into their bedroom. Ruth watched it for what seemed like hours.

Eleven years after the eclipse, at the end of the century, Patrick Mercer hardly thought about his ex-wife. She crossed his mind at his mother's funeral, and he scanned the pews for her, but she'd either missed the short death notice in the paper or decided to stay away. He certainly wasn't thinking about her as he drove to the university; he wasn't thinking about anything but his carefully rehearsed lecture. Patrick was no public speaker. At the museum he had little contact with anyone other than staff, and even when school groups visited they were always more interested in dinosaur bones or mummies than old books. The woman from the university, however, had been very persistent.

'The students would really benefit from your expertise,' she'd said. 'There's nobody in the art history department with your specialised knowledge.'

'I'm not sure I could relate,' said Patrick. 'I'm close to retirement, you realise.'

The woman was delighted. 'Wonderful, yes, passing the torch and so forth,' she said. 'Thanks so much. Bye now.'

Some of the students had positioned small tape recorders to catch his voice. Patrick tried to ignore them. He cleared his throat, tapped his notes into a neat pile. Before him was a tier of faces, rows and rows of them, pens poised.

'Light,' he began, 'is the enemy.' He'd spent weeks planning his opening statement, had imagined the students sitting up and looking at him with interest. Now, though, in the cavernous lecture theatre, his voice sounded thin, unsteady, quite different from how it had in his bathroom. He swallowed. 'Medieval manuscripts, by and large, were made for dark places: churches, monasteries, libraries. Even those in private collections were obviously never exposed to electric light, and little sun entered the medieval window. Indeed, one of the reasons for the rich illumination on so many manuscripts was to make the pages sparkle in the dark.'

The side door swung open and a spotty young student slipped into the lecture theatre. He made his way to a seat, crouching and scuttling, trying to avoid the beam of the overhead projector. It caught him anyway, threw his hunched shadow at the screen.

'Sorry, excuse me, sorry,' he whispered. The door sighed itself shut.

'One of the museum's most recent acquisitions,' Patrick continued, 'is a beautiful but damaged thirteenth-century manuscript. It contains the only known copy of the life of one Saint Hilla of Regensburg, and following extensive restoration is now being translated from the Latin.' He paused. He didn't know why he'd mentioned Hilla; she wasn't in his notes, and ordinarily he avoided discussing his translations while they were still incomplete. 'Incorrect storage,' he said, scanning his notes. 'Incorrect storage can lead to damage by light, mould, fire, water, silverfish, worms, rodents and moths.' He displayed the first transparency: an Italian book of hours which had suffered in the sun. 'Manuscripts are most often bound in leather. The pages are also made of animal skin. Think about how easily our own skin is damaged, and you'll realise why proper handling of these artefacts is so important.'

Pens were racing across paper. Patrick paused to allow the students to catch up with his voice. His notes said *smile now*. He smiled. 'My point is: a book can provide a link to other lives, a window to another time. It can *illuminate* the past—' he waited for a laugh, which was not forthcoming '—and it's up to us to preserve that past.' He smiled again.

When his mother had died, Patrick had telephoned the university.

'It's not that I don't want to do the lectures,' he said.

'It's up to you, of course,' said the woman, 'but I know our students have been looking forward to hearing your insights. There's nobody in the art history department with your expertise.'

So, for the next fortnight, Patrick had rehearsed in front of the bathroom mirror. 'The illuminated manuscript,' he'd told his foggy reflection that morning, 'is a window. It offers us a glimpse back in time in a way no other artefact can. When we open a text written by a medieval hand—' here he'd opened his flannel at himself '—we open a window to the past.' He'd splashed his razor in the basin, cut the surface of the steaming water and, as he ran the blade across his skin, tried to hold his hand steady.

He hadn't slept well at all. Projected into his dreams were the transparencies he'd chosen for the lectures: hugely amplified details from illuminated bibles and psalters and books of hours and saints' lives. A monkey played the bagpipes for him, dogs bit their own tails, angels picked lilies. Then things became unpleasant. Ornate initial letters writhed and sucked; a zoomorphic S curled around him, squeezing his ribs so the air rushed from his mouth; an ivy-leaf border wrapped tight tendrils about his fingers. As he ran from the mass of leaves a G pulled him into its maw, bending his body to match its lizard curves, and just as he was working himself free of the pages, just as he was shaking his gilded limbs to return to the real world, someone closed tight the cover.

A student in the front row put her hand in the air. Patrick hadn't been expecting questions, but she was staring right at him, waiting.

'Yes?'

'Is it true,' she said, 'that the museum sold one of its most valuable bibles in order to pay for the multimedia wing?'

'Ah,' said Patrick, 'yes. No. A bible was sold, but it's not unusual for an institution like the museum to, to, rotate its collection. The manuscript containing Hilla's life, for example, is a new purchase—'

'But the bible money is funding the multimedia wing, isn't it?' said the girl.

'The multimedia wing,' said Patrick, 'is an exciting new concept in museum design.'

'Do you like it?'

'Pardon me?'

'Do you like the multimedia wing?'

'Actually,' said Patrick, 'I haven't had a chance to explore yet.'

'I think it's an eyesore.'

Patrick thought of the sold bible. It had been one of his favourites: a rare ninth-century manuscript with a jewelled binding, tinted pages scattered with gold and silver. He had made his feelings known, of course. He had written a letter, collected some signatures. He was close to retirement, though. The bible was sold.

'As I mentioned, most manuscripts are made of animal skin,' he said. 'Strictly speaking, parchment is obtained from sheep or goats, while vellum comes from calfskin. Although much less common, the skins of deer and pigs, and even hares and squirrels, were sometimes used.' On the overhead projector he placed a border detail showing squirrels. 'While very durable, this natural material does present some problems when it comes to storage, display or restoration.' He glanced at his watch. He had no desire to discuss manuscript care, to outline the tedious facts of dust, mould, temperature control. What he wanted to describe was the joy he felt when examining a border strewn with dragonflies, strawberries, cornflowers, moths, when trying to trace with his eye a gospel's endless interlacings, when holding a glittering prayer book no bigger than a house key and once worn on the belt of a noblewoman. He wanted to explain the unique scent of parchment, that thick perfume that clung to the fingers for hours. He longed to quote from Hilla's delirious conversations with God, to tell the legend of Columba copying Finnian's psalter.

'Humidity levels,' he said, 'are important.'

At the end of the hour the students began shifting in their seats, putting away pens and pencils, shutting folders. Patrick collected the slippery transparencies together. 'Next week we'll talk about moths,' he said, and switched off the overhead projector.

'I used to visit you at the museum,' said a soft voice. 'Those were happy times, weren't they?'

Patrick lost his grip on the transparent unicorns, ivy leaves, serpents, lilies; they slid across each other like sheets of ice.

'Rosemary?' He frowned, as if something about her face confused him, although there was nothing puzzling about it, nothing mysterious at all. It was far too familiar a face. 'What are you doing here?'

'I finally took your advice,' she said. 'I'm studying again. Only part-time, but it's going well.'

She was wearing some sort of ridiculous, fluttering dress. No more Hedley's blazers, then, no more sensible trousers with pockets so shallow they held only half a cold hand: this must be her student look. Nearly sixty, and she was dressing like a student. The black fabric billowed around her like smoke. Her hair was grey.

'I'll be graduating next year.'

'Good for you,' said Patrick, looking at his watch.

'It said in the prospectus that you'd be giving some lectures. I've really been looking forward to it. Gosh, you look great. How long has it been?'

'It's been years, Rosemary,' said Patrick. 'Eleven years.'

The other students were moving past, threading out the door and away to coffee, the library, home. Rosemary lowered her voice.

'I was dying to tell everyone that we used to be married. They'd never believe it, you know, that I'm single and independent. Without children. All mature students get tarred with the same brush. I'm sure they think I'm a bored grandmother.' She paused, knotted the microphone around her tape recorder as if trimming a gift. Then she touched the back of Patrick's hand, her voluminous sleeve spilling on his skin. 'I'm sorry about your mum. I did want to go to the funeral, you know, but—'

Patrick took his hand away, smoothed the transparencies into a pile again. One on top of the other like that, the angels and lilies and letters and unicorns and monkeys blurred into a dark mass.

'Are you okay, is there anything I can do?'

'I'm fine,' said Patrick, looking at his watch again. 'I'm just off to her place now, actually, to sort through some things, so I should be getting on.'

'Yes, of course,' said Rosemary. 'I thought your lecture was brilliant, by the way.' She slipped a piece of paper into his hand. 'Give me a ring, we could get together for a drink some time.'

Although it was autumn, the sun was unbearably bright outside the lecture theatre. Patrick peered into the shimmering blue sky, felt the corners of his eyes tense. He climbed into his car. What in God's name, he thought, was Rosemary doing in the class? How dare she turn up uninvited, a stale gust of smoke, the wicked fairy at the christening?

At least she hadn't come to the funeral. It had been a small affair, peopled by those who really had meant to visit Doreen, but just hadn't had the time.

'She was never the same after the fire,' said a cousin who, despite having ignored Patrick's mother for years, had numerous opinions on her mistakes in life. 'It was the loneliness that got to her,' she said. 'She lived too long. She should have remarried after Graham passed on, that's what she should have done.'

'They lost everything, you know,' he overheard another relative saying. 'It broke her heart. You don't get over something like that.'

'It was the boy, wasn't it? Playing with a magnifying glass.'

'She never mentioned it. Tried to pretend it was all forgotten. Very unhealthy.'

Patrick placed his folder of transparencies, his lecture notes and Rosemary's phone number on the passenger seat. He remembered the fire. It had got into his eyes and it was still there now, a dark after-image that sometimes sprang to life at night. It's not your fault, it's nobody's fault, his mother had said, but he knew better.

He flipped down the sun visor against the glare. He could feel the heat seeping through the roof of the car, softening the vinyl, making the steering wheel difficult to hold safely. The sun was just a star. But although there were millions of other stars in the sky during the day, they were invisible, drowned by the sun. Get your moles checked, his mother used to scold him every time he visited her. Have you had your moles checked? She avoided the outdoors when the sun was shining. It's dangerous, she said, and you know it. And of course, Patrick did. He'd known it for years, ever since the fire, and every time his mother mentioned the dangers of the sun he wanted to tell her that he hadn't meant any harm, hadn't dreamt he could cause such damage with a star and a piece of glass.

As he started the car he thought he saw Rosemary in his rear-view mirror. She was with a group of friends, laughing, sliding on a pair of sunglasses that were far too young for her, probably revealing that she used to be his wife. She never could keep a secret. He glanced in the mirror again, but the woman had turned her back and was walking away, and maybe it was just someone who looked like her.

He accelerated away from the university, the tree-ringed campus disappearing behind him. He found himself taking the turn-off to his mother's, although he hadn't really intended going there. He'd been delaying the solitary visit, reluctant to sort through the clothes, the china, the shoes lining the wardrobe like motionless lizards. But now his car was whizzing under the sign to her suburb, not even slowing down, and there was no time to change his mind. Telling Rosemary he was going there had somehow made it true.

He sped past fields dotted with sheep, cattle, goats, pigs, the occasional cluster of deer. He tried to recall what venison tasted like. It was fashionable now, and often appeared on the menus of up-market restaurants. Patrick rarely ate out, though; he couldn't justify spending that much on food, which was gone in an instant, and besides, he had to think of his retirement. He never took taxis, never bought flowers. The most valuable thing he owned was his manuscript, probably German, probably twelfth century, which described how to produce other manuscripts. *You must now know what bones are proper,* its author advised. *For this purpose take the bones of the thighs and wings of fowls or capons; and the older they are the better. When you find them under the table, put them in the fire, and when you see they are become whiter than ashes, take them out, and grind them well on a porphyry slab. On parchment you may draw or sketch with the above-named stylus, first rubbing and spreading some of the powdered bone dust over the parchment, scattered thinly and brushed off with a hare's foot.* Patrick occasionally let guests take a look at the manuscript, but was careful to show them how to handle it properly.

At the supermarket a few weeks back there had been a venison promotion. A young woman in a white smock and a white hat had been standing behind a cardboard stall, the sort that would, Patrick imagined, fold away like a toy at the end of the day. As each shopper passed she said, 'Would you like to try some Deerly Beloved venison, ma'am?' or, 'Sir, can I interest you in our new Deerly Beloved venison?' And she extended a paper plate with little cubes of meat on it, each one pierced by a toothpick. Patrick had watched the other shoppers taste the venison, smile and move on. They were so relaxed about it, so brazen. He'd rushed his trolley past, avoiding eye contact with the venison girl, although the aroma of the meat was delicious.

His car hurried on towards his mother's house, jolting slightly as it reached the bridge. On either side was a row of thin bars, like a cage to keep out the river. Grazing animals flickered behind them; projections from an old film, a trick of the light. He thought he saw hares and squirrels. The sun was so bright on the grass that it hurt his eyes, and beneath his chilly feet, under the metal floor of the car, the tyres, the asphalt and the concrete, was the water. He thought he could hear it rushing, and he was rushing too, going far too fast. He would be retiring soon. Then he could slow down. He thought of Saint Hilla, who had lived on holy water and communion wafers for weeks at a time. The animals flickered and shook, the grass burned his eyes, the river cut into the ground and he had to get to his mother's house, his old house. His smooth-soled shoe pushed harder

25

against the accelerator and then there were no more animals, no grass, no river, no bars; speed blurred them to a ribbon. And above the sound of the icy water and the rumbling of the engine there was another sound, a noise in fact, and it was the side of the bridge collapsing as the car struck it, and the bars fell away like kindling. And then Patrick was falling, the car a loose carapace around him, and unicorns, letters, angels, ivy leaves fell and fell, and his lecture notes fell, and everything he'd just said was all mixed up, and the water tumbled closer, rushed to him, all jumbled with sky and unicorns and words, and Rosemary's phone number flitted, a white moth, and then the sun burst, and it filled the car.

Every contact leaves a trace. Colette re-read the letter and tried to remember if she knew a Patrick Mercer, whether he was someone who should be familiar to her, whether she might have met him when she was overseas. *As you will have heard*, the first line assumed. She wondered how concerned she should be about his hospitalisation, his serious condition, his bruises and grafts. His unconsciousness. There was her own name at the top of the letter, added by hand in the space after *Dear*, and her own address—her mother's address—on the envelope. *We're asking all of his friends to send letters which can be read out to him, or tapes.* Surely, she thought, she wouldn't have forgotten a friend. She ran her finger over the stamp as if doing so might provide her with a clue. She checked inside the envelope for something she might have missed, some other document which explained everything. On the back was an English address she didn't recognise. Perhaps, she thought, she'd been at school with him. Most of her year were overseas now, New Zealand having become too small for them. She studied the tiny alpine scene on the stamp. There appeared to be a figure standing on the mountain, legs astride. An English explorer, perhaps, anonymous in his fur lined cladding, about to plant a flag into the snow. Colette held the envelope right up to her eye, so close she could smell the sour white paper, but the explorer was inked over with a blurry date. It dirtied the whole mountain, and she couldn't be sure he was there at all.

Her mother's key turned in the front door, and Colette pushed the letter between the pages of a magazine.

'How's the packing going?'

'Fine.'

'I'm glad you'll have your brother looking after you. Make sure you take him along when you're flat-hunting. There are some odd people around.'

'Yes, Mum.'

'I bought you a new duvet cover. Your old one goes with the curtains, so I'd like to hang on to it.'

Colette wished her mother would stop giving her things. She'd been trying to sort through cupboards and drawers for days, culling her belongings, ridding herself of dolls, picture books, cheap music boxes; the encumbrances of childhood. She couldn't wait to move up country, couldn't wait to leave behind her like a bad dream the cold south and all its clutter, its many layers of insulation. She took the soft parcel. The duvet was pictured on the bag, all flounces and roses and gaudy butterflies. 'Thank you,' she said, and didn't open it. She pulled another cardboard box from its hiding place at the back of the wardrobe, sighed, shook her head. 'Mother,' she said in her strictest voice, upending the swollen carton, 'is it necessary to keep my first pair of shoes? A brick from the Victory theatre? Mr Stott's funeral leaflet? It is clutter, Mother, and your life would be so much cleaner without it.' She snatched a selection of objects and dropped them at her mother's feet for emphasis. She had no wish, she said, to be reminded of her own birth, a felled tree, the loss of a tooth.

'I'm sorry you find my life unclean,' said her mother, catching a cracked leaf before it touched the floor. 'I'm sure, in the north, there are clear surfaces in abundance.' She handed her daughter a pile of clean underwear. And, knowing that in a long thin country the distance between north and south is considerable, she unzipped Colette's pack—it folded open like a flower—and slid some family photos into an inside pocket.

That night Colette lay wide awake in her old room, in the bed that matched the curtains. Her eyes itched and streamed, her chest hurt and she sneezed and sneezed. She wasn't sick; there was nothing wrong with her. It was the dust that caused her discomfort, the minute particles she'd raised during the day. They hung in the air, scraps of her past, irritants that filled her empty room and kept her from sleeping. She scratched at her eyes. Her mother had never been a tidy person, but after Colette's father left, all housework ceased. She refused to throw anything away. She surrounded herself with piles of washing, newspapers, mending; she nestled in the centre of her mess like a rat. Colette never brought friends home.

She wondered why her mother bothered about the duvet matching the curtains when the rest of the house was in such confusion; when dust furred every surface, even the slippery leaves of the rubber plant. And the duvet didn't match the curtains, anyway. It had been washed too many times and the flowers—daisies, violets—had faded, as if bred in the dark. Colette pulled at a thread and it unravelled in her hands, and she kept pulling and pulling until it broke, and her fist was filled with undone flowers. She imagined the whole house unravelling, carpets and curtains and bath-mats and cushions and even clothes fraying and unspooling. And then she imagined opening all the doors and windows and letting a gale inside, letting it pick up all the messy, grimy threads so it could whisk them away like tumbleweed.

In the north, when she found somewhere to live, she would paint her walls white. She would find a room in an old house, somewhere with high ceilings, tall windows. Bare wooden floors, perhaps. She would polish her antique furniture with beeswax and position it out of the sun. Selective buying using money her father sent at birthdays and at Christmas meant she now owned a walnut dressing-table, a low nursing chair, a Scotch chest—good, expensive pieces which responded to care. She had no time for the glassware and china her mother hoarded. Dinner sets were all right, but Colette couldn't see the point of fussy vases and ceramic birds and horses and winsome children. She reached a hand behind her head and felt the bars of her white iron bedstead; cool, smooth. In the north, she would buy white sheets and white pillowcases and she would wear white shirts which she would hang out to dry by their hems, not their shoulders, and they would billow on the line like sails, like a string of ships.

Colette scratched at her eyes again, which only made them worse. She lay on her hands, her knuckles like stones in the small of her back. Finally she turned on the light and began flicking through a magazine. From its glossy pages, from its articles on finding a man, pleasing a man, keeping a man, slid the letter. She read it once more, noting the polite appeal for donations to help meet *a number of costs*. Perhaps, she thought, there was no Patrick Mercer. Perhaps this was the work of some con artist, someone who had gleaned her address when she'd used her credit card or entered a competition or answered a survey. She wouldn't reply. Even if Patrick Mercer was real, she disliked the thought of sending news about herself across oceans, her life being used to generate sparks in a stranger's brain.

There wasn't much to sort through the next day, just her dressing-table. She turned out her sock drawer and picked through the contents, discarding several pairs which she hadn't worn for months, but which her mother deemed still useful. Bunched up like a mean thought was a nightdress given to her by an ex-boyfriend. It was too short and too blue, and the lace chafed her. Once, when she had worn it all night, there had been scratches on her chest in the morning. She stuffed the flimsy garment into the rubbish bag. She didn't know why she'd held on to it; she hardly thought of Justin now. She continued clearing her room, throwing away little pieces of her life. Like a thief she emptied earrings and bracelets into a pillowcase. She discarded sachets of lavender that had lost their scent, shook a jersey not worn since last winter. It smelled slightly musty, but she would rinse it out at her new flat, when she found one. She folded the arms across the chest and rolled it into a tight woolly bolt.

Paris. Justin had bought the nightdress for her in Paris, in one of the cheaper chain stores.

'Nobody has to know it's not from the Champs-Elysées,' she said, squirming against him in the thin blue silk. 'We'll tell everybody it's from the Champs-Elysées.' But she wore it only a few times because it always made her feel sad, not quite good enough.

She and Justin hadn't stayed together for long after that. She'd left him overseas, in London, which was as far as they got on their round-the-world trip. She couldn't believe he wanted to work in a pub instead of coming back to New Zealand to resume his law degree.

'Don't you want to be able to afford nice things one day?' she yelled, aware of how ugly she sounded.

'There's nothing in New Zealand I want to afford,' he said, and that was that.

Dear Patrick, she composed in her head as she continued sorting and packing, *this is embarrassing to confess but I'm not sure where we met. I think it must have been when I was travelling the year before last. I'm back in New Zealand now, and about to move up north, where I'll be finishing off my history degree after the summer. What I should be doing is earning some real money, but two thirds of a BA isn't worth much. Hopefully I'll be able to find a holiday job.*

Patrick was real, of course he was. She must have met him when she was overseas, but she had no idea where, or under what circumstances. She sealed the letter from his Friends inside the last box. Then she closed her empty drawers and her empty wardrobe and looked at the reflection of her old room in the mirror. She'd always hated the fact that she could see herself when she was in bed, but there wasn't enough space to arrange the furniture differently. Some nights she used to cover the mirror with a sheet, as if someone had died. Once upon a time, she remembered her father telling her, people covered their mirrors to protect the dead, to keep them from glimpsing their departing souls and taking fright. Colette began filling out address labels, watching her hitcher's thumbs—her father's thumbs—curling away from her hands. She was very like him to look at, her mother often told her. Sometimes, she said, it was as if he were still there. Colette addressed label after label, directing her belongings to her brother's flat, writing her name so many times it became unfamiliar.

Malcolm liked to read in bed until late, until he couldn't hold his eyes open any longer. Their bedroom was at the highest point in the house. It had a turret overlooking the harbour, and although the view was spectacular, it could be cold. He'd switch on his bedside light and lean into his pillows, tucking the sheet around himself so that Ruth didn't complain of the draught. Then he'd read and read, folding the evening paper into portions the size of fat letters. They inked the sheets, but Ruth had given up trying to remove the marks. The twenty-first century was almost here, she said, and she had better things to do with her time. Reading bedtime stories to Daniel, for instance. She knew he was a demanding child, but she was sure he'd love a story from his dad now and then. And besides, she said, repeated exposure to phonemes developed a child's auditory cortex, resulting in greater brain capacity. They had to accept the fact that Daniel wasn't like other children, that he needed all the help he could get, especially to prepare him for starting school the following year. Malcolm felt stupid doing the voices, though. He was hopeless at mimicking a lion, a tree, a car. Ruth was much better at make-believe. And so, in the evenings, when Daniel wouldn't settle, Malcolm was left to read the paper and to cover the sheets with ink. Mostly it dissolved in the washing machine, but now and then a ghost showed against the cotton, shadowing Malcolm's side of the bed like an intruder's fingerprints. And sometimes, he knew without seeing, ink lay smudged under Ruth's cool feet.

'Are you still reading?' she'd mumble late at night, squinting at him as if she'd forgotten something. 'It's time to sleep now. It's dark. Go to sleep.' She didn't understand Malcolm's hunger for information, his need to watch the world for signs. She didn't understand that he read to identify danger.

'It's important to know what's going on,' he told her. 'How do you expect to get by, if you don't know what's happening around you?'

But Ruth closed her eyes, turned her back on the bedside light. She never read the paper now.

'A periodicals librarian who doesn't read the news,' said Malcolm, 'makes no sense.'

It just depressed her, Ruth said, all those robberies, guns, deceptions, wars. There was enough sadness in the world without having to read about it at bedtime.

When he was collecting the first photos of Daniel on his tricycle, Malcolm bought a plastic key-ring and had a copy of Laura's bush-walk photo made. He knew it wasn't a true representation of her, but then, few photos were. It disguised the puppy fat around her chin and jaw, laid shadows along her cheekbones. It made her older. And Malcolm took comfort in that, because as long as this version of his daughter existed, he could believe there was a chance for the other one, the real one, to grow older.

There was something unsettling about cutting a photograph. He was tampering with the past, trimming it to fit his current require-ments. He removed a very narrow strip from one side. At least, he thought, there were no other people in the photo, nobody from whom he had to separate his daughter. She was surrounded by nothing but bush. That was where he'd felt most at ease with her; under the close-knit canopy, the dangerous sun diffused by leaves, she seemed to relax. On walking holidays she led him and Ruth along tracks that wound and branched like green veins, going slowly so her aged parents could keep up, she said, but she was always pausing to feel some bright moss, to run her finger over spores clustered like Braille on the underside of a fern.

He cut away another strip of bush, careful not to damage Laura, the glossy paper curling at the touch of the blades. He could almost smell the damp foliage, fallen trunks alive with insects, the wood so soft that it broke away like cork in your hands, and the leaves rotting underfoot. In drier spots you could find their skeletons, as fragile as the wings of dragonflies, and if you held them up to the light they broke the sky into a jigsaw. Malcolm sliced away another strip, and another, and ribbons of bush were falling around his feet, and he kept cutting and clearing until he reached Laura. And then there was no more bush, and only she remained, isolated, out of context. She was the right size now. He slid her into the plastic cover, then prised the double ring apart with a coin and attached his keys. She would come everywhere with him. She would unlock doors, start the car. She would fit in his pocket or the palm of his hand like a lucky charm, sealed under plastic so that no water could get in, and no dust. And at night, she would deadlock the door of their house, and they would be safe.

The man didn't have much luck with girls. It didn't seem to matter what he did—asking for a light, paying them compliments on their figure, buying them drinks all night, hinting at his skill between the sheets. The ones who did agree to go out with him knocked him back after a couple of dates at the most.

One night, at the pub, he tried to chat up a girl sitting at the bar.

'Have you got a mirror in your pocket?' he asked her, but she turned away and kept talking to her friend, who was a bit of a dog. 'Hey,' he said more loudly, 'I said, have you got a mirror in your pocket? Because I can see myself in your pants.'

She didn't even laugh. She just grabbed her bag and shifted away from him.

Summer had arrived early, and there had been no rain for weeks. Even though Malcolm insisted on watering the garden every evening, the soil was cracking like old skin, the zucchinis swelling, turning to marrows overnight. Daniel refused to eat them, and Ruth was sick of the sight of them too. Things were going to waste. Heavy-headed roses shed their petals at the slightest touch. Even the birds sounded tired.

When Ruth unlocked the front door each afternoon, a wall of trapped heat rushed against her. She dropped her bag on the couch, shucked off her sandals, opened every window.

'Draw Daddy another picture,' she'd say to Daniel, sitting him down with paper and crayons and sometimes, if he'd been good, paints. Then she peered into the bathroom mirror and dabbed her face with cleanser, rubbing it in with the pads of her fingers. She did this very gently, as the magazines suggested. Dragging the skin, especially the delicate area round the eye, caused premature ageing.

'Why don't you leave some windows open during the day?' Malcolm said when he got home. He was standing at the front door as if he couldn't bear to come inside, fanning himself with the newspaper.

'Run and get your new picture, Daniel,' said Ruth.

Malcolm was already taking the glasses from the cabinet. He twisted the ice-cube tray, shook out several cold nuggets.

'Do you know how insecure these old windows are?' she said. 'If they're open even a crack, someone can walk right in.'

Malcolm sighed. 'Some of the upstairs ones, though, they'd be all right. You can get special locks for them.'

Ruth clinked the ice-cubes in her glass, her fingers tracing patterns in the condensation.

'Here,' said Daniel, handing his father a buckled picture. Two sheets of greaseproof paper had been ironed together with a sprinkling of crayon shavings in between. 'Like this,' he said, and held the picture up to the light so the slivers of wax shone.

'Very pretty,' said Malcolm. 'Is it a boat?'

'Yes!' shouted Daniel. 'A boat, a boat!' And he ran around the couch. 'Mummy thought it was a house.'

Malcolm put his head on one side, assessing, deciding. 'No, of course it's not a house. Look at these yellow bits, they're the sails, and those are the masts, and there's even a porthole right here.' He glanced at Ruth. 'I'll pick up some locks tomorrow, shall I?' Then he said, 'Aren't you a clever boy.' And he sailed the boat slowly across the glass, and Daniel's eyes followed it, and Ruth finished her drink and went to the kitchen.

She twisted the roots off the lettuce as if wringing a bird's neck. The outermost leaves were thick at the base, and a darker green than the others. Here and there along the edges they were brown and crisp, like paper starting to burn. The good leaves she plunged into water. They kept rising to the top and floating, frilly green boats, and she pushed them under again and again to rid them of the grit from the garden. The water circled her wrists like silver bracelets. She remembered seeing her mother standing at the sink in summer, her wrists held under the cold tap. It cools the blood, she'd explained. Ruth sank her arms deeper into the water, past the hot creases of her elbows. The lettuce leaves bobbed around her. She waited for her blood to cool, and she thought about locks, and window-pane oceans, and boats made of coloured wax.

She couldn't sleep that night. It was too hot to have even a sheet over her, but she felt exposed, unsafe without any sort of covering. She remembered staying with her grandparents when she was a girl. All the beds in their house had had layers of blankets on them, heavy wool coloured like the insides of chocolates: soft pinks and greens, thick creams. She remembered the weight of the blankets on her, their close weave, the furry smell of them. The satin binding was smooth and cool like her grandmother's fingers, the wool itself rough like her grandfather's cheek when he kissed her goodnight. Nobody had blankets like that any more, she thought. Nobody wrapped beds tight like gifts. Ruth slept under feathers now, and dreamt of birds, of being so light she might float away, but she missed the safe weight of childhood. And sometimes she still dreamt of Laura.

She was careful not to wake Malcolm. She wandered from their turret bedroom to the kitchen, from the kitchen to the lounge. She stood in every room in the house, observed the night from seven different angles. Last of all she checked Daniel, who was curled in his usual tight ball, fists clenched, untouchable. Only Laura's room she didn't enter, although she could have, quite easily. She could have grasped the door handle, pushed her way in. She could have brushed her fingers over clothes in the wardrobe, held the pillow to her cheek, pulled the curtains to keep out the night. Or she could have just stood there for a while, touching nothing, not even sitting on the smoothed bed. But she didn't go in. She rushed back to her room, suddenly scared, expecting to find something dreadful if she did open the door. The man who took Laura, or her own terrified reflection.

After Malcolm had fitted the locks, Ruth agreed to leave a few windows open during the day. Each morning she slid them up just a crack, smaller than a hand-span. All except for Laura's room; that remained closed.

As soon as she got home she knew that things had been disturbed: the dried flowers on the window sill were knocked over, Malcolm's papers skewed. Pieces of Daniel's jigsaw puzzle—Big Bird, from *Sesame Street*—were scattered around, patches of orange and yellow littering the floor like fallen leaves. She heard a rustling in the next room and froze.

'Who's there?' she called, motioning for Daniel to keep still and quiet. She inched her way across the kitchen. One piece of puzzle had made its way under the table: a fragment of wing, the feathers almost indistinguishable from the tail plumage. Daniel always got into difficulty with that one. He was really too young for such a confusing puzzle.

She pushed open the lounge door. Nothing was disturbed, as far as she could tell. 'Is there anyone there?' she said, her voice brittle in the uncarpeted room. The new window lock was still in place, the gauzy curtains moving in the breeze. Daniel's boat picture, held to the glass with one piece of tape, fluttered now and then. There was no one here.

Ruth was about to kick off her shoes when she noticed a spatter of white on top of the television. It was on the floor, too, and on the rug. Bird droppings.

She opened the window as wide as it would go. There was a smudge on it, where the bird must have flown into the glass. She peered under the couch, behind the chairs and curtains. She even lifted the rug and looked underneath, although she knew there would be nothing there but dust. The bird could be anywhere in the house.

She worked her way through each room, finding more droppings here and there, but no bird. In Daniel's room it had speckled the dressing-table. The poor creature must have caught sight of itself in the mirror, Ruth realised, and taken fright. She filled a bucket with warm water and began to clean up.

'Why are you washing the wood?' said Daniel.

'There was a bird in here,' she said. 'He made a wee bit of a mess and Mummy's just tidying it up.'

'A big bird?' he said, coming over and inspecting the surface.

'Mind the bucket, Daniel.'

'Was it Big Bird?'

'No,' said Ruth, drying off the dressing-table with one of Malcolm's old singlets. 'Just a little sparrow or a starling or something. But he's gone now.'

'Why?' said Daniel. 'Why didn't he stay?'

———

In bed that night, Malcolm lay on her so heavily that the air was pressed from her lungs. It was as if the hot weather had made his flesh more dense; as if there were no spaces in him. Ruth thought she could hear something in the bedroom. Was the bird still trapped there, in a corner perhaps, beating its wings under the bed like a patient ghost?

'Shh,' she said, and placed a hand on Malcolm's shoulder. She listened for the movement of wings, for feathers rustling like bedclothes.

'What is it?' said Malcolm. He was completely still now, and whispering, as if he had heard something too. 'Am I hurting you?'

Ruth closed her eyes and shook her head. Malcolm began to move again, and the wooden bed creaked, and Ruth kept her eyes shut so tightly she could see patterns: snowflakes magnified many times over. And with each creak she thought of thin bird-bones locking into place, preparing for flight.

15 November 1999
Dear Colette,
*   Patrick has been making slow but steady progress. His fractures are healing well, and we hope it won't be too much longer before he regains consciousness. Thank you all for your letters and tapes. He has heard them several times over, and we're sure they're making a difference. The balance in his account is growing steadily, too, for which we're sure he will be grateful—even if he is a little gruff at first! We all know how uncomfortable he can be in the face of generosity, but please continue to help him in whatever way you can.*
*   Yours,*
*   The Friends of Patrick Mercer*

It was the first piece of mail Colette received in the north. On the envelope her old address had been crossed out with one swift diagonal line, and in her mother's untidy hand were the words *Please forward to*, followed by her brother's address. Colette sighed. Just the address would have done. Her mother was always saying too much, providing unnecessary detail. She risked nothing.

That night Colette lied to her.

'I'm having a lovely time,' she said. 'All the courses look so interesting, it's hard to decide what to take. And transferring won't be a problem, they said at Registry.'

'And the flat-hunting, how's that working out? Have you found anything?'

'Not yet. I've seen a few, but they're all pretty untidy.'

'Have you been taking Dominic with you? What does he think?'

'Oh yes,' lied Colette, 'he's come with me to all of them, don't worry. We're having a great time.'

'Have you thought about Christmas?' said her mother. 'When do you think you'll be here? It'll be nice to have my two babies home again.'

'We'll probably just come down for a couple of days,' said Colette. 'We thought we'd spend New Year up here.'

'Oh,' said her mother. 'You're not homesick, then?'

'No, not at all. Dominic's here. And my allergies are much better.'

And Colette wasn't sad to have shifted, to have left behind the place of her birth, to be separated from her mother. She didn't miss the cold south, the wood-smoke that got into her throat and her hair, the frequent asthma attacks. In the north, she could breathe properly. The following year she would be able to walk to university without a coat, sit outside at lunchtime. She could see her brother whenever she wanted to, go out with him and his friends, until she had some of her own. She'd made the right decision to move, she knew, but despite the warmer climate, the lush foliage, she felt a gloominess she couldn't identify. It filled her head, pressed itself against her temples, her ribs.

'You sound down,' said her mother. 'Are you sure you're all right?'

'I'm a little bit tired, that's all,' said Colette, thinking of the walk she'd taken that afternoon. She'd wandered down the street to see where it led, taking careful note of signs so she wouldn't get lost. *Give way*, she read to herself. *Children crossing*. The sound of her shoes was huge in her head. *Stop. Wait.* There was danger everywhere, and what good was a signpost? It was just another thing to hit.

'I'll be fine once I find some summer work,' she said into the telephone.

'What you need is iron. Girls these days don't eat properly, they don't get enough red meat. You should have some lamb's fry.'

'The real name is liver,' said Colette. 'I abhor liver. You know that.'

'Do you?' said her mother. 'I must be thinking of Dominic.'

'Yes,' said Colette, 'most likely.'

Her mother always thought of Dominic. As a child, Colette had suspected she only ever wanted a boy. Later, when she could exercise adult reasoning, she believed that her mother loved him more because he was so like his father in temperament, so like the person who had left them. She had made Dominic belong to her. And then he left too.

'You can come and visit any time you like, Mum,' he'd said. 'You can get cheap flights if you book ahead.'

She had never visited her son, though. She had stayed in the south in her cluttered house and had focused her attention on Colette.

'I can't understand why he moved so far away,' she said. 'He could have studied chemistry down here, couldn't he?'

Colette's brother had always liked reading about men overcoming enormous odds. As a boy, his bookcase was punctuated with stories of survival, courage, wilderness improvisation. Sailors drifted in damaged lifeboats for weeks, mountaineers endured blizzards, plane-crash heroes administered inventive first aid. The thing the stories had in common was that they were all true; he wasn't interested in anything made up. When he poked fun at Colette's teen-romance novels, she told him he had no imagination.

'Imagination?' he said, eyes wide. 'What sort of imagination do you think it takes to build a shelter from branches and leaves? To survive two weeks in a snow cave?'

Once, he'd insisted on sleeping in the garden. He'd made his own shelter from sheets and long-handled garden implements, and had even stuffed a pillowcase with hay intended for the rabbit. He ignored Colette when she told him that real explorers didn't use pillows, and had placed it at the head of his sleeping bag.

'I don't know,' said their mother. 'I'm not sure I want you out there all night.'

But Dominic had shown her his shelter, demonstrated the door flaps and the straw pillow, and eventually she relented, and Dominic got his way. Colette had looked out the window once, when she woke in the night, and there was a faint glow soaking through the walls of the makeshift tent, and Dominic's silhouette was huge against the family sheets. That was all she remembered, except for hearing her mother getting up throughout the night and sliding open the back door to check he was all right.

Patrick was hot, he was burning up. He could feel the heat of the flames against his face, almost touching his skin, his eyes and nose stinging, his throat rough. He was crying but the fire evaporated his tears before they ran down his cheeks. And there was something in his arm, a thin hard something right in the crook of his elbow. He could feel it every now and then as he moved.

He opened his eyes and looked around. In every direction there was nothing but white, and above him hung a liquid-filled bag on a hook. He was very cold and had no idea where he was, or why his head was throbbing, or why, for that matter, he was so under-dressed. He fingered the stiff, scratchy gown. He must look ridiculous. He shivered. Was that snow, that soft cold substance beneath his feet? Was there anyone around who could give him directions to his mother's house? Was there anyone here at all? Remain calm, he said to himself. Now was not the time to panic; panicking would only make his head hurt. Above him the sun was a pale disc. Children were wrong, he thought, to draw the sun with a big, smiling face. He wished he had his duffel coat with him. He was annoyed with himself: for not having the coat, for being cold, for having a headache. For getting so lost. He must have taken a wrong turn somewhere. Nerves, probably. Although he thought the lecture had gone quite well, he was still shaking. That annoyed him too.

His priority, he decided, was to find his car. If he hurried, he might still make it to his mother's house before dark. He climbed to the top of a gentle slope and turned slowly, scanning the horizon for any sign of the vehicle. The snow must have fallen very quickly. It had been fine when he'd left the university, he was sure, but now he couldn't make out any landmarks at all, just drifts and folds and banks of snow. He knew he shouldn't have bought a white car; he'd wanted the gold but it cost more.

His head was still throbbing, and he realised he must have been wandering for hours. He lifted his wrist to see the time but his watch was gone, and in its place was a plastic bracelet. He raised it to his face and read his own name. It occurred to him that dusk should have fallen a long time ago, but the snow was still glaring under the wan sun. It was beginning to hurt his eyes, and he wondered if night would come at all, if the sun would ever set. Perhaps it would simply circle the horizon, always in his eyes, and the day would never end. He was so cold. He sat down in the snow and waited for someone to come.

'How do you determine the original source of a medieval text?'

Patrick opened his eyes to find a group of animals staring at him: sheep, calves, deer, goats, their eyes huge in the white landscape. Behind them the ice stretched forever, a blank page.

'Well?' said an old ram at the front of the group. 'What about the popular image of the lone monk toiling over a manuscript. A myth, by and large, wouldn't you say?'

'Ah,' said Patrick, 'that's an interesting question. Yes. There has been considerable debate on that very question.'

'He's stalling,' muttered the ram.

'He doesn't know!' hissed another towards the back.

'For many years scholars have—' Patrick began, but was drowned out by his audience.

'He doesn't know, he doesn't know!' they shouted.

'Hey Longbottom!' yelled an athletic young buck, 'I thought you said they were sending an expert. We've all paid our fees, and this is the rubbish we get. Some old pensioner.' He thrust a hoof at Patrick. 'He wouldn't know his arse from a plate of porridge.'

The old ram smiled. 'The brochure did, I agree, promise an expert,' he said, 'and as you have so descriptively expressed, Parksy, it appears Mr Mercer—'

'Doctor Mercer,' said Patrick in a low voice.

'—it appears Mr Mercer here would not know his arse, as you say, from a bowl of porridge.'

'I believe it was a plate of porridge, Longbottom,' said a sleek doe.

'Thank you, Melanie, you are correct, of course. Vigilance, my friends! You let a plate become a bowl and all of a sudden you've got pandemonium.' He paused, smiled at Patrick. 'However,' he continued, 'in these days of cutbacks and general belt-tightening we must all make do with what we have, be it plates or bowls or second-rate speakers. I'm sure I need not remind you all of the disastrous consequences of last year's squirrel gag.'

The young buck sniggered.

'Enough!' said Longbottom. 'Let's give the man a chance to redeem himself. Mr Mercer?'

Patrick cleared his throat. 'I wonder,' he said, 'if there might be something else I could wear.'

'Something else you could wear?' bellowed Longbottom. 'What do you mean, something else?'

'Just a jumper, perhaps some socks—'

'Oh some socks! Mr Mercer here has cold tootsies!' The animals laughed. 'You've been issued the regulation gown, have you not?'

'Yes, it's just it's rather—'

'Good God, man, you're wearing more than we are! You don't see young Parksy whining for jumpers and woolly vests, do you? You'll need to be made of sterner stuff than that, I'm afraid, Mercer. Something else to wear, indeed!'

Patrick took a deep breath. 'The issue of source material,' he said, 'is a thorny one. Often we are dealing with texts that have been reproduced over many hundreds of years. Bibles, for instance, or saints' lives—' He stopped. At the edge of the group, Parksy was batting a live fish between his hoofs like a cat toying with a mouse.

'What's wrong now, man?' said Longbottom.

'I'm sorry,' said Patrick, 'but—' he gestured at Parksy '—it's very distracting.'

'Fling it, Parksy,' barked Longbottom. The fish was flicked back into the water. 'Mr Mercer, if you please.'

'Prod him.'

    'What?'

    'See if he moves.'

    'He's not pretending, you know.'

    'If you won't, I will.'

    'Shh!'

    'What?'

    'He said something.'

    'I didn't hear anything.'

    'Something about a vest.'

    'That'll be the morphine talking.'

Patrick had been talking for close to an hour, he estimated. Although he hadn't touched on a lot of what he'd prepared, he didn't want to risk boring his audience, and it was impossible to gauge whether they were still interested or not. He put his hands behind his back in what he hoped was a confident pose, but he could feel the gap in the back of his gown. He folded his arms across his chest instead. 'Are there any questions from the floor at this stage?'

'I have a question, young man.' A plummy-toned nanny goat raised herself as far as her figure would allow. Her chest wobbled as she spoke, and Patrick couldn't help thinking of Mrs Morrin, who had lived next door when he was a boy, and whose reading glasses had hung from a chain against her enormous, upholstered bosom. 'You mentioned zoomorphic ornamentation—I wonder if you would tell us in a little more detail the sorts of illustrations one might encounter. Zoomorphically speaking.'

'Well,' said Patrick, 'it's a vast field, as you can imagine. Not only did medieval artists pepper their work with known animals, they also painted creatures from classical mythology, and beasts entirely of their own invention. The matter is further complicated when you realise that, even when they were drawing on the natural world—'

'I thought you said they painted.'

Patrick sighed.

'My lovely wife is correct, Mr Mercer, you did say they painted.'

'Yes. They painted. My point is, even when they—took inspiration from the natural world, very often they had never set eyes on the animal in question.'

'You mean they just *imagined* what an elephant, for instance, might look like, and then made it up?'

'Precisely,' said Patrick, pleased he was finally getting somewhere.

'Outrageous,' tsked the nanny goat.

'Do you think he can hear us?'

'I don't know. No.'

'He looks so emaciated.'

'So would you.'

'It's a shame about his hair. He had such lovely soft hair, even after it went grey.'

'Maybe we should have a conversation.'

'I don't think he's feeling that chatty.'

'Us, not him. You and I should have a conversation.'

'I thought we already were.'

'About him. Things he might recognise.'

'Um. All right, museum, illuminated manuscript—'

'That's not a conversation.'

'I feel stupid.'

'Nobody can hear you.'

'Then what's the point?'

'Paper,' said the doe in a silky voice. 'Perhaps Mr Mercer could tell us something about paper production.'

'Of course,' said Patrick, and smiled at her. If he could get Melanie on side, perhaps Longbottom would settle down a little. 'Although paper began to be used widely only after the fifteenth century.'

'Well what did they use before then?' said Longbottom. 'It said in the brochure that you'd cover manuscript production from the fifth century. They can't have made books without paper, can they?'

Laughter rippled around the group. Even Melanie was smirking.

'Well,' said Patrick, 'paper was used earlier than then, but—'

'Oh, so it was, was it? Just forgot for a minute, did we?'

Patrick bent so that his face was level with Longbottom's nose. He caught a whiff of fetid breath. 'Parchment,' he said. 'That was what they used before paper caught on.'

'What's that you say? Parchment? Never heard of it.'

'Parchment, or vellum. There is a slight technical difference between the two, but basically they're the same material.' And then Patrick told them how the skins were scraped of fat and hair, how they were immersed in lime, scraped again, stretched and dried. There was a flesh side and a hair side to any page of parchment, he said, and it was usually possible to tell which was which.

When he finished, there was silence. He scanned his audience, waiting for comments, perhaps a question or two, but the animals just stared at him. One or two lambs and calves began crying.

'But that's barbaric,' said Melanie quietly. 'Longbottom, this is appalling. Must we listen to these horror stories?'

'Sir, we are outraged,' said Longbottom in a pale voice. 'You come here supposedly to entertain us, it's billed as a lively and informative talk for the whole family, and then you force us to listen to these, these atrocities.'

'But I don't—'

'Silence! You have said quite enough, sir.'

'I'm afraid I don't quite—'

'I said silence!'

Patrick shivered. While he'd been talking he hadn't noticed the cold, but now the snow was biting into his toes, the wind numbing his nose, his ears. And his head was pounding again.

'Are you cold?' said Longbottom. 'Perhaps you'd like a nice woolly coat, how would that be? And some cosy fur-lined boots?'

The animals began to approach him, fanning out to form a semi-circle. They struck the ground as they moved, sending up clouds of snow, thousands of icy slivers.

'I've offended you,' said Patrick. 'I'm not sure what I've said, but I'm sorry. I'm sorry.'

The animals moved in closer, hoofs churning the snow. It whirled around them, a haze of silver and white, blurring their outlines. They could have been rocks, Patrick thought. Angry, advancing rocks. He crouched down into a ball, made himself as small as possible. Perhaps they would not find him in this white storm; perhaps it would bury him before they reached him. By now he could see only the snow. He closed his eyes, and could still see nothing but white. He felt himself being lifted, and through the blizzard he could just hear a voice, below him now.

'Mummy, that wasn't true, was it? What that man said, that was just made up.'

'Yes, darling, it was just a story.'

'I thought so.'

'This house is getting run down, you know,' Ruth said in bed one night.

'Mm,' said Malcolm, his face shadowed by newspaper.

'The doors need sanding, and the downstairs carpet's badly faded from the sun. Most of the windows stick. The oven's temperamental. The paper's coming away in Daniel's room. And all the ceilings need repainting.'

They both looked up. The ceilings were one of the house's most interesting features: plaster scalloping and garlands and elaborate central flowers. They reminded Ruth of wedding cakes.

'They need a bit of attention, I suppose,' said Malcolm. 'I could do a few repairs over summer.'

'We don't need a place this big,' said Ruth. 'When I'm back at the library full-time I won't be able to keep a place this big clean.' She studied the scalloping, followed the pattern around each corner. 'The room in best shape,' she said, 'is Laura's.'

'That's because it's not used.'

'Exactly.' Ruth's eyes traced the outline of a flower. The light fitting hung from the centre, its bulb a bright stamen. 'Maybe we should move,' she said.

Malcolm took a long, slow breath. 'Maybe we should.'

The next morning Ruth bought a paper on the way to work, and at lunchtime, in the staffroom, she turned straight to the real-estate pages, leaving the other sections neatly unread. Jan, her boss, watched her, but made no comment. *Be quick*, the advertisements cautioned, *won't last*. And she would be quick, she decided, otherwise she and Malcolm and Daniel would never move. They would stay forever in the old house, the high-maintenance house with its vast garden, its warped windows, its turret that watched the sea. Ruth ringed several advertisements, without any idea what OSP or H&I or sunny ROW site meant. There was no glossary. And perhaps the abbreviations were common knowledge, and everybody else was familiar with them, these shortcuts that made life simpler. Since Laura had gone, Ruth sometimes felt as if she'd been lost too, as if she were living in a place where she no longer knew the rules or the language. She remembered being faced with a choice of three new yoghurts at the supermarket once. She'd stood there staring at the different cartons, picking them up and putting them down again, reading the labels as if they would provide her with advice.

She folded the newspaper and rinsed her coffee mug. 'I'm just popping downtown,' she said to Jan. 'Shouldn't be too long.'

'What sort of place are you looking for?' said the real-estate agent. 'A family home?'

'Well, not a large place,' said Ruth. 'My husband and I are just finding our old house too big. But we'd like to move right away, as soon after Christmas as possible.'

'So you're wanting somewhere low maint, two or three brms,' said the woman. She began writing on a pad. 'There are some gorgeous townhouses around.'

'Do they have gardens?' said Ruth. 'My husband loves to garden.'

'Some of them do, smallish plots. Although of course that will increase the price.' She scribbled away for a moment. Ruth wished she could see her notes. It felt like a visit to the doctor, as if her defects were being recorded, her frailties assessed. The woman looked up and smiled. 'How many children do you have?'

'Just one, at home. He starts school in March.'

'But you might have others staying from time to time?'

'Yes,' said Ruth. 'It's possible.'

'They never really leave, do they?' said the woman. 'I can't get rid of my thirty-year-old. He still brings his ironing round.' She laughed. 'Three brms, then,' and she noted it down on her pad.

Ruth nodded.

'Any animals?'

'Just a cat. We used to have a labrador, but that was years ago.'

'Dogs are a lot of work,' said the woman. 'Mind you, cats can be fussy too, can't they? What's yours called?'

'Fluffy,' said Ruth. 'My son named it.'

'Here's a trick for you.' The woman leaned across the desk, as if to whisper. 'When you do move, butter Fluffy's paws once you get to the new place. It'll stop him from running away.'

Someone was reading to him. A woman, there was a woman reading to him in a hushed voice usually reserved for the terminally ill, or children at bedtime.

'But in those days, after that tribulation, the sun shall be darkened, and the moon shall not give her light, and the stars of heaven shall fall, and the powers that are in heaven shall be shaken.'

The voice reminded him a little of his mother's. He wished she would be quiet, just leave him alone. But on she droned, on and on: 'Take ye heed, watch and pray: for ye know not when the time is.' Perhaps she thought she was helping. Perhaps, because of his work, she assumed he was religious. In the Middle Ages, he recalled, it was customary to read saints' lives to the afflicted. The scrapings of manuscripts were mixed with water and administered to victims of snake-bite. The Book of Durrow was used to cure sick cattle; the finger bones of an Irish scribe who had copied countless gospels performed a miracle after his death. 'And what I say unto you I say unto all, Watch.' Perhaps the woman wanted to save his soul, or lull him to sleep. 'Are there not twelve hours in the day?' she asked. 'If any man walk in the day he stumbleth not, because he seeth the light of this world. But if a man walk in the night, he stumbleth, because there is no light in him.'

Patrick thought of the legend of Saint Columba; how he'd copied Saint Finnian's psalter illegally and how, in the church at night, his fingers had shone as he wrote. 'And there are also many other things which Jesus did, the which, if they should be written every one, I suppose that even the world itself could not contain the books that should be written.' Patrick imagined copying a book by hand. Mistakes would be inevitable. He wondered if Columba had made mistakes, whether Finnian's copy was accurate. He tried to ignore the voice, the story-time, nearly-time-for-lights-out voice that sounded like his mother's. The woman had no idea what she was reading. It was outrageous. Who knew what the real story was? How could anyone ever believe what they read?

Patrick's mother was a small, careful person, deliberate in her actions. Unlike her son, who left behind him a trail of crumbs, books, toppled trains and soldiers, she left no wake.

Patrick knew this hadn't always been the case. He had seen school photographs of her, when she had been captain of the athletics team. Her limbs were long and muscular and in one picture she was stretching out a baton, relaying to the viewer some schoolgirl message. In others she flew across hurdles, cradled the heavy shot to her cheek like a violin. And there she was on a bicycle, the outline of her knees showing through her skirt, her hair a rippling pennant. It seemed she was never still. In many of the photographs— -which Patrick had labelled *young* in his mind, although they were very old—parts of his mother were smudged. Her hair and her cheeks smeared the pictures, her arms were blurred wings. None of the photos was an original, of course; they'd all been lost in the fire. These were copies, mostly taken from Aunt Joyce's collection, a few from his grandmother's. They weren't as sharp as the originals, and they felt different, too; whereas the old paper had been thick, textured like skin, these were thin and slippery, difficult to hold. They showed every fingerprint. And there were gaps: here was Patrick as a newborn, then all of a sudden he was starting school. Here was his mother at school, there she was married.

Her wedding photograph was one of the few in which she was perfectly still. She was tiny inside the frame, insignificant against the ornate dress. It was heavy with beading and embroidery, and the train had been swept around her ankles and spread in front of the wedding party like an extravagant blanket, as if, after the photo had been taken, everyone would sit down for a picnic among the stitched butterflies and flowers and tiny, gold-flecked birds. Patrick imagined her walking up the aisle in the massive garment, the train slowing her, keeping her steps steady, ladylike, no relay races here. She had been sewn into the dress, she'd told Patrick once. Her mother had insisted. It gave a better line than catches and buttons and hooks and eyes.

'Your grandmother stitched me in herself,' she said, 'and she pricked me with the needle, by accident, but there was just a tiny spot of blood and it didn't show through.'

There was no blurring in photographs of Patrick's mother after the fire. She could sit still for hours, it seemed. Sometimes she did. Patrick blamed the fire for his mother's slowing down. And the fire was nobody's fault.

Patrick's father wore a pocket watch which his wife had given him on the day they were married. The chain could be seen glinting in the wedding photograph, while hidden in the waistcoat was the thick golden disc that sat under his ribs and ticked like a second heart. Sometimes, on special occasions, he would open the back and show Patrick the tiny mechanism that made it work. Patrick was always surprised at the neatness of it. Hours and minutes never felt tidy to him; they leapt and raced like hares. He wondered if his own insides were that neat.

'This is the hairspring,' said his father, pointing to a tight coil, 'and this is the escape wheel. And here's the part that makes the sun and moon pictures move.'

The pictures were Patrick's favourite part of the watch. When the sun was in full view, the moon couldn't be seen at all, and vice versa. It made him shiver as if he knew a secret when he thought of a hidden moon, a hidden sun, moving behind the golden workings. His father insisted they were useless.

'Purely decorative,' he said. 'A man knows if it's night or day without having to consult his watch. Your mother liked them.'

Patrick peered at the watch side-on to see the sun slip away.

'Do you think,' he asked his father, 'there's a time of day when you can't tell if it's morning or evening? If you were shut in the dark for a week, say, and then let out, could you tell what time it was?'

But his father didn't answer. He simply pocketed the watch and said, 'Bed.'

The bed had been made too tightly. Patrick moved his leg, tried to untuck the sheets with his foot. The woman's voice stopped.

'He seems restless.'

'Should we ring for the nurse?'

'Let's just plump his pillows for him. Here, tuck the sheet in on your side, it's coming loose. Right—my substance was not hid from thee, when I was made in secret, and curiously wrought in the lowest parts of the earth. Thine eyes did see my substance, yet being unperfect; and in thy book all my members were written, which in continuance were fashioned, when as yet there was none of them.'

Patrick was on a train with his father. They were on their way back from a seaside holiday, and his mother must have been there too, somewhere, but Patrick was leaning against his father and the motion of the train was lulling him almost to sleep, except he didn't want to go to sleep, he wanted to make the holiday last and last, and sleeping was a waste of time. His father was dozing, cupping his pocket watch in his hand, and Patrick kept himself awake by watching the second hand move round and round the white dial, and outside the train everything became dark, and Patrick saw the moon rise in his father's palm.

When his Aunt Joyce visited she took his chin in her hand and told him how quickly time passed.

'The year has flown by,' she said, examining his face. 'Here we are in September already, and the trees are starting to turn. What do you want to be when you grow up, Patrick?'

'A clockmaker,' he said, because it was the first thing that sprang to mind. 'I want to be an horologist.' And Aunt Joyce turned to his mother and said how wonderful, Doreen, a doctor in the family.

After that, Patrick felt obliged to borrow library books about clocks. He studied pictures of the Glockenspiel in Munich, with its feasting aristocrats and its jousting knights, and the Peacock Clock, with its chirping cricket and singing owl, and the Torre dell'Orologio in Venice, with its two bronze giants who struck the bell on the hour. His favourite, though, was the Strasbourg Cathedral clock, which was as tall as a three-storey building. Its parade of figures included the three wise men, who bowed before the Virgin Mary every hour, Jesus, who appeared regularly to bless the twelve apostles, and a metal rooster which crowed and flapped it wings at noon. Patrick saw pictures of birdcage clocks and coffin clocks and clocks that showed the phases of the moon. He saw the metal weights used to regulate time, and he learned how it was once measured by sun and by shadow, by the wastage of lamp oil, the burning of candles. He learned how fire clocks gauged the hour by the ashes produced, how the Chinese added mercury to their water clocks to stop time freezing. The first mechanical clocks were believed to describe the movements of the universe, the workings of God; they were toys for the rich, who had the least reason, in Patrick's opinion, to keep track of their days. Clocks could indicate the feast days of saints, the positions of stars; clocks could predict eclipses. Galileo, Patrick discovered, conceived of a pendulum by watching a cathedral lamp swaying and timing it by his own pulse. A French man called de Villayer used his sense of taste to tell the time at night: when he reached for the hour hand in the dark, his fingertip found one of twelve different spices positioned on the dial in place of numbers. At the end of the eighteenth century, Patrick read, an exporter sold defective cuckoo clocks to China. When the deceitful vendor arrived with a second cargo, he convinced his furious customers that the clocks were indeed in working order, and that the cuckoo was a very unusual bird which sang only at certain times of the year. When the season was right, he assured them, every cuckoo in every clock would open its throat and sing.

Then Patrick's friend Andrew was given a set of Meccano for his birthday, and Patrick was invited round to see it. *The finest hobby in the world for boys*, said the instruction manual. *Try building models entirely of your own design. In doing this you will feel the real thrill of the engineer and the inventor.*

'Mine makes five hundred and forty-seven models,' said Andrew. 'More, if you count the ones I invent myself.' And he told Patrick about a Belgian boy, Marcel de Wilde, who had constructed a model of the Barendrecht Lift Bridge in Holland.

'He'd never even seen it,' said Andrew. 'Only in photographs. It took eight thousand pieces of Meccano.' In the picture he showed Patrick, Marcel de Wilde was crouching beside the towering model, adding the finishing touches. He was wearing shorts, and a sleeveless pullover which did not look home-knitted.

'I've decided to make a clock,' Andrew announced a few days later. 'And I've joined the Meccano Guild. If I can get someone else to join, I'll be presented with a Recruiting Medallion.' He showed Patrick the Guild information in the manual. *Its primary object is to bring boys together, and to make them feel that they are all members of a great brotherhood, each trying to help others to get the very best out of life.*

'Well?' said Andrew.

'I'll have to ask my father,' mumbled Patrick.

Day by day, after school, the clock took shape. Andrew did most of the construction himself, but now and then he let Patrick help. When it was finished it would work just like a real one, Andrew said, and he showed Patrick an article about a Meccano clock made in France. It was nearly twice as tall as the man standing proudly beside it in the picture, and it displayed the movements of the planets, the time in all parts of the Earth, the day of the year. Inside there was one wheel, said Andrew, which made a complete turn once every two thousand, five hundred years. 'He got the idea from the clock at Strasbourg Cathedral,' he said. 'It's one of the most famous clocks in the world.' And he began telling Patrick about the bowing wise men, and the crowing metal rooster, and Patrick said nothing. He opened the instruction manual and read while Andrew talked and talked.

If you are ever in difficulty with your models, or you want advice on anything connected with this great hobby, write to us. We receive every day hundreds of letters from boys in all parts of the world, and each of these is answered personally by one of our staff of experts. Whatever your problem may be, write to us about it.

'There's nothing new about Meccano,' Patrick's father said that night. 'It's been around for years. I used to play with it myself. Terrible waste of time.'

'But it's the finest hobby in the world for boys,' said Patrick. 'And if you come up with your own models, you feel the real thrill of the engineer and the inventor.'

His father, however, refused to buy any.

It didn't take long to convert the house. To speed things up, Malcolm did a lot of the simpler work himself, after the builders had finished each day. He hardly had time to eat dinner. Ruth tried not to watch as he peeled off layers of wallpaper, the patterns as familiar as old photographs.

'It doesn't have to be perfect,' he said, sanding away cracked paint. 'We'll probably get students in. I should be finished in a few weeks.'

They lived upstairs for the first fortnight, while the bottom storey was done, then moved downstairs so the rest could be completed. They had to shift the Christmas tree, and the ornaments shook and fell as they carried it, leaving a trail of stars and bells and angels and snowflakes on the stairs. Daniel didn't mind the disruption; for him, whose memory was so short, it was an adventure, a camping holiday. The rooms filled with dust. It was astonishing, Ruth thought, how quickly a place could be divided in two.

In the new year, the day before they moved, Malcolm arrived home to find his wife kneeling in the hall, pulling the tape off sealed cartons. Their possessions surrounded her in unsteady piles: books, linen, newspaper-wrapped china. Malcolm had to pick his way through them to get to her.

'I thought we were meant to be packing,' he said, kissing her on the cheek.

'Where's Laura's bear, have you seen Laura's bear?' Ruth dragged a new carton to herself and plucked at the tape with her fingernails.

'I saw Daniel with it the other day. I thought you'd given it to him to play with.'

Ruth stared at him. 'Why didn't you say something?'

'I thought you'd given it to him. It was a nice idea, I thought.'

'Why didn't you ask me? You know how hard he is on toys. How rough he can be.'

Malcolm smoothed the end of the tape back down. 'He wasn't doing anything to it.'

'Remember what he did to the truck Mum gave him? And the koala Phil sent over?'

'I thought it was nice he had something of Laura's. He doesn't have anything of hers at all.'

Malcolm reached for his wife, but Ruth was rising to her feet and his fingers slipped down her back and into air. She strode towards Daniel's room, brushing a pile of crockery with her foot as she passed. A teacup teetered to the floor. The handle broke away and spun across the polished wood like a question mark. Ruth didn't stop.

'Daniel,' she said, very slowly, 'Mummy wants to find Laura's bear and I think you might know where he is.'

Daniel didn't look up from his colouring book. He was gripping an orange crayon in his fist and scribbling over outlines of houses, dogs, beach scenes. Everything was orange today; there were pages of it.

'Bear, bear, bear,' he said, colouring an ice-cream cone orange.

'Sweetheart,' said Ruth. 'Listen to me. What have you done with Laura's bear?'

Daniel stopped colouring. He studied the crayon, dug his thumbnail into the wax.

'Mummy will be very upset if he's gone missing. We're moving tomorrow, we have to find him. Do you know where he might be hiding?'

He shook his head.

Ruth crouched slowly down to the floor and took the crayon from him. 'Lying is a very, very bad thing to do,' she said, 'and you'll always be found out in the end.' She stroked Daniel's hair. He tore a corner off the ice-cream page and pressed it into a tiny, tight ball. 'Mummy knows when you're not telling the truth, sweetheart.'

Daniel rolled and rolled the paper pellet between his finger and thumb. 'He was all dirty,' he said. 'He needed a bath.'

Ruth swallowed. 'A bath.'

'His ears were dirty. And his tummy. I washed him.'

Laura's bear was balanced on the edge of the bath. A pool of water had trickled down the side and spread across the floor. The bear slouched, heavy with water.

'Oh,' whispered Ruth. 'Oh, oh no.' She knelt to the floor, touched the wet fur.

'Mummy, your knees are getting wet,' said Daniel.

Ruth didn't answer. The more she touched the bear, the more he curled in on himself. He couldn't even hold up his head.

'He's just a little kid,' shouted Malcolm. 'And you tell me often enough that he's different, that we need to be patient with him.'

'It's the dishonesty that bothers me,' said Ruth. 'The sneakiness. He wasn't going to tell me, you know.'

'It was an accident,' said Malcolm. 'Accidents happen.'

And Ruth was quiet then, because she didn't want to talk about accidents with Malcolm, not with Daniel so near by.

It was an accident, the man told himself. The girl shouldn't have offered him a ride if she didn't want company. She shouldn't have come inside for a coffee, giggling and flicking her hair, licking chocolate-cake icing from her fingers. She shouldn't have sat so close to him on the couch.

'Let go,' she whined, 'you're hurting me.'

'Hey,' he told her, 'I was only being friendly.'

'That's okay,' she said, without looking at him, 'but I really need to get going. I'm meeting a friend, we're playing tennis. My boyfriend.'

'It's bad manners,' said the man, 'not to finish your cake.'

Stories survive. Details survive. The colour of a jacket, threads of conversation or song, the aroma of a meal—such details can survive years. But Colette had no recollection of Patrick, despite searching her memories of overseas again and again. There was no evidence of him in her photo albums, nothing in her address book. At her new flat, which she'd found advertised on the library noticeboard right after New Year, she examined the pages where old addresses had been erased and new ones written in. Here and there under the glow of the naked bulb she could make out lost acquaintances, discarded friends, their indentations still visible. There was nothing to suggest a Patrick Mercer. How, she wondered, could he have left no impression? How could there be no trace?

When she was little, when Dominic was reading his survival books, his amazing stories of endurance, Colette wrote letters. She collected pen-pals all over the world—France, Italy, Australia, Fiji, Japan—and every few weeks she received news about pets, holidays, favourite colours. Twice a year, she also heard from her father, who never had much to say. His letters consisted of questions rather than news: was Colette doing well at school, did she like her new bike, how tall was she now. Writing back felt like homework. *If a father leaves a mother and flies to Australia when his daughter is five and his son is six, how old will they be by the time he returns?* The letters she looked forward to most came from America, from her cousin Nina. When Colette saw photos of her, she imagined herself wearing Nina's clothes, walking Nina's dog, playing Nina's piano. She saw herself in the Rocky Mountains, at the Grand Canyon. Nina had been born in America. Colette's Aunt Pam had married a Californian entrepreneur and had never been back to New Zealand.

'We're too boring for her now,' said Colette's mother. 'We're too ordinary.'

Every year, on her Christmas card—always a winter scene—Pam wrote that they would all be more than welcome to come and stay.

'She always likes to rub it in,' said Colette's mother. 'She knows we could never afford a trip like that. Not now.'

Although Colette had never spoken to her cousin, she imagined they would be instant best friends if they met. Nina sent her hologram stickers and bubblegum cards and instructions for magic tricks, which Colette performed for Dominic; usually her mother was too tired to watch. Once Colette received a letter from Nina that was blank apart from a handwritten note at the very bottom saying *Iron Me*. When Colette did so, writing appeared; words the colour of dead leaves covered the page. For a while she and Nina corresponded in lemon juice, composing acid little notes about the shortcomings of other friends, parents, siblings. Colette enjoyed deciphering Nina's invisible messages. There was nothing wrong with having secrets.

She hadn't stayed in touch with any of her pen-pals; she couldn't even remember their names. Nina had stopped writing too, or Colette had, she couldn't remember which. The only news of her came at Christmas, on Pam's snowy cards: Nina was dating a Swiss boy, Nina had been accepted for law school, Nina was seeing a lovely young dentist.

It was possible, Colette supposed, that Patrick was an old pen-pal. She wondered what he looked like.

She inspected her new, empty bedroom. The only piece of furniture in it was an oak wardrobe which was there when she moved in. She rather liked its leadlight windows, its iron key which turned almost silently. Not that she would ever lock it; to a burglar, a lock signalled valuables, and the door would most likely be smashed open. Colette had heard of too many antique boxes and cabinets and desks being destroyed in break-ins. She stretched out on her sleeping bag and admired the ornate white ceiling. She didn't mind that her things were still at Dominic's, that she had been sleeping on the floor for the past three nights. It was interesting, she thought, how little was necessary in order to survive. She ran her hand over the carpet. She could see where pieces of furniture had stood, where the pile had been thinned by bare feet.

'It's quite a find,' she told her mother. 'Dominic said I wouldn't find anything better. Well, he was probably keen to get rid of me.'

'And is it in a good part of town?'

'It's close to university and it's cheap, which is the main thing. I still haven't found any work.'

'And your flatmates, what are they like?'

'Nathan. He seems nice. He works most nights, so I haven't seen much of him.'

'And it's just the two of you, is it?'

'There's a downstairs flat as well, with three or four students. It's really very safe.'

During her first few days there, when Nathan was out, Colette explored the place, picking up objects that weren't hers and turning them over and over. Nathan, she decided, had reasonably good taste. He had chosen sensible spots for his furniture, arranged the kitchen intelligently. She read the bottoms of plates and bowls, where the maker's name was stamped into the clay, or painted on in delicate gold code. She opened the fridge and stared at the contents: frosted bottles, meats wrapped in foil, a jar of olives with garish red centres, a bowl of cold plums. She felt the chill from the open door pouring over her legs and her feet like ice water, like thawed snow, and eventually the fridge shuddered and hummed and she closed it again, her fingertips leaving misty prints on the chrome. She examined the contents of drawers, tugged at stiff handles. Unvarnished sections of the kitchen floor suggested the removal of peculiar, obsolete fittings. The flat was the upstairs half of a turn-of-the-century home, and in the lounge, a modern cupboard covered what must have been the internal staircase. The bathroom was immaculate: matching toilet, bath and hand-basin, streamlined cabinets, a border of pale shells stencilled just below the ceiling. In other rooms, though, fire surrounds had been covered with green and pink bricks, and at some stage the chimneys themselves had been sealed over. Colette considered the various casualties they might contain—spiders, mice, perhaps the bones of a bird.

Nathan had taken the best room: a circular turret that watched the harbour. His was the only view of water; the other rooms faced into the bush, suffusing the flat with a faint green light. It reminded Colette of a neglected aquarium. Outside her bay window, tree ferns and flax lapped at the glass. This was exactly the type of flat she'd been looking for, she told herself. Sometimes, though, when she traced the patterns on the high ceilings, the plaster scrolls and flowers, they seemed heavy enough to fall. She couldn't wait for her lectures to start.

When the rest of her things arrived from Dominic's, Nathan helped carry them down the track to the house.

'Be careful,' he said. 'Bones have been broken coming down here.'

'How do you know?'

'Look how steep it is. There must have been accidents.'

They piled the boxes in a corner of her room. Already it was looking cluttered. She could hear Nathan running up the track again, fetching more boxes, his footsteps thudding the damp earth. Things would be fine, she told herself, once she was unpacked and settled. She would get used to flatting. The rent was cheap; she was paying less than Nathan. Still, she envied him his round room, his unencumbered view of the sea. She pressed herself into a corner between the oak wardrobe and the wall. Every now and then, she discovered, when the wind blew enough to move the trees, she could make out a triangle of ocean. And for some reason, although she had never lived by the sea, this comforted her.

'It's a pointless space,' said Nathan from the doorway, and Colette jumped. 'You couldn't fit anything there.'

'I suppose not.'

'And if you move the wardrobe along any further it'll block the light, and it's dark enough in here already.'

Colette made a small noise of agreement. She didn't want to tell Nathan about her tiny ocean view, her secret patch of harbour. Instead she said, 'We had a corner like this in our old house, in the kitchen. The Naughty Corner. My parents didn't believe in smacking, so if we misbehaved we got sent to the Naughty Corner and had to stand facing the wall until we were sorry.' She could still remember the glossy green paint filling her vision, the furrows the brush had left, the smell of the hardboard underneath. She had stood there for hours sometimes. She'd never been sorry.

'She has to learn to share,' her mother said.

'She's five years old, Anne. It was only a chocolate bar.'

'It's the principle of the thing.'

Colette's father made his voice very quiet, steady. 'You're a fine one to talk about principles.'

'I can't imagine you misbehaving,' said Nathan. His eyes scanned the available space. 'We could always move it to that wall, I suppose,' he said, crossing the room in a couple of strides, testing the weight of the wardrobe.

Colette squeezed out of the corner. 'No,' she said. 'It's fine there, it's the best place for it.' Nathan was still grasping the wardrobe, hugging it to himself like an old friend. 'Honest,' said Colette. 'Do you want something to drink?'

There were no clean glasses, so she poured the juice into teacups. She eyed the unvarnished shelves which didn't quite meet the wall, the oddly shaped bench. 'They've really butchered the place,' she said.

Nathan laughed. 'I think he did a bit of a DIY job. They seemed keen to get it rented. I'm sure I was the first person they saw. Remember the Laura Pearse case?'

Colette nodded. It had been all over the papers when she'd been at primary school. Her mother had stopped letting her walk home by herself, insisting on picking her up from the school gates. All the parents had been anxious; every afternoon a row of cars snaked along the curb, each driver scanning the throng of emerging children, searching for their own. Colette and her friends had hated Laura Pearse for that.

'Dominic was allowed to sleep in the garden all night,' she'd whined to her mother, who muttered, 'That was before all this business.'

'They're her parents,' said Nathan. 'This is where she grew up.'

Colette stared at him. 'How horrible.'

'They seem all right, as far as landlords go. She'd like to get rid of the place completely, I suspect. She waited outside while he showed me round.'

Colette drained her cup, then pushed another box into her bedroom with her toes. It fell on its side, lolling on the mottled carpet. 'There's just one more. I should be able to manage.'

'It's no trouble,' said Nathan, and held the front door open for her. She had to squeeze past him to get out.

It was cool away from the sun, and the air smelled of crushed onionweed. As they made their way back down the track Colette could distinguish a few of the white, bell-shaped flowers in the undergrowth. Her foot slipped on a loose stone. She slid her fingers further under her side of the cardboard box, and a CD clattered over the moss.

'Chopin,' said Nathan, nodding, approving.

Beside them the house rose above the track, taking up the sky.

When she began to fill her new room with her old possessions, she discovered the cache of photos in her pack.

'Ha!' she snorted, and when Nathan appeared at her door she held them up to him like a fan. 'My mother,' she said, but she pinned the pictures to her bedroom ceiling anyway, where the plaster was flat. They surrounded the flowers and scrolls like an audience.

'Let me hold the ladder for you,' said Nathan.

Now and then Colette could feel his warm forearms against her calves as she moved above him, arranging her relatives, pieces of her history. She flinched then; she hadn't shaved her legs for days. As she climbed down she was careful not to touch him, holding her breath until she reached the floor.

'A comely bunch,' he said, looking up. 'Good genes.'

'Well, that's it for now,' said Colette, suddenly uncomfortable to be standing underneath her relatives with this stranger, but Nathan didn't move. 'I'll give you a call if I need any more help. Thanks.'

She inspected her work. Her great-grandfather stood behind his seated wife early in the twentieth century, grasping her shoulder as if to keep her from rising, his lips hidden by a fat moustache. His wife held Colette's infant grandfather stiffly on her knee. Dominic was graduating, all teeth and gown, leaning forward to have his hand shaken by the Chancellor. Colette's mother, hugely pregnant with Dominic, frowned at the camera, and, in a later, thinner picture, sat on a twiggy beach shielding her eyes with her hand. Colette herself didn't appear in many, except for the very tip of a nose—that may or may not have been hers—celebrating her mother's fortieth birthday. And a blurred shot of her in a too-small swimsuit, taken when she was about sixteen, running along the same twiggy beach. There were none of her father. She folded the ladder away. Her neck hurt.

They observed Colette at night, the people in the photos, and whispered to one another. Isn't she brave, they said, leaving home like that? The north is so big, it is so far away. But she made the right decision, oh yes. There is nothing down here for the young. She will do well. She will go far.

Only her mother was silent, squinting against the thin southern sun.

———

Dear Colette,
   Patrick's leg came out of plaster just before Christmas and the pins have taken well. The physiotherapist says he is her best patient, because he does everything she says and never answers back! He is lucky to have such wonderful care. Please keep writing and visiting; we're always delighted to hear from you, and we know Patrick is benefiting from it too. We are, of course, keeping all your letters and tapes so that he can enjoy them properly when he comes to.
   Many thanks and best wishes,
   The Friends of Patrick Mercer

'I wish I would get some mail,' said Nathan, eyeing the letter. 'Nobody ever writes to me.'

Colette slid the envelope under the newspaper and turned to the jobs page, moving her index finger down column after column.

'Two years of university, two thirds of a history degree,' she said, 'and I'm qualified for nothing. I won't be able to afford the textbooks, at this rate. Why is everything so expensive up here?'

'You could try the owners,' said Nathan.

Colette looked up, keeping her finger on the same spot. *Girls wanted,* said the ad, *must be open-minded, attractive, under twenty-five.*

'When he showed me round the place, he said they needed someone to mind their kid.'

'But I thought Laura—'

'They've got a four-year-old son. They had to take him out of day care. He's a handful, I think.'

'Call me Ruth,' said the woman, extending a hand. Colette supposed this meant she had the job, and smiled. The woman strode into a lounge with bone walls and swept her arm in front of her. 'This is where you'll be spending most of your time. He likes the polished floor. And that rug.'

Colette nodded and said, 'What a lovely colour scheme,' but the woman was already pushing open a door into the dining room. On a mahogany sideboard sat an incomplete tea set and a cluster of photographs framed in silver. There were one or two portraits— Daniel on a tricycle, Ruth and Malcolm on their wedding day— but mostly the frames contained landscapes. There were mountains and rivers, frost-covered plains, stony beaches. At the back, slightly away from the others, was a picture of teenage girl surrounded by trees and ferns. It was faintly familiar to Colette.

'I love your sideboard,' she said. 'They're hard to find in such good condition these days.'

'It doesn't go with the new house,' said Ruth. 'I'd like to get rid of it, but it belonged to Malcolm's mother.' She hurried past the gleaming mahogany. 'You've looked after children before?' she said over her shoulder.

'Oh, yes. I used to nanny for a family with a Down's girl.' A lie. 'And I often minded my little cousins, down south.' Also a lie.

'Mm. Until he starts school we'd need you from ten till three, Monday to Friday. From March, we'd want you for a couple of hours each afternoon. We're still renovating the kitchen, I'm afraid, so you'll have to pick your way around the ladders and things. My husband insisted on replacing the oven, he likes to bake bread. He has jelly with bananas most afternoons. Daniel, I mean. Sliced lengthways.'

'Of course,' said Colette, eyeing the sleek surfaces, the marble and chrome, and thinking of her mother's cluttered rooms.

30 January 2000
Dear Colette,

Please promise me you'll look after yourself. I read so much in the paper about the crime rate up there. It worries me. Please promise you'll be sensible. I'm sending you a cheque so you can do some self-defence classes. You must learn to protect yourself. I don't want you to walk around afraid all the time, but I just read so much these days.

Patrick was the only one at his school who looked forward to the dentist's visits. Some of the younger children cried when they heard she was coming to examine their teeth, to search for imperfections and decay. Miss Phipps assured them in a loud voice that there was no need to be frightened, really no need for such a noise, but it made no difference.

Unlike the girls in his class, with their small mouths and pale smiles, the dentist wore bright red lipstick and was always pleased to see Patrick.

'What a fine set of teeth,' she'd murmur as she leaned over him in her white tunic. 'This won't take long at all.'

Her own front teeth were flecked with gold and she hummed as she worked. Patrick found himself wishing for cavities.

His mother made sure they were at the surgery half an hour before his appointment. The dentist smiled hello at him, her golden front teeth sparkling, then ushered into her shiny room another boy. Patrick waited on a smooth wooden bench that squeaked and moaned whenever he moved.

'Don't fidget,' said his mother.

He studied the posters on the wall. His favourite one showed cartoon teeth racing one another to a giant bowl of fruit and vegetables. Underneath it were the words *Make sure you have a winning smile*. Behind the closed door, he knew, the other boy would be settling into the crook of the dentist's chair and waiting to be raised to her probe, her glaring light, her coin-sized mirror, her cool, cool hands. Now and then Patrick heard crying as the drill buzzed, and he knew then that the boy would emerge with a bee made of cotton wadding and gauze. The dentist fashioned them herself, and although he'd never cried in front of her, Patrick had three bees; a family group which hung from his bedroom ceiling. When he woke at night he could make them out in the dark, hovering above his bed like tiny ghosts. Occasionally, too, the dentist awarded samples of mercury. Patrick had never been given any, but his friend Andrew had. It shimmered and trembled in its little box, separating into dozens of beads no bigger than pinheads and then, always, clustering together again.

'My only desire is to be with him. My head buzzes with the demands of this world, but I long to devote my days to prayer. At the church I kneel for hours, watching the dark glint of the cross until I taste gold on my tongue. I rejoice to see the skin on my knees raw and sometimes broken; it is a sign of my devotion to him, and it deters my suitors.'

'I will be all things to you, my precious bride, my chosen one. I will never leave you. Resist the advances of earthly suitors, I am a jealous bridegroom and will tolerate no rivals.'

'I wish I had been born plain, so that no man would admire me. I refuse all adornment although I know it pains my mother. She talks of my wedding banquet, and asks me which flowers I should like to wear in my hair, and suggests roses for love, and ivy for fidelity. My suitor brings me gifts: small boxes of roses and violets, a silver ball, sprigs of lavender tied with ribbon, cooked figs. But I desire no man, no earthly gifts or pleasures.'

It was outrageous. Patrick wished they would stop; he couldn't bear to hear his translation mangled in their mouths. They had no feeling for the words, no sense of the music. They might as well have been reciting a shopping list. But on they read, not noticing his sighs, his grimaces.

When the bell rang, Miss Phipps clapped her hands and said, 'All right, children, quickly and quietly please.' There was a fire drill every few months, and the whole school had to line up in the courtyard and wait while the roll was called. 'Leave everything,' Miss Phipps commanded, tucking her handbag under her arm as Patrick's class filed outside. 'Take nothing with you, there's no time.'

Outside, the rows of children peered at the classroom windows, willing flames to appear, but when the bell had stopped ringing and they had all answered to their names, everyone filed back to class and life continued as before.

'He is closest to me just before sleep. I see him at the foot of my bed, and he casts a glow like a candle in a still room. He speaks to me as a lover, calls me by name, tells me secrets. Sometimes he is silent and watches me from the doorway, his eyes never leaving my face, and on other occasions I do not see him at all, but I feel his breath on my cheek and I smile. Some nights he does not come. Hour after hour I wait, examining my conscience to discover how I have offended him, why he is punishing me. I place my blanket on the floor, no matter how cold the weather, and I pray for him to come to me. Sometimes I think the walls will cave in with the force of my desire for him.'

'I want you to desire only me, to long for me above all else. You must shun all things pleasurable; you must fast and pray, and give away your fine clothes.'

'I think of him constantly. I do not eat; I am weary of this body and long to be free of it. Once I wore flowers in my hair, I covered myself with gowns of silk and braid and my shoes were stitched with gold. I had many suitors; they brought me gifts to win my heart.'

'I will give you a love so fervent that you will hunger for no one and nothing but me. I love you so much that I do not see your flaws. No husband loves his wife as perfectly as I love you.'

'My father asked me to bring him a loaf of bread, and as I was standing at the larder I felt the devil enter me. I do not know how long he had possession of my body, but when he left me there were no figs left; every one had been devoured. I wrapped the bread in my apron and hurried to my father, and when I opened it, the loaf was gone, and wildflowers fell at his feet.'

The thought began in the soles of Patrick's feet like a chill from cold ground. Up it crept, through his knees, his thighs, moving under the tight sheets and into his stomach, his chest. The thought was: they had been in his house. These strangers, these faceless readers had gone through his belongings like thieves. They had taken his translation notes and goodness knows what else. He closed his ears to their drone.

The man had left her on the floor while he thought. The car was the most urgent problem; it was in his driveway, squat and red like a boil. He pinched the bridge of his nose but he could still taste the blood, metallic in the back of his throat. He finished the girl's piece of chocolate cake. Then he reached into her pocket for the keys.

As he drove to the river an idea formed, clotting and congealing with every twist in the road. He parked under willow trees which curtained the view of the traffic. Their roots were like a net, he recalled, and could catch at feet, hold a swimmer under. He left the Mini locked, so it wouldn't look abandoned. Then he went back to his flat and the girl, and waited until it was dark.

Malcolm wrapped the chicken bones in newspaper while the sink filled with water. Around his fingers the rubber gloves felt like old skin, like something discarded, reptilian.

'I've found a girl, I think,' said Ruth.

He looked up from the steaming water. 'A girl? How old is she?'

'I don't know, twenty, twenty-one. A third-year student. Our new tenant, as a matter of fact.'

Malcolm kept scrubbing the pan in wide circles, although it was already clean. 'What's she studying?'

'Ah—history? Something artsy. She came round to meet Daniel today. Yes, history.'

'It doesn't have much to do with child care, does it? Nursing would be fine. Or medicine. Even education.'

'You'll scrub the non-stick off, you know,' said Ruth. 'It's poisonous underneath.' And she took the pan from him.

A twenty-year-old girl, thought Malcolm. Twenty-one, perhaps. She was little more than a child herself, and yet Ruth was happy to leave Daniel in her care.

'I'd already had a baby at her age,' said Ruth. 'And she seems very mature. And she's had experience with special-needs children, she used to look after a Down's girl.'

'She's a complete stranger,' said Malcolm. 'There have been cases.'

That night he thought about the 1988 eclipse. Although Laura had been excited about it, Malcolm hadn't bothered to see it. I have to go into the office, he told her, it's nearly the end of the financial year. I'll see it next time around.

Then, a few days later, when the house was full of police, reporters, acquaintances who wanted to help, when the phone kept ringing and ringing, he realised he'd never have another chance to see a total solar eclipse, not without leaving New Zealand.

Malcolm had helped the police look for Laura by day, and by night he had tried to think of new places to search. He had stayed up late while Ruth slept without dreaming, her eyelids stilled by a white pill. The house changed at night time; it shifted on its haunches, settled into the dark. Malcolm jumped at every creak. His teeth chattered, although it was the end of summer and still warm. In the lounge he kept the fire blazing, aware of the waste, and tried to remember every piece of lonely country he knew, every dense gully, every isolated beach. He went over and over different landscapes in his mind, recalling scenes he'd photographed on bush walks, family holidays, long drives.

'Have you tried here?' he asked the police, indicating on the map a new pocket of bush, a fresh stretch of coast, each time moving further away from the wind turbine.

'We think your daughter was simply in the wrong place at the wrong time,' the detective inspector told him, but he wouldn't say where that wrong place was.

'She liked it here,' said Malcolm, his finger covering valleys, national parks, miles of ocean.

Ruth's pills wore off early, before the sun was up, and she rose and made coffee and brought it to Malcolm. Then she bathed and dressed, and waited for news.

'The library told me to take as much time off as I need,' she said. 'Jan's rostered some more students on, isn't that kind?'

Malcolm's boss had also told him not to come into the office, but he still went to work for a couple of hours each day. It was important, he decided, to try and maintain a routine, and accounting was comforting work; there was always a right answer. At home, there was no routine. He was never asleep at the same time as Ruth. Since the day Laura went missing, their bodies understood different schedules; it was as if they were living in opposite time zones, foreigners to each other.

At the office, nobody knew what to say to him, so they didn't say much.

'We weren't expecting to see you here,' they mumbled. 'You mustn't come in till you're ready.'

At morning tea they talked about the weather, the traffic, the new photocopier. All newspapers were stuffed into briefcases, desk drawers. Laura's name was never mentioned, and the fact that she'd been missing for a week, a fortnight, almost a month was only obliquely acknowledged.

'How's Ruth?' they asked. 'Poor Ruth, such a difficult time for her. Do give Ruth our love, won't you?'

The receptionist, whom Malcolm had never liked, was especially cheerful.

'Nick's decided to buy the Alfa,' she said one morning, dropping a leaky teabag into the sink. 'We did another test drive last night. It's silver.' And everyone looked up from their mugs as if they were interested, because everyone had seen that morning's headline: *Hopes Fade of Finding Laura Alive*. The receptionist began describing the car, glancing over at Malcolm now and then. 'It's got power steering,' she said, 'and Nick said the colour went with my eyes, but I'm not sure what he meant because my eyes aren't silver, are they, they're amber.'

Even Phil was distant, avoiding Malcolm's office, rushing past him with his head down, his arms full of papers.

'You should stay at home,' he said. 'You should be with Ruth.'

There were many unconfirmed sightings. Dozens of people had seen girls resembling Laura, girls with her jersey or her hair. The police would investigate all of them, of course, but Malcolm and Ruth should know that most information from the public was useless.

'You'd be amazed at the calls we get,' said the detective inspector. 'All sorts. A lot of the time people just want to talk to someone, but they've no idea how difficult they make our job.' Malcolm and Ruth must try to keep things in perspective, he said, not get too excited.

Malcolm wasn't excited. He remained completely calm. He understood that every call counted, that any one of them might be vital. And he understood, too, that people wanted to feel useful in the face of calamity.

'Busybodies,' said Ruth. 'Don't they realise they're slowing everything down? Do they think the police have time for their false information?'

Malcolm still remained calm. He did not take Ruth by the shoulders and shake her, he did not raise his voice. There is no such thing, he said quietly, as false information. There is just information, and some of it is helpful and some of it is not.

The girls, though. The ones like Laura but not Laura. Malcolm tried not to think about them. He refused to imagine them safe at home with their families, going to school, going to the pictures. How dare they, he thought. How dare this group of imposters muddy the water, walk around as if they hadn't a care in the world, walk home alone at night if they wanted to, all the while looking like his daughter?

'We'll let you know if there's any news,' said the detective inspector, 'just as soon as there's any news at all. We're still following up a lot of the sightings.'

And Ruth said what Malcolm had been trying not to think: 'Does every girl look like Laura?'

On the train, on the way home from work a month after Laura had gone, or maybe six weeks, someone stroked Malcolm's hair. Just as they were pulling into a station, and passengers were buttoning coats and folding away newspapers and snapping shut the brassy clasps on briefcases, someone placed a hand on his head. He spun around in his seat but there was nobody behind him. People were filing out one by one, politely making their way to the overbridge that spanned the tracks like an insect. Some were already hurrying along its high metal back, striding towards crisp news tucked in the letterbox, casseroles in the oven. He recognised nobody.

Malcolm stared at the window as the train slid away from the station. Not at the platform, not at the grim track-side houses, but the window itself. It was a trick he used in order to keep his head clear; if he watched the view outside he felt the world was slipping away. He concentrated on the logo at the bottom of the pane: two fish, curled into one another in a cool embrace. Eventually, though, his eye picked out the space between them, and they were no longer two bowed fish, but a capital S, a trademark. *Pilkington's Safety Glass*, said a tiny inscription. S for Safety. Like the pair of silhouette faces that suddenly become a white vase, the fish were defined by emptiness, by the clear ocean between them. They would never touch.

The train crossed the river, the sound of the wheels amplified by the space beneath, thrown back by the water. Dozing commuters jolted awake at the noise. Whoever had touched his hair had done so by accident, Malcolm decided. Perhaps the train had jarred a little, perhaps there were too many passengers jostling to get out. Perhaps it wasn't even a hand that stroked his hair. Perhaps it was an elbow, or a shoulder, or maybe a wrist, the soft, blue-etched inside of a wrist.

Despite the discomfort it caused Ruth, Malcolm read the newspaper every day, and the habit continued even when it was obvious that Laura was never coming back. Most of the local news wasn't so bad. It was only every now and then that violent crime occupied the headlines, but those stories stayed with him.

One June night in 1994, a little boy went missing. Malcolm read about it in bed. He scanned the top section of the front page, sensed his skin shrinking at the words: *foul play suspected, parents distraught, a community waits*. He felt very cold and small all of a sudden, too small to be up so late and reading such dreadful things. He shifted his weight from hip to hip but couldn't get comfortable against the pillows; his body no longer fitted into the hollow it had created. Cold air rushed under the covers and Ruth stirred, pulled the sheet to her face. Malcolm saw it then, on the bottom half of the page: a picture of Laura. One he'd taken on a bush walk, just before it had started to pour with rain. And he thought, how strange, a little boy disappears and they print Laura's picture. It was a trick he would come to recognise over the years, a way of filling space, selling news. It wasn't just Laura they used; every time a child disappeared the ghosts of others were invoked. That was how Malcolm came to think of them, the whole gallery of lost children: ghosts. He studied the picture of the missing boy, the new ghost. He brought the page closer and closer to his face until the child was a mass of dots, grey, black, charcoal, his smile lost in the spaces, all meaning gone. He'd done the same thing with pictures of Laura, six years earlier, when she'd been the lead story. He'd held her too close, lost focus.

He put the paper away then. He didn't want to read any more that night, didn't want to keep folding and refolding Laura as he scanned stories about rugby and the road toll and heroic pets. All the while he'd been reading about the boy, he thought, Laura had been folded against his knees, rubbing off on the bedclothes, his every movement blurring her. He switched out his light. Ruth slept on, and he was glad. She'd been mentioning having a child, and although Malcolm had told her no, although he'd pointed out that she was forty-one years old and that no child could replace Laura, she continued to raise the matter. He climbed from the bed, backing out like a toddler, feeling for the far-away floor with his toes.

It was cold in the lounge, and every now and then the old sash windows shuddered. Ruth had wedged paper around them, but the panes still moved when it was windy enough. Malcolm put his hand to the glass. He hadn't been up at night like this for years. The garden was grey, blue, the moon a tusk. He contemplated writing to the family of the missing boy. He could tell them, for instance, to give themselves time, not to return to work too soon, not to put on a brave face for the sake of family, neighbours, colleagues.

When Malcolm took his hand away from the lounge window, there was a faint image of his palm against the glass, his fingers in bony sections just like an X-ray. In the kitchen he rinsed the newspaper ink from his hands and imagined he was washing away bruises. When he woke in the early morning, Ruth told him there had been an accident. She was pregnant. She thought it was a boy, and she liked the name Daniel.

The man knew they'd had another child. He saw an article in the paper when he was visiting his mother. The funny thing was, it didn't show the new baby at all. Instead, there was a half-page picture of the girl. It was quite a nice shot; she was wearing tennis gear, her little white skirt resting just at the tops of her thighs.

The night before Ruth returned to the library full-time, just after her son began school, she laid out her work clothes. She was exhausted; Daniel had taken a long time to fall asleep.

'I can play with you every day when I get home,' she'd told him. 'And Colette has all sorts of ideas for games, doesn't she? You have fun with her, don't you?'

She could feel Malcolm watching from the bed as she draped jackets over skirts, matched blouses to belts.

'You'll look fine whatever you wear,' he said. 'Anyway, you're only increasing your hours. It's not as if it's a new job.' And he went back to his newspaper.

Ruth hadn't read a paper in twelve years. She couldn't understand why Malcolm wasted so much time poring over the news; he read enough for two. Sometimes, in bed, he'd rap the newsprint like the skin of a drum, saying, 'Listen to this.' And Ruth would say, 'Not now, I really don't want to hear about it now. If the world ends, we'll know.' She had learned to fall asleep with the light on.

Once, in the middle of the night, she woke to find Malcolm still reading.

'You can't just bury your head in the sand,' he said, without lifting his eyes from the page. 'What do you do at the library? Doesn't Jan think it's strange?'

'They get things wrong,' said Ruth, 'or they make it up.'

It's hard to believe you could have a fifteen-year-old daughter, Mrs Pearse.
I was quite young when I had her.
Early twenties?
I was nineteen.

You're close in age—are you also close emotionally?
We discuss most things—clothes, school-work, movies, boys.
Boys?
She's a popular girl. She always had some boy or other ringing her.
Was there anyone special?
Laura goes out with lots of people. Like I said, she's a popular girl.
Popular.
Yes, very sociable.
Would you say she was mature for her age?
She reads a lot. She always did well at school.
And what about on weekends? Does she like getting dressed up, going to parties? Putting on a bit of make-up?

At the library, the news was treated with care. It was a fragile thing, something that could crumble to dust at the touch of human hands. It deteriorated in sunlight, needed protection from silverfish and moths and acidic fingertips. It was stored underground, tied into months, stacked into years. If an old issue was requested, Ruth would have to go down to the newspaper basement where, she knew, Laura was also stored. The papers towered well above her head, and she moved between the aisles with care. One false move, she imagined, and she would be buried.

She was far more at ease with the microfilm collection; there was something reassuring about the rows of white boxes. To Ruth they suggested order: pharmaceuticals, perhaps, or neat botanical specimens, or butterflies mounted on pins. Inside the boxes, each page of news was preserved, reduced to the size of a postage stamp. Illegible to the naked eye, but if necessary it could be reconstituted. And then it could be viewed like a movie, like something made up.

In the library staffroom there was usually a copy of the morning paper. Jan never offered it to Ruth, and never commented on its contents. When the new bindery assistant started work, though, she kept asking Ruth if she wanted a section.

'I thought you of all people would be interested in the news,' said Nicole. She peeled open a yoghurt and licked the foil like a child.

'What does that mean?' said Ruth.

Nicole frowned, glanced at Jan. 'Well,' she said slowly, 'your job. Periodicals.'

And Jan said, 'Oh, I'm sure Ruth has enough to do with newspapers without reading one at lunchtime.'

Some lies are not discovered. In 1994, after Laura had been missing for six years, Ruth lay in bed one weekend morning and said, 'I want another child.'

Malcolm opened his eyes, stroked her hair. After a moment he said, 'We've been through this, love.'

'I know. But I've changed my mind. I want another one.'

Malcolm's hand kept moving over her hair; long, even movements that might be used to calm a frightened animal. 'I'm not able to go through that again,' he said. 'I don't want a replacement.'

When she got up, Ruth took a long bath. She wet her hair and washed it, working the shampoo into a thick lather. As a little girl, Laura had loved bath time. She'd make shampoo horns with her fringe and squirm from Ruth's reach when it was time to get out, a slippery, soapy devil. Every now and then Ruth would let her use one of the bath pearls which sat in a cut-crystal dish on the windowsill: small soft globes filled with scented gel that melted in water. After they had dissolved and Laura had climbed from the bath, her hair hanging in rats' tails, her skin pimpling in the cold air, Ruth would pull the plug. Sometimes, as the water disappeared, she'd see the empty bath pearl as it floated to the drain. She caught one in her fingers once, and it felt soft and warm, like skin, and it smelled like oranges.

From the bath, Ruth could hear Malcolm making breakfast. Pancakes were his Sunday-morning speciality and sometimes, if he felt like it, he made soft brown bread for lunch. All her friends told her how lucky she was. Their husbands couldn't boil an egg, they said, not if their lives depended on it. When he made pancakes, Malcolm cracked eggs with one hand. It's all in the thumb, he'd say, tapping them on the side of the bowl and flicking them open, but Ruth had never been able to master it. She always crushed the egg, ruined the batter with shards of shell.

She didn't feel like pancakes that morning. She didn't feel like anything at all. The water around her had cooled to the temperature of blood. When you bake bread, Malcolm had told her, the water has to be at blood temperature, otherwise you kill the yeast. He'd shown her the test: you had to shut your eyes and lower your fingers into the bowl, and if you couldn't feel the difference between the air and the water, you were safe. Ruth closed her eyes and sank to rinse her hair, and it was true, she didn't notice the point at which her skin left the air. The water rushed into her ears and that was all she could hear, just the hush, hush of the water, and Malcolm was gone, he was miles away across the ocean.

She checked the day on the sheet of pills. Sun. They circled right around until they met their own beginning, a month of pills, a bracelet of days, and some days were real and some of them were only sugar. She shouldn't worry if she skipped a sugar day, the leaflet said, but taking them would help her maintain a routine. And Ruth did take the sugar pills, had done so for years, because she knew that it was useful to trick herself like this; it was safer. It also helped, the leaflet said, to tie the pill-taking to something she did every day, so Ruth took her pill, either real or fake, after she'd cleaned her teeth each morning. It was easy.

She pushed the Sun pill from the foil—it was a real one—and held it between her thumb and forefinger. It was tiny, no bigger than a cluster of cells. She listened. Malcolm was still busy in the kitchen. She dropped the pill down the toilet, where it floated for a moment then sank, a small pink pebble. Every morning from then on, after she'd cleaned her teeth, she flushed one pill away. She imagined them travelling through underground pipes and finally washing into the sea. Perhaps, she thought once, she was rendering certain sea-dwelling creatures infertile, but when she considered the sheer volume of water, and the smallness of the pills, she realised this was unlikely. So she kept flushing them, disposing of a lie a day, and Malcolm had no idea, none at all.

Ruth's salt theory began with the moon. She'd told nobody about it; she knew it had no scientific basis. She kept it to herself the way someone might keep a shell or a pebble tucked in a pocket, in the silky lining next to the heart, to be taken out every now and then and contemplated.

She first noticed the salt cravings when she was pregnant with Laura, and over the years she realised they intensified right before her period. Malcolm sometimes caught her munching potato chips or popcorn or salted peanuts and he'd say, 'Aha. That's enough of that, I think,' and take the food away.

'I am not a child!' Ruth had yelled at him once. He'd just looked at her, then taken the bowl of nuts and said, 'We'll just pop these away, shall we?'

From then on, she kept her salt consumption hidden. She knew Malcolm was only concerned for her health, but she couldn't explain to him the urgency she felt when the craving began. Besides, a little bit now and then didn't hurt. She sprinkled it on her meals before she took them to the table, before she'd even tasted the food. She kept packets of salted nuts in her desk at the library and, for emergencies, in her handbag. Sometimes, as she passed the kitchen, she dipped her fingertip in the salt and licked it, as if tasting cake mixture.

One restless night, she'd risen from bed and paced round and round the turret, eating cashew nuts. She'd been flushing her pills away for almost three months. Laura had been gone for six years. Another year and she'd be officially dead. Ruth could see right down the hillside; the roofs of the houses were propped-open books, each containing a different story. The moon was almost full. From the turret she could see the silvery ocean. Turrets, she recalled, were built on Victorian houses so wives could watch for their husbands returning from sea. She felt the salt gritty on her fingers, working its way under her nails, and when she finished the bag of nuts she held her hand up to the light. The salt grains were luminous. The moon, she thought, controlled the salty tides. Her body retained water right before a period. The more salt she consumed, the more water she retained. Laura could be in the sea somewhere, under the glowing moon. She licked her fingers.

She could never put her theory into words. It existed at a physical level, like the body's knowledge of pain or heat. Malcolm wouldn't understand. That was all right. By the next week, she was pregnant.

Daniel was fourteen days overdue.

'We'll have to induce you,' the doctor said, and Ruth had no choice. As they wheeled her into the stuffy delivery room she recalled something she'd owned as a child: a glass globe, the size of an orange. It was filled with water, except for a tiny bubble of air at the top, like the space in an egg. Inside, surrounded by pine trees, stood a plastic Santa Claus. Ruth didn't know who had given her the globe or what had happened to it, but she remembered shaking it and shaking it at Christmas time, making it snow in summer. And she remembered believing that each night, when no one was looking, the Santa floated to the top and breathed, taking into his plastic lungs enough air to last a day.

They gave her invisible gas for the pain. Malcolm held her hand and told her everything would be fine, but Ruth didn't want the baby to be born. She wanted to keep him just a little longer.

And then she was holding him, her yellow baby, his skin the colour of sunlight, and the nurses were taking him and tagging the crease of his wrist and saying he'd be fine after a few sessions under the lamps, and Malcolm was stroking her hair.

'You've done so well,' they told her, plumping pillows and tightening sheets. 'You should be very proud of yourself.' And although they were smiling and Malcolm was calling her darling and photographing her and his son rather than endless icy landscapes, she knew she was holding a flawed child, an unlucky exception.

She and the baby had to stay in hospital for a week following the birth. Nothing serious, Malcolm told people, just a little jaundice. Flowers filled her room. She lay for hours gazing at roses and carnations, at pollen-filled daisies, sprigged curtains, buttercup-yellow walls. The nurses wore enamel name-tags in the shape of dinosaurs or sunflowers or pieces of fruit, and the doctors encouraged her to use their first names. The baby cried and cried. Ruth longed for a blank room, plain bedding, anonymous staff. Somewhere as empty as an unmarked page. The place where she'd had Laura had been like that.

Friends and acquaintances visited and fussed. They commented on her hair, her complexion, told her she looked wonderful. No one lingered. No one mentioned the fact that, on her sixth day in hospital, her daughter had been missing for seven years. You need your rest, they said. We mustn't keep you. Some deposited gifts on the edge of the bed and backed out the door, explaining they were no good with hospitals.

'If there's anything else we can do,' they said.

No. There was nothing.

Seven years. Ruth had thought she'd feel worse, but she was too exhausted; the baby had been crying non-stop for the first six days of his life. Now, though, he was silent.

'Tired himself out, has he?' said the nurse. 'Maybe Mum can get some rest too.'

Ruth drifted in and out of sleep. The bundle in the cot lay so still that whenever she woke she had to check he was still there.

After an insipid lunch, she made her way down the corridor to the snack machine and bought potato chips and nuts. Today, she decided, she would give in to her salt cravings. She knew it was unwise. She knew how it got into the blood, how it could clog the arteries, damage the heart, but she needed it. She ate as she made her way back to bed and each time she swallowed she felt a tide rushing through her, shaking in her head like waves. In this country, there was no escaping the sea. She remembered her schoolteachers telling the class what to do if a tidal wave hit. The telephone book had even carried tsunami advice, printed in capitals and accompanied by cartoon waves, tiny palm trees: MOVE TO HIGH GROUND. KEEP AWAY FROM STREAMS FLOWING TO THE SEA. NEVER GO TO THE BEACH—IF YOU SEE THE WAVES IT IS TOO LATE TO ESCAPE THEM. Ruth knew that such warnings were useless, that no one could survive the ocean. She chewed and swallowed, chewed and swallowed. Was salt water bleaching the bones of her daughter? Was it corroding her fingernails, her painted toes? Was Laura in the sea?

Although it hurt, she ran back to her room. The baby was fine, of course he was. He hadn't moved. Even when Malcolm came to visit, and woke them both, the baby didn't jostle his arms and legs and screw up his face.

'Is there something wrong with him?' said Malcolm. 'It's like he's a different child.'

There were more bouquets waiting at home. They occupied the hall, the lounge, the bedroom. Some had even been placed, unwisely, in the kitchen, and were already wilting.

'I borrowed some vases from Mum,' said Malcolm, sliding Ruth's neat blue suitcase on to the bed. 'I'll unpack for you, shall I?' And he flicked back the clasps.

The bundle against Ruth's chest started to stir then. It opened its tiny dark eyes for a moment and moved its lips. It dribbled.

Ruth smiled at it. 'Daniel,' she said. 'Are you a Daniel?'

Malcolm held up a nightdress. 'Machine or hand wash?'

There was some interest in the birth. Two women's magazines requested an interview with Ruth, and three newspapers phoned.

'Thank you,' Malcolm told them, 'but this is a family time.'

One paper did a story anyway, a weekend feature announcing *Life Goes On.*

'This is a family time,' says father Malcolm Pearse, but what sort of family life is possible when a daughter has disappeared without trace?

There was a photograph of Laura playing tennis. It covered half a page.

Malcolm telephoned the paper from work. He was calm, he was polite. He wouldn't give them another story, no *Father's Anguish* or *Wounds Still Raw.* He hoped he made himself understood.

After that, he and Ruth and the new baby were left alone. They no longer struggled to pretend things were normal, because they were. Meals were cooked and consumed, clothes washed, worn and washed, curtains opened and drawn. Ruth took leave from the library to look after Daniel, Malcolm received a substantial pay-rise. They renovated the bathroom, bought a bigger car, a new cat. They went on holiday to Bali and Hong Kong; they spent a week in Sydney. Daniel went to day care, Ruth returned to work part-time. Things were so normal that they no longer noticed the sly staring in the street, or if they did, they no longer mentioned it to each other.

Paper is not strong. It can be cut, torn, crumpled, burned. It can be ruined by water, consumed by silverfish, pitted and corroded by moths and worms. It can be wrapped around gifts to embellish good intentions and thoughts that count, then ripped open in a moment and discarded. It can be blown away by a breath of wind.

In the silent dining room, the night before she returned to work full-time, Ruth stared at the bush-walk photograph. It was a piece of paper, nothing more. It wasn't even a good likeness. The dense trees and ferns had made it overexposed, and Laura looked paler than she really was. Her freckles were dissolved, the smattering of spots on her forehead had disappeared and her tiny eyelid scar was invisible. Laura had liked it; she'd called it her cover-girl picture and pinned a copy to her wall.

'Do I really look like that?' she'd asked, so Ruth had said yes, because she wanted Laura to think herself beautiful. But it wasn't a good likeness. She should have told the police, insisted they use a different shot. It turned her daughter to moonlight, this picture.

Ruth went to the kitchen. The non-stick pan hung on its special hook, the kettle rested on its stand, the copper-bottomed pots glinted like gongs in the dark. Everything was in the right place. Even Daniel, she told herself, was where he should be, tucked up in bed, safe. He would come to love Colette. She would be like a big sister. In the pantry Ruth found half a packet of peanuts, and she swished them around in her mouth. The salt dissolved and trickled down her throat and she realised she wasn't hungry at all. Peanuts were one of the most high-energy foods, and energy was the last thing she wanted now. She wanted calm, the ability to lie still. She wanted her feet to stop twitching, her fingers to stop flickering as if practising scales. She wanted to slow herself down. She spat the peanuts into the sink. They rattled like teeth.

When she arrived home the next day, Ruth found Colette sitting at the kitchen table reading a magazine. The breakfast dishes had been done, the bench tidied and the tea-towel placed precisely on the rail.

'Where's Daniel?'

Colette looked up. 'Hi! I'm finding out how to remove yellow stains from a wedding dress.' She held up *Woman's Day*.

'Is he on his own?'

'He's asleep,' said Colette. 'He even suggested it himself. He was no trouble.'

'Asleep?'

'Mm. Can I get you a coffee?'

Ruth was already heading towards the hall. 'Please,' she called.

In Daniel's room the curtains had been drawn and Ruth could just distinguish her son's face. She held her cheek close to his mouth to feel his breath. Then she tucked the sheet around his chin and returned to the kitchen.

'So how was the first full day back?' asked Colette.

'It was fine.' Ruth watched the girl opening cupboards, arranging cups, pouring water. It was odd that she seemed to know exactly where to find everything; in this new house, Ruth herself was still learning the co-ordinates of her possessions. 'Quite good, actually. But they're computerising the accounts system at the moment. It's really slowing us down.'

'It'll be worth it, though,' said Colette. 'It'll make life much easier.'

'I suppose so,' said Ruth, remembering when the library had no computers at all. She thought of the old card catalogue, the rows of dark wooden cabinets. They were in the basement now—level zero—along with all the books that hadn't been issued for twenty years or more, and the newspapers. Jan had asked her to go down there that afternoon for an urgent request, and she'd pulled open one of the long, narrow drawers. She'd supported its weight with one hand and had run the other along the cards, across their furred edges. The library still had to produce a new card for every new book, in case the system went down. A power cut, even one blown fuse and the whole thing could be demobilised.

I'm so glad you've enrolled in self defence, wrote Colette's mother. *When do you start? Soon, I hope. And how wonderful that you've found a part-time job, I imagine you'll need a bit of extra pocket money now that you're paying rent. They sound like a nice family. Such a shame about their daughter, I remember her being in the news and how worried we all were, still you just never know what life has in store for you, perhaps their little boy is some comfort. How are you finding your lectures? What is Nathan studying? I'd like to hear about your new friends. I suppose with work and study and now your evening classes you don't have much spare time, but I'd love to hear from you if you do get a moment.*

There was one man in the class. Colette wondered what his reasons were for being there; for one ridiculous moment she imagined him planning an attack, researching the techniques that could be used against him. He was a slight person, and she noticed that all the other class members were especially gentle when paired with him. Even the tutor, who often chose Roland for demonstrations, was less aggressive with him than with any of the women.

In one exercise, when he grabbed his partner from behind, the woman—a young mother—simply crumpled. For a moment nobody knew what to do, least of all Roland. He let her go and stood back in surprise as she sank to the floor. The other pairs froze in various positions of attack and defence while the woman lay whimpering on the padded mat. Then the tutor strode over to her and patted her on the back, saying, 'All right, then.' The woman stopped coming to classes after that.

One morning Colette woke to find her bed covered with photographs, as if there had been a quiet snowfall during the night. As she inched back the duvet she discovered that some pictures had worked their way into her bed. She had been sleeping on them, and when she picked them up in her weak, morning hands she found that they were warm, that they had taken warmth from her own skin. She thought of the landscapes on Ruth's sideboard, the silver-framed stretches of snow and ice. She shook her sheets then, and beat her mattress to be sure she hadn't missed any pictures. As she bent to make her bed she felt something sharp cutting into her side. When she lifted up her pyjama top there was a photograph stuck to her skin. She peeled it away. Herself, aged about sixteen, running. And it was then, while she was still half asleep, that she remembered where she had seen the other photo on Ruth's sideboard: it had been in the papers and on the news for weeks, many times, years before.

'Of course,' said the lecturer as he distributed the essay questions, 'at this level you're expected to start thinking for yourselves. You're welcome to come up with your own topic, but you'll need to discuss it with me before mid-year.'

Colette scanned the photocopied sheet and found nothing that interested her. The birth of the trade union movement, the Depression, the perceived threat of Japanese invasion during World War II: she had exhausted every one of the topics before. She wanted to learn something fresh about the past, to feel the texture of new information between her fingers. It was possible, she supposed, that the questions were deliberately dull, designed to bore students into exercising their creativity. While the lecturer talked about the unacceptability of hand-written work and the impossibility of extensions without a medical certificate or proof of bereavement, Colette invented possible topics. She imagined turning up at his office to discuss Hairstyles of the Suffragists, or Twentieth-Century

Representations of the Sheepdog, or From Dripping to Vegemite: an Analysis of Post-Colonial Sandwich Spreads.

At the library the microfilm collection filled shelf after shelf. Colette weaved in and out of the rows as if negotiating a maze, reading dates, names of newspapers. They suggested an almanac, a comforting natural order: there were *Stars, Times, Evenings, Mornings.* She thought of the amount of news the boxes contained, tried to visualise the robberies, sales, wars, elections, murders, births. Every row was the same as the last; a brick wall, well over her head. She slowed down in 1988. She couldn't remember what time of year Laura had disappeared, but suspected it had been in the summer. She recalled stuffy car-rides, her mother tuning the radio to the news and shushing her and Dominic at any mention of Laura's name. Colette stopped in the second week of January. The time of her own birth; it seemed as good a place as any to begin.

The library was totally quiet. There were no gossiping groups filling in time between lectures, no patient explanations of chemistry or statistics. Colette heard nothing, not even the sound of pages turning. As she withdrew the box she felt uneasy. Who was she, after all, to be poking around for information? Ruth would be horrified if she knew. She'd never once mentioned Laura; the photograph in the dining room was the only clue that she'd ever been part of their family. Colette's hand brushed the metal shelf and she felt a snap of electricity. She had always been susceptible to shocks. If she brushed her hair for too long it floated about her head like seaweed. She avoided wearing man-made fibres. Once, when she'd removed a polyester jersey in the dark, she'd seen sparks leap from her body.

'Touch the glass when you've opened the door,' her father told her as she climbed from the car. 'To ground yourself.' But then he left for Australia, and there was no one to tell her how to protect herself, and although his car-window trick still worked, Colette didn't understand why.

She should go home, she thought, just leave the reels of newspapers on the snapping shelves. But she was holding the January box now, and there was a gap in the row, a hole in time big enough to slip a hand between, small enough, perhaps, to stop up with a palm. She stood very still and listened, and everything was quiet, of course it was. She was in a library doing some research, because that was what students did, and she was studying history, after all, and had every right to investigate the past, and the ground had not opened beneath her feet, and the sky had not fallen in. She took the box and ran and ran past walls of white bricks, through tight corridors of news.

Colette switched on the viewer and loaded the film, easing it between the squares of glass. They reminded her of laboratory slides, and she thought of school science classes, where she had seen skin cells and hair and grains of pollen under a microscope. She had been amazed at their secret shapes, and also a little afraid of the complexity of the world.

There was a dial which controlled the speed of the film, and she discovered how to move from page to page slowly enough to read headlines and skim pictures, how to pause on a particular story and how to position it for photocopying. If she felt like it, she found, she could send the reel spinning, the back-lit pages a blur of grey, whirring past too quickly to make sense. Perhaps, she thought, this was something like the images people saw as they died.

She didn't find Laura until the beginning of March. After that, though, with each issue, her pictures grew larger, the headlines blacker. Several times the photograph from Ruth's sideboard appeared; Laura stared out from the bush, an older version of Daniel. And soon, a week or so later, there was a photograph of Ruth and Malcolm. They were sitting in a room Colette recognised as her own, but the walls were covered with tennis posters and dog posters and the bed was wedged head-first into the arc of the bay window. Ruth held a toy bear on her lap. Colette fed the viewer with silver coins, and in a matter of seconds she received warm, dark pages that were difficult to read, but not impossible.

As she descended the stairs she saw Ruth one flight down, chatting to a colleague. She turned on her heel and ran back up, then caught the lift to the exit level, avoiding eye contact with the other students. Nobody took the lift one floor, especially not down. For a moment she considered affecting a limp, but thought better of it. Her avoidance of Ruth was bad enough; there were only so many lies a day could accommodate. As she left the stairwell she heard Ruth's voice floating down from the landing.

'She's a third-year student,' she was saying. 'He seems to have taken to her. As a matter of fact, he told me he wants to marry her. Of course, it's early days yet.'

Colette hurried away, the copies of Laura heavy in her bag.

'I'll be God.'

'You were God last time.'

'Which means I'm familiar with the role. A certain consistency must be maintained.'

'It might help Patrick if we swap.'

'Now, page twelve, wasn't it. Here we are. No bread can satisfy this longing, no water can quench your thirst for me. Page twelve. Up the top.'

'Only if we swap next time.'

'Yes yes, we will, next time.'

'Promise.'

'I promise. Page twelve.'

'Right—food and wine taste only of earth. I fast until I am dizzy with bliss and can hardly move. My father tries to tempt me with plates of figs and nuts, but I refuse all nourishment.'

'Ignore those who advise you to eat; their only goal is to distract you from me. Continue to devote yourself to prayer, and I will come to you.'

'My stomach is a dark traitor, vulnerable to the devil's suggestion, and I fear it constantly. When the devil seizes me, my own will is snuffed out. I watch my body eat as if watching someone else, someone who is familiar to me but over whom I have no power. Even though my stomach threatens to split and my jaw aches from chewing and my throat is raw from swallowing, I cannot stop. My eyes terrify me; they take on a glassy lustre, like those of a corpse.'

'My love for you is a fire. You are right to spurn the attentions of earthly suitors; their tongues are made of glass, their promises fragile things, transparent and easily broken. Until one is able to live in a state of perfect love, every love should be held suspect. I will hold you so close you will forget your own body.'

'He holds me so close to his body I cannot feel my own flesh. I am told I lie on the cold stone floor and am seized by convulsions, but to me these moments are very still; he is the centre of my desire and I cannot move for pleasure.'

'By sustaining the body, you sustain corruption and kill the soul, but if you fast and pray, I will reward you.'

'A group of noblemen came to my father's house and asked to see me at prayer. My mother was uneasy about it, but told me she could not refuse such powerful men. Because I love her I relented, and the men came to my room. I thought they would be content to watch me from the doorway, and perhaps to pray a little, but they entered and began to touch my dress, my hair, my face. One of them fell to the floor and kissed my feet, while another demanded I kiss his hand. Who am I to kiss a nobleman? Yet I did as he asked.'

'I give you a golden ring to wear to show you are my bride. Each day at noon I will send you an angel who will feed you with his own hands.'

'My mother insists I eat. She treats me like an infant, swooping morsels towards my mouth as if they were birds, and twittering and cooing to me. But still I refuse this food which has taken flight; if I ate it I fear it would spread its wings inside me.'

'Your suitors will fall away from you like dead leaves, but your true bridegroom will wrap his promises around you, and you will feel warm, as if sitting by a fire.'

'I wear his ring on my finger. My body aches with longing for him and my days are filled with waiting. I am consumed with waiting.'

'In you I have hidden a great treasure. Others may—'

'Colette,' said Patrick.

'—try to tempt you away from me, but—'

'Shh! Did he say something?'

'Colette,' said Patrick.

'I think he said Colette.'

'I've been sending the newsletter to a Colette. She was in his address book.'

'You never told me that.'

'Why would I?'

'He had an affair with her, on a trip to New Zealand in 1976. He told me about it years later, after quite a few glasses of wine. He thought it wouldn't matter by then. She was married, of course.'

'So was he.'

'Quite.'

'Patrick? Patrick, can you hear us? Are you there?'

28 February 2000
Dear Colette,
    You'll be happy to know that Patrick has started to regain consciousness. Although he is still quite drowsy, he is a little more alert each day and is having speech therapy. He also has movement back in his hands, and is being taught to write all over again.

Perhaps because there were two in his surname or perhaps because it was easy to form, lower-case e was Patrick's favourite letter. It suggested an ear open to secrets, the coil of a shell, the fluttering start of life. To begin with, his letters were as shaky as a child's. The pen was too thin in his hand, like a piece of straw, a matchstick, and it slipped and slid from his grasp, covered the page with blue nonsense. All colours were laid on twice in manuscript illustrations, he recalled. *At first very thinly, then more thickly; on letters but once.* He formed another e, wishing he could write in a colour other than blue. He thought of the medieval instructions for tempering Spanish green: pure wine was added, with a little juice of the iris, cabbage or leek if shadows were needed.

'Good,' said the physiotherapist, as if she could read his scrawl, 'very good.'

The next time she came she brought him a pen thickened with rubber grips, swollen like the spring bulbs his mother had planted each autumn.

'Now,' she said, 'I want you to write your name.'

The first time Patrick had learned to write, it had been a struggle.

'His hand is lazy and untidy,' Miss Phipps told his parents. 'If he doesn't show significant improvement he'll be held back a year.'

Every day after school, Patrick wrote out alphabets, copying the letters from a master page provided by Miss Phipps. He bent his face so close to the paper he could hear his own breathing. He made his letters so perfect it became difficult to tell which was the master page and which his copy. That was what his mother said, and Miss Phipps was pleased with his work too, but his father made him keep copying.

'One more,' he'd say, peering over Patrick's shoulder at the completed alphabets. 'We can't have you falling behind.'

Patrick kept writing until his father said he could stop; sometimes he was still copying when it was dark.

'Am I dumb?' he asked one evening, and his mother, who never shouted, shouted, 'Who told you that? Did you say that, Graham?'

'We can't have him falling behind, Doreen,' said his father.

Patrick wasn't held back, though. In fact, he was top of his class that year, and every year, and he devoured any book he could lay his hands on.

'You've molly-coddled him, Doreen,' said his father. 'We've got a sissy on our hands.'

In the new house, Ruth had found a space for almost everything. Sheets and towels were folded to fit new cupboards, Daniel's bike was slotted in the garage with Malcolm's gardening things, the ironing board had its own hook. The spare bedroom held a single bed and a chest of drawers suitable for a guest to use, and Malcolm's mother's tea set, minus one cup which had been broken in the move, was displayed on the dining-room sideboard. The silhouette picture, however, was a problem. Although it had been one of Ruth's favourites, it was wrong in this open, airy house.

One day when Laura was off school with chicken pox, a woman appeared on their doorstep. She looked about eighty, Ruth thought, although her voice belonged to someone much younger.

'I am a silhouette artist,' said the woman. 'Is there anyone you'd like me to portray? Would you like to see some of my work?' She opened a crumpled plastic bag bearing the words *Mansfield's— Jewellers of Distinction*. 'My portfolio,' she said, fanning several silhouettes before Ruth like a deck of cards. There was a little boy, his high child's forehead framed by curls. There were two young women face to face, mirror images of each other. 'Twins,' said the woman. 'The space between them makes a vase, do you see?' Another depicted a girl in a lace blouse, every ruffle picked out, wisps of hair curling at the nape of her neck.

'They're very good,' said Ruth.

'I also do pets,' the woman said, 'provided they don't talk back. I had to do a budgie once. "I love you," it kept saying. "I love you, I love you, do you love me? I love you."'

'We don't have any birds,' said Ruth, 'just a labrador and a very old cat.' She studied the young boy. Even the eyelashes were distinguishable. 'These really are beautiful.'

The woman withdrew another silhouette from the bag; her trump card. 'Have a peek.' It depicted a middle-aged woman with short, wavy hair, a straight nose, a long neck. It looked familiar to Ruth, but she didn't know why.

'Well?' said the woman.

Ruth frowned, shook her head.

'I shouldn't be telling you this, really—' the woman glanced over her shoulder '—but Her Majesty was one of my best sitters. Never moved a muscle.'

It couldn't hurt, Ruth decided. Laura had been bad-tempered all morning, pronouncing as boring every activity her mother suggested. She'd tied her Barbie doll's hair in knots, broken a glass, scribbled across the pages of two library books. She'd stabbed herself with her embroidery needle, dotted blood across her bedspread.

'Come in,' said Ruth. 'My daughter could do with the company.'

At the kitchen table the woman produced a sheet of black paper from her Jewellers of Distinction bag. She took Laura's face in her hands, combed soft fingers through her bed-mussed hair.

'What a pretty girl you are,' she said. 'You're going to be quite something in a few years.'

Laura was shy at first and wriggled in her seat, scratched her spots.

'You'll only make them worse,' said Ruth, and Laura pulled a face and scratched even more at her arms, her chest, her back. 'Do you want some more ointment? Shall I get the ointment, would that help?'

'It smells funny,' said Laura, frowning and picking at a spot on the back of her hand where the pink cream had caked and dried.

'Don't scratch, love, you'll leave scars. And try to sit still for the nice lady.'

The silhouette artist gently turned Laura's head to the side so she was facing Ruth. 'Such a strong profile,' she said. 'Such regal lines.'

'What's regal?' said Laura. The woman was rummaging in her plastic bag and appeared not to have heard. 'Mum, what's regal?'

'It's like royal, sweetheart.'

'Do I look like a princess?'

Ruth took in her daughter's pallid skin, the shadows under her eyes, the swollen spots, the cracking bottom lip. 'Yes, sweetheart, you do.'

The old woman took a pair of very fine nail scissors from her bag, the kind with curved blades that follow the shape of a fingertip. Then she began to cut. She held the paper right up close to her face, and Ruth couldn't see her as she worked, only her hands as they trimmed away strips of paper and let them fall like black leaves to the floor, and Laura stopped talking and stopped scratching and was very still, and although she was looking straight at her mother, Ruth had the impression she was looking right through her, seeing something else entirely: herself as a princess, a royal beauty.

'My daughter had hair like yours,' said the woman.

As the black fell away Ruth saw the shape of Laura forming, and the silhouette artist's own face becoming more and more visible. She turned and turned the piece of paper, adding more detail each time: the eyelashes, the flared ends of the hair. With one last cut she defined the curve of the throat, then placed the finished silhouette on the table.

'Is that me?' said Laura, smiling. 'Is that what I look like?'

'We hardly ever see ourselves in profile,' said the woman. 'It's always a surprise. Like hearing your own voice.'

'That's you all right,' said Ruth. And it was.

After the woman had gone, Ruth cleared away the paper from the floor. Smaller scraps covered the table top, as fine as hair, and Ruth recalled how, as a girl, she had always taken her own clippings home from the hairdresser's. She hadn't liked the thought of leaving behind pieces of herself. She cupped her hand and swept the paper cuttings into her palm. These would make an image of Laura too, she thought, if she pieced them all together. A negative.

The silhouette artist would be dead by now, Ruth supposed. She held Laura's likeness against the walls of the hall, the lounge, the dining room, but it was wrong. It was nothing but a shadow; a black hole where her daughter once had been. She couldn't look at it.

A few days later, Daniel brought it in from the garage. 'Look what I found,' he said. 'It was on the ground.'

Before Ruth could answer, Malcolm was saying, 'Do you like it, Daniel? Would you like to have it?' And Daniel was saying yes please, yes please, and they were positioning it on his wall, above his bed, where it hung like a night-time window. Ruth sometimes heard him talking to it, saying good night or good morning, telling it stories. Malcolm never observed these odd little speeches, and Ruth never mentioned them, but she couldn't shake the feeling that Daniel was filling the frame with himself, taking over the outline of his sister.

Colette had already thrown her jacket on her bed and had started brushing her hair when she saw the letter. It was propped against her pillow, as white and smooth as the clean sheets, the stamp perfectly aligned, her name and her old address dead centre.

14 March 2000
Dear Colette,
If you are one of the friends who has been to visit Patrick, we'd like to thank you for your help. He has been making real progress over the last couple of weeks and his doctors are confident he will continue to improve. Please keep coming, even if it's for just a few minutes
We're also grateful to those of you living further afield who have sent letters. We read them to Patrick over and over—he never gets tired of listening to them.
A special thanks to those friends who have made donations to Patrick's fund. The money will make a big difference to him when he is out of hospital.
Warm wishes to you all,
The Friends of Patrick Mercer

Colette slipped the letter into her dressing-table drawer with the others. There was quite a pile of them now, all the same size, hidden like love letters under coiled tights, cotton pyjamas. At the back of the drawer was a pouch tied with ribbon—a sachet of lavender she'd bought at a craft fair with Justin because she'd wanted a memory of the day. She placed it next to the letters, then covered them with soft cotton, as if tucking someone into bed. Poor Patrick. She loathed hospitals, with their sour, sterile smell. The scent of lavender reminded her of summer, gardens heavy with bees and sun and flowers. She should write to him, she knew, but if she did she would be exposed as a stranger, not a friend at all, and the letters would stop coming.

She'd heard her mother on the telephone once, crying. 'You can't just disappear from our lives,' she was saying. 'We never hear from you. What am I supposed to tell them?' She sniffed, blew her nose. Her voice became louder. 'Oh, you'd love them to know, wouldn't you? You'd love them to know it's all my fault. I'm surprised you haven't told them yourself. No, wait, you only write once a year.' She was silent once more, sobbing, listening. When she spoke again her voice had wilted. 'Please come home,' she said. 'Colette and Dominic miss you. I miss you. It was a stupid, stupid mistake. Please come back.'

In the kitchen, Nathan was slicing mushrooms. 'Did you have a good day?' he said.

'It was all right.'

'I saw you at the library. I did call out.'

Colette placed a mushroom in her mouth, the hood like skin against her tongue. 'I mustn't have heard you.'

The front door was open, and her dress lifted in the breeze. She felt her legs become rough with goose pimples and she struggled to hold the fabric down, clutching at the billowing cotton, snatching floral handfuls. She remembered her mother telling her that in the fifties women had sewn coins into their flaring hems, or sometimes small stones.

'I hope you like lasagne,' said Nathan. 'There's quite a bit of it.'

'Did you put my mail on my bed?'

Nathan opened the oven, grimacing at the rush of heat. 'Well,' he said, sliding the lasagne in gingerly, careful not to burn himself, 'who do you think put it there?'

'It's just I have a thing about people being in my room when I'm not there. You know.'

'Oh,' said Nathan. 'Sure. Well. I'll leave it on the bench from now on then.'

'It's nothing personal. It's not that I think you'd, you know—'

'No,' said Nathan. 'That's fine.' He pushed the oven door shut. 'You need your privacy. It's fine.'

They ate dinner watching the news. Nathan was quiet, and when Colette asked him about his course or the neighbours or his previous flats he responded with one-word replies, his eyes never leaving the television screen.

After dinner she returned to her room and spread the photocopies of Laura on her bed. The quality was poor, and although she could make out most of the text, the pictures were little more than blots. They showed a person, that much was apparent, but it could have been anybody: an old man, a toddler, someone her age. Or a teenage girl. The pages felt heavy with ink, heavier than normal paper. Colette recalled a television programme she'd seen about a blind man who could identify playing cards by their weight: the higher the card, the more ink used. He'd held them so lightly on his palms, his eyes staring into the middle distance, beyond the glare of the camera and the sceptical audience, and one by one he'd sensed the weight of a king, a knave, a cluster of diamonds, a single heart. Colette ran her fingers over the dark images. The more she looked at them, the less human they became, and had she not seen them enlarged and illuminated at the library, or framed in silver on Ruth's sideboard, she would not have been able to say what the patches of grey and black represented. A tree, a mountain, thickening storm clouds. A swirl of tea leaves in the bottom of a cup; something by which to tell the future.

The next day she studied Daniel's face, watched him pushing a toy ambulance across Ruth's Persian rug. He was a little like his mother around the mouth, she thought, and he had Malcolm's colouring, but there were no conspicuous similarities, nothing that bound him to his parents. The person he most resembled was Laura. In the dining room, Colette peered at the bush-walk photograph and wondered what he would make of his missing sister as he grew older.

She wondered whether Ruth and Malcolm would remark on the likeness, or whether they would note it only silently.

'Colette!' called Daniel, his voice quivering. 'Where are you? Colette!'

He was crying, holding the broken ambulance. Plastic patients were scattered across knotted birds and flowers.

'It's all right,' she said, 'it doesn't matter. We'll go out, shall we?'

And they walked hand in hand through the dining room, past his sister, who watched from deep in the bush.

'Here we are,' said Colette, stopping at the top of the path. 'Your old house. I suppose it still looks the same, from the outside.'

Daniel released his small, thick hand from hers and headed down the path.

'Hey, wait a minute,' she called, but he was already halfway to the stairs, dodging protruding roots and slippery patches as if he knew the terrain by heart. 'Be careful,' she said, more to herself than to him; by now he was out of earshot.

He was waiting at the top of the stairs for her, the front door already pushed open.

'It must feel like home to you,' she puffed, sinking into a chair. 'Sort of, anyway. I'll get us a drink in a minute. What do you want? Milk? Juice?'

'Yes please,' called Daniel, running his hands over the kitchen cupboards, the bench, the smooth stove. He went into the bathroom, and Colette could hear him turning the taps on and off, lifting the heavy glass lids from bath salts and replacing them with a clink. He had lived here for five years, she realised. Her claim to the place was two months. Still, his prying fingers made her uneasy. When he went into her bedroom, she followed him.

'Do you want to see a photo of me at the beach? It's just around here somewhere—'

Daniel was examining a stain on the wallpaper.

'Hmm,' said Colette, shifting books and papers. 'Don't know where it's got to. Next time, okay?'

'Okay,' said Daniel.

'This is where I keep all my books for university.' Colette showed him the shelves she'd made from bricks and planks of wood. 'They're all right, aren't they? Until I can afford some nice antique ones. And this is Mr Fuzz.'

Daniel scrutinised the teddy bear for a moment, gave it an experimental prod.

'My mother made me bring him up here, to keep an eye on me,' said Colette, and pointed to the bear's one glassy eye.

Daniel fingered the empty socket. 'Like a belly button,' he said.

Back in the lounge he stared at the cupboard that covered the old staircase, pulled at the door handle.

'Like this,' said Colette. 'Twist and then pull.'

He leaned inside, then looked up at Colette, frowning. He ran his hands over the shelves and made a small cry; two minor-key notes like a bird before rain. He shut the cupboard, looked around, then headed for the door to the turret room.

'No, that's Nathan's room,' said Colette. 'We can't go in there.'

But Daniel had already opened the door.

Nathan was lying on his bed, jeans pushed down around his knees. He scrabbled for the blankets, pulled them over himself. 'What the fuck—' A photograph fell from his hand and landed face-down on the carpet.

'Sorry,' said Colette. 'I tried to stop him.'

'Just get out.'

'Sorry. Yes. Daniel, come on.'

The boy was staring at Nathan, eyes wide with alarm.

'Daniel?' Colette took his arm. He started to cry then, huge sobs that filled the musty room. He hid his face in the crook of his elbow.

'For Christ's sake, will you just fuck off?' shouted Nathan.

Colette dragged Daniel away. His cries grew even louder, and he followed her blindly, stumbling over his own feet.

'It's all right, everything's all right,' said Colette. 'Nathan's just in a bad mood, that's all. It's not your fault.'

'My fault,' repeated Daniel.

'We'll go home now, shall we? We can paint if you like.'

Nathan's door flew open and he pushed past them. When he slammed the front door the whole house shook.

'He was a bit upset, I'm afraid,' said Colette. 'Well, very upset. It was all quite awkward.'

Ruth stubbed out a cigarette, squashing it against the ashtray more times than were necessary. 'Why did you take him there? Why did you put him through that?'

'Sorry,' said Colette. 'I didn't mean him any harm. I'm sure he'll be okay, after he's had a sleep. He probably won't even remember it.'

'Oh he'll remember it. You'd be amazed what he remembers. He's not stupid, you know.'

'No. Of course not. I didn't mean—'

'I haven't smoked in years,' said Ruth, emptying the ashtray, opening all the windows. She put a hand to her temple and shut her eyes. 'Just don't take him there again, all right? He's not like other children.'

Colette ate dinner in her room. She could hear Nathan moving around the flat, helping himself to food, scraping his plate, rinsing the dishes. He turned the television on and watched the first few minutes of the news, then flicked through the other channels. He rustled the newspaper, flushed the toilet. Around eleven o'clock it grew quiet, and Colette emerged and made some toast. She winced as she dropped the jam spoon and it clattered to the floor. Nathan's door opened.

'Oh, you are home,' he said. 'What's up? Not feeling well?'

'Not very.'

'Do you need any—'

'Good night,' said Colette, and went back to her room, closing the door behind her.

She couldn't fall asleep that night, nor for the next few nights. She thought she heard running outside, quick footsteps drumming the garden. She gripped the sheets, buttoned her pyjamas right up to the collar. She had a sense of waiting for someone to enter the house and find her alone in bed with only photographs watching over her. The stranger would unfurl a hand at her like a star, his fingers fast at her throat.

When she looked out her bay window, though, there was nobody outside. From certain vantage points the antique panes of glass warped the view, and if she shifted her head even slightly it did seem as if something were moving in the bush.

Silly girl, said the people in the photos. Who does she think is there?

Colette shut the curtains and pulled the covers up to her chin. This is an old house, she told herself. They are old windows. Glass was a liquid, she recalled, and if left for long enough it sank and thickened, and played tricks on the eye.

'Why do they keep sending this junk? We've written at least three times telling them we have no use for it.' Jan gulped her coffee. 'I mean, if it were in English, perhaps. But Russian? How many Russian entomologists are there on campus?'

'None, I expect,' said Ruth, staring over the staff-room balcony at the students swarming below.

'They're like tiny insects, aren't they?' said Nicole.

'Hey, there's one of my tenants.' Colette was walking past, head down, alone. 'In the green jacket and the jeans.'

Jan craned her neck over the balcony. 'This is the girl who looks after Daniel, is it? She'd be quite pretty if she did something with her hair.'

'Daniel wants to marry her,' said Ruth. 'He adores her.' She watched as Colette passed directly underneath them.

'She looks very young,' said Nicole.

'She's twenty-one.' Ruth sniffed the cigarette smoke that floated up from the throng of students. 'She has such good skin. I want her skin.'

'I could never leave a child with a stranger.' There was a note of accusation in Nicole's voice. 'I saw this American programme once. They set up hidden cameras and filmed nannies doing the most appalling things. Hitting the children, ignoring distressed babies. Going through underwear drawers.'

'I had a student nanny once,' said Jan. 'Nightmare. Invited her boyfriend over when we were away. Left used condoms in the bath.'

'She's very good with Daniel,' said Ruth. 'Very good. He adores her.' She watched Colette walk downhill towards the harbour and disappear from view. 'We'd hate to lose her.'

'I'm sorry I was sharp with you last time,' she said. 'I was just worried about Daniel. He hid himself in Malcolm's wardrobe. I couldn't find him for ages.' She stopped. 'He's not like other children. I'm a bit over-protective sometimes.'

'No harm done,' said Colette.

'No. No harm done.' Ruth let this echo for a moment. 'How do you manage to be so relaxed?'

'Me?' Colette laughed. 'Dominic will love that!'

'Well, you are.'

'I haven't slept for the past four nights.'

Ruth looked down at her hands. 'I hope you're not, I hope you're, you know, looking after yourself.'

Colette laughed again, more cautiously. 'This isn't a birth-control talk, is it?'

'No, I mean, well, we worry about you, Malcolm and I. New to the city. And now this business with Nathan. You don't have to stay in the flat because of us, you know.'

'It's a great flat. Great location. Five minutes into town, two minutes up to campus—'

'You've done wonders with Daniel, even Malcolm's noticed. We'd hate to lose you.'

'I'm fond of him.'

Ruth clasped her fingers together. 'But you have to protect yourself,' she said. 'You have to be so careful, these days.'

'You're beginning to sound like my mother,' said Colette. 'Or my Gender Relations lecturer. She keeps telling us how dangerous New Zealand is now. Do you know, as recently as the 1950s, most people didn't bother locking their doors at night? I'm thinking of basing an essay round that.'

'It has possibilities,' said Ruth.

'I've been going to self-defence classes, actually. Mum's idea.'

'Good,' said Ruth. 'That's good.'

'Going out again tonight?' said Nathan.

'I won't be late.'

'Most mysterious. You're hardly ever here these days.'

Colette swung her satchel on to her back. 'Leave the outside light on, okay?'

After self defence that night, the class went out to the pub.

'I've never had this many dates,' said Roland, and bought everyone a drink.

Colette noticed that he was paying a lot of attention to Tracey, one of the younger women, and after a while the two of them rose to leave together.

'Hey, Trace,' said one of the class members, sniggering, 'even if it's less direct, take the most well-lit route.'

'Don't get into an empty train carriage,' said another.

'Tuck long hair inside your collar.'

'Walk confidently, stand up straight.'

'Make yourself appear as large as possible.'

'Hold your keys between your fingers like a knife.'

'The eyes are a vulnerable spot.'

Roland and Tracey grinned and left.

'Don't forget to go for the groin,' someone called.

Colette stumbled home late, a little bit drunk, taking a shortcut through the park. She felt invincible. She knew how to defend herself, should the need arise. Which points of the body to target. She could bring a man down in three simple moves. Her voice alone, she told herself as she climbed the stairs to the front door, could be sufficient to dissuade an attacker. She would simply fix him with a look, tell him loudly and firmly NO NO NO, foil his every move. She would have a silver whistle arranged between her lips and, between her fingers, a key with which to unlock his eyes.

Nathan had already gone to bed. Colette stumbled over the magazine rack and giggled. She knocked her toothbrush into the bath. She would clean her teeth in the morning. That would be all right. Everything would be all right. Perhaps, she thought, she would write a letter to Patrick. She left her clothes where they fell, and when she dropped into bed she slept so soundly that she couldn't even remember her dreams.

In summer, at Aunt Joyce's, Patrick thought he could see fireflies in the garden. They remained with him long after he'd returned to his parents' house; dots of illumination on his dim holiday memories, like irregularities on an X-ray. He stayed outside for hours watching for them, while inside the house his aunt and his mother and father drank bitter coffee and discussed the world. He sat very still, hoping the grown-ups would forget he had not gone to bed. The stone seat chilled beneath him, drawing moisture from the earth like a tree, and the goldfish were lazy in the pond, tails drifting like silk handkerchiefs, and the birds grew mournful, then silent. He believed the fireflies were spelling out messages, the secrets of flowers, trees. Always, though, just as he made out a letter here, a word there, his father or his mother or his aunt turned the porch light on and drenched the garden in a bright domestic glow, and the fireflies rolled away like scattered beads.

'Come in now, Patrick,' the grown-ups called, and he would leave the garden behind, because teeth had to be cleaned and pyjamas donned and cheeks kissed. Sometimes he looked out the bedroom window to see if the fireflies had come back, but all he ever saw were the occasional beams of a passing car. When he closed his eyes, though, he could see them, their bright trails indigo on his retinas, like ink. And as he was falling asleep he moved his lips to read the words: *stay outside, stay out all night.*

He always slept in his cousin's room; she spent the summer holidays at her father's.

'You're not a bad swap for her,' said Aunt Joyce, tweaking his ear the way his mother never did.

Patrick didn't remember Faye, although there were photographs of the two of them together as toddlers. Every year his mother said, 'It's such a shame Faye's not here. They used to play together so nicely.'

Faye's bedroom was white. She had white curtains and a white bed and a soft white rug on the floor. It reminded Patrick of a dental surgery.

One year, the year before the fire, his mother said, 'We're going to spend Christmas with Aunt Joyce. Faye will be home from school, of course, so you can catch up with her. And we're meeting a man called Ronnie.'

Ronnie was Aunt Joyce's new friend. He was very wealthy and Patrick would have to be on his best behaviour. People like Ronnie did not suffer fools.

A bed was made up for Patrick in the sunroom, which Aunt Joyce called the conservatory even though it contained no plants. His parents had Joyce's guest suite, but when she was out he heard his mother describing it as just a large bedroom with a washstand in one corner. Patrick had never slept in a room made of glass, and that night he tricked himself that the conservatory walls weren't there at all, that they had melted away into the cold garden.

'In summer you could watch for your fireflies from your bed,' his mother said, but Patrick, who had just seen Faye walking past in her nightdress, didn't answer.

On Christmas Day, Faye smoothed the damask cloth over the table, tweaking each corner so the folds were even. Then she took six matching napkins—as big as kites, Patrick thought—and folded them into elaborate flowers. She placed one on each plate; water lilies adrift on fluted ponds.

Aunt Joyce sat at the head of the table, with Ronnie to her right. Outside, the winter sun caught on the lilies and made them transparent as paper. Patrick's mother had made a lily centrepiece— her little contribution to the dinner, she said—and the scent mingled with the smell of roast beef and goose.

'I'm not very hungry,' she said as she sat down. 'It seems silly, doesn't it, to have all this food for only six people.' She took a few thin slices of meat, a dribble of gravy, one potato. 'You've gone to so much trouble, Joyce,' she said, 'but I don't have much of an appetite, I'm afraid.'

Ronnie filled four goblets with wine. 'You'll like this, Graham,' he said. 'Good and full on the tongue.'

'Marvellous, yes,' said Patrick's father, taking a tiny sip.

'Can we have some?' said Faye. 'Because it's Christmas?'

Patrick's mother said, 'Oh, I don't think—' but Aunt Joyce said, 'Half and half, then,' and brought a jug of water and two more goblets.

'This is what they do in France,' said Faye. 'They're allowed to drink it from the time they start school.'

Aunt Joyce's wine goblets were silver on the outside and gold on the inside. The stems were turned and grooved like the legs of a chair, and swelled in the middle to a fat bead. The wine made the goblets fog up like winter windows. Patrick held his by the stem, like a pen, but it tipped forward and spilled all over the tablecloth.

'Well that was clever, wasn't it,' said his mother.

Faye laughed.

'No harm done,' said Ronnie. 'At least it wasn't the really good stuff.' He winked. 'We'll have that later, Graham,' he said, and he mopped away the excess.

Patrick's mother dabbed her mouth with her napkin, then began folding the white damask into smaller and smaller rectangles. Her face was very solemn, as if there had been some sort of disaster and she was preparing a bandage. She lifted the tablecloth and slid the napkin underneath. 'To stop the wood from marking,' she said, and Patrick knew she was right to do so but for the rest of the meal all he could see was the mound under the cloth, upsetting Faye's careful smoothing. Nobody refilled his goblet.

As they ate, Faye talked about a restaurant they'd been to for her last birthday. It was French, and the chef had presented her with a special pudding just because she was turning thirteen. He'd made her a basket from sugar and water—imagine, she said, just sugar and water—and filled it with cherries and chocolate mousse. Around the edge of the plate, piped in chocolate, were the words *Bon Anniversaire Faye*. 'That means happy birthday Faye in French,' she said, and reached for the platter of roast beef.

'I think you've got enough on your plate, dear,' said Aunt Joyce, catching her daughter's arm. 'She's grown so much this last term,' she said. 'She hardly fits any of her clothes. Ronnie almost didn't recognise her when he met her from the train, did you Ronnie?'

Patrick wished he could be taken to a restaurant on his birthday, and presented with a pudding in his honour. He tried to picture the basket. Was it solid and crunchy, the way sugar went when left in the bowl too long? Was it clear, like toffee, and dotted with tiny air bubbles? Thick and rough, sparkling like morning frost? As Faye spoke, he watched her cup her hands to make the shape of the basket, twirl her finger above her palm to indicate the sweet filling. Perhaps, he thought, Faye's special pudding, made for her because she was turning thirteen, resembled a spider's web, the clear threads snapping on the tongue like glass.

'This is very good, Joyce,' said Patrick's father, helping himself to a little more, arranging the food in neat sections on his plate. When eating, Graham Mercer liked to include a portion of everything with each mouthful. He often recommended the method to guests.

'I begin with the meat and I work clockwise around the plate,' he would explain. He was able to judge perfectly the quantities of food and was never left with a mound of parsnip, say, or orphan beans. At the end of each meal he said, 'Perfect,' more pleased with himself and his rationed mouthfuls, it seemed, than with the food itself.

When everyone had finished, Aunt Joyce produced a platter of chocolates. There were lemon baskets, scallop shells, cherry clusters, walnut swirls, white-on-dark cameos, all resting in crimped paper cases.

'From Carnaby's,' she said, and Patrick's father, who had been trying to pick a strand of goose meat from his teeth, stopped and said, 'Well now.'

'Just one for you, Faye,' said Aunt Joyce.

Carnaby's Chocolatier sold handmade confectionery by the ounce, like gold. White-gloved women with covered hair weighed each customer's selection, then folded the pieces into foil bags. Tongs were used at all times; deft silver fingers that caused no melting, left no prints. In rows, in glass cabinets, the chocolates were displayed like pieces of jewellery intended for the décolletage, the wrist, the throat. Patrick had been with Aunt Joyce when she'd bought her Christmas selection. She'd held his hand on the way there and he didn't mind, even though these days he shook away his mother's fingers when they grasped for his.

While Aunt Joyce waited at the counter, Patrick wandered towards the back of the shop and was surprised to find that it opened on to a dance floor. There were no windows, but the walls were covered with mirrors, bevelled and scalloped like pralines, and in one corner a bar curved, a beckoning finger. Sugary glass orchids and leaves formed chandeliers which shook as Patrick walked beneath them. He closed his eyes and breathed in the scent from the shop, and it was as if the whole place were made of sugar, and he imagined the people who came here to dance, the sweetnesses exchanged every night. He saw the costly glint of silver, gold, the slow unwrapping as coats were abandoned, gloves peeled away. He saw shoulders bared and glowing like marzipan. He didn't like the taste of marzipan; it was sweet and bitter at the same time, like wine was: something adult, something acquired.

'Come away now, Patrick,' said Aunt Joyce, and she took his hand again and led him back to the street.

'What was that room at the back of the shop?' he asked on the way home, and she said, 'It used to be a cocktail bar. Your mother liked going there.'

———

When Christmas dinner was over and the grown-ups had slouched in their armchairs to let the afternoon pass, Faye said, 'Be my hands.' She led Patrick to her mother's bedroom, opened the top drawer of the dressing-table and selected lipsticks, eyeshadows and small, heavy jars. At the back of the drawer, thin vials of perfume glinted: amber, topaz, citrine. 'You have to keep it in the dark,' said Faye, 'otherwise it goes off. It starts to smell like cats' piss.'

Patrick had never seen so much make-up. His mother, he realised, used only the basics: pressed powder, mascara, red lipstick, and some cornflower-blue eyeshadow for special occasions. She called them her face, but here there was enough make-up for countless faces, a different one every day.

'What's this?' he said, touching a metal device with his fingertip. It resembled a pair of scissors, but instead of straight blades it had a curved, sharp clamp. It was vaguely orthodontic.

'Look,' said Faye, and pressed it to her eye.

Patrick gasped, snatched out his hand to stop her.

'It's a lash-curler, silly. It makes your eyes bigger. It's an optical illusion.' She positioned herself in front of the full-length mirror. 'Stand behind me,' she said.

She took Patrick's hands and pulled them around her, then clasped her own hands behind him. He peered over her shoulder and was pleased to see how convincing his arms looked attached to her body. He waved at the mirror, reached up and smoothed a finger over Faye's eyebrow. She laughed, and he fluffed his hands through her hair, flicking it forward so it rested over her shoulders and chest.

'You've got nice arms, for a boy. Not hairy.' She cocked her head to one side. 'Do you think I'm fat?'

'No,' said Patrick.

'Mum thinks I need to lose weight. She says I've inherited the Stratford thighs. Ronnie doesn't like big women.'

'I think your thighs,' said Patrick and swallowed, feeling them against his own, 'are very nice.'

'Hmm,' said Faye, 'I wonder what make-up I should wear for my date tonight.'

Patrick held a thoughtful finger to her cheek.

'I don't want to look common—a light dusting of powder, I think, to start with.'

Patrick reached for the powder compact. It was gold, with a complicated geometric design engraved on the lid. Inside was a small velvet pad already caked with make-up. There was a ribbon across the back, and he hooked his fingers underneath it and began dabbing powder on Faye's cheeks.

'I mustn't forget my jaw-line and my neck,' she said. 'It's very important to blend, otherwise you get tidemarks.'

He ran the pad up and down her throat.

'Eyeshadow next. The gold will match my gown.'

There was no applicator, so Patrick used his fingertip to apply the shimmering powder. It was like pollen, he thought. Faye's eyelids felt so delicate he was afraid they would dissolve under his touch. At the small of his back he could feel her clasping and unclasping her hands.

'Eyeliner completes the look,' she said.

Patrick's hands groped across the dressing-table for the pencil. It was difficult to hold, almost too thin, and had been sharpened with a knife; he could feel the ridges where the blade had sliced at the wood. 'It feels very sharp,' he said, but Faye sighed and said, 'It's not a real pencil, silly, the lead's soft, like crayon,' so he rested his hand on her cheek and began to outline her eye. It was disorienting, watching himself draw in the mirror. Faye stood very still, and he could feel her breath on his fingers. His hand looked unfamiliar to him; he no longer recognised the curve of his wrist, his sharp knuckles. It was Faye who was holding the pencil, Faye who was deciding where to draw, where to add colour and shadow. She blinked, and the tip jabbed her eye.

'You idiot! Why don't you watch what you're doing?' She wriggled away from Patrick, and suddenly he was alone in Aunt

Joyce's bedroom, and there was powder spilled on the floor and on the pale ash dressing-table, and it was getting dark outside.

Faye didn't speak to him for the rest of the day, and at the supper table she rubbed her eye and frowned a lot. Nobody else seemed to notice anything was wrong, and Aunt Joyce didn't mention any tampering in her room. Patrick concentrated on his hands. He could see a residue of golden dust on his fingertip, embedded in the grain of his skin. He could still make it out that night in bed, if he held his finger under the light. He closed his eyes and imagined he was in the sweet-shop ballroom with Faye, and that the conservatory windows were mirrors. Light bounced off the glass as he danced with her, flickers of purple, licks of red and orange. By morning the eyeshadow had disappeared from his skin, lost somewhere in his sleep.

Ruth had tried to ignore it. In warm weather, she'd told herself, it was normal; she was simply shedding her winter coat. As summer ended, though, as the evenings turned cooler and the leaves began to drop, she continued to find blond strands everywhere in the new house. They wove around the bristles on her hairbrush, they clogged the plugholes, clung to cushions and curtains, wound themselves so tightly around the vacuum-cleaner head that she had to cut them away with nail scissors.

Her hairdresser told her not to worry. People lost up to eighty a day without even knowing, she said, waving her scissors through the air, and Ruth had plenty left to lose, and where had she bought her gorgeous earrings? Up to eighty hairs a day, thought Ruth. For a family of four, that was two thousand, two hundred and forty hairs a week. Almost ten thousand a month. She wondered where it all went, why the human race wasn't knee-deep in hair. It didn't decompose quickly. It was one of the last parts of a person to remain. Even bog bodies, buried for centuries, had hair.

'Stress or poor nutrition is most often to blame,' said the doctor. 'Have you lost a lot of weight recently? Are you dieting?'

'No,' said Ruth. 'We've got a beautiful kitchen in the new place. If anything, I'm eating better than I ever have.'

'Shifting house is one of the most stressful activities we ever face, of course,' said the doctor. 'Quite apart from strangers traipsing through your home, and the packing and unpacking, and the whole financial side of things, it can be hard to part with a place that's been an important part of your life.'

'Oh, but we haven't sold,' said Ruth. 'We've converted it into two flats and we're renting them out. Malcolm did a lot of the work himself.' She stopped, ran her hand through her hair. She didn't say that Malcolm had worked on the house night after night. She didn't say that he'd spent almost no time with Daniel, that they'd hardly seen him at all, he'd been so busy with the conversion. Splitting their old life in two. And she didn't say how quickly it had happened.

'Alterations,' said the doctor, 'can be very demanding.'

Ruth said no to the pills he suggested, but promised to buy a relaxation tape which had, he assured her, worked wonders for his wife.

That night, when Malcolm was reading the paper and Daniel had gone to bed, Ruth lay down on the lounge floor. She could hear the hiss and whine of the tape as it started to spool through the stereo. She hadn't listened to a tape in a long time.

'They won't even be making them in a few years,' Laura had told her once, and had explained to Ruth the miracle of the compact disc. 'The CD,' she'd said, holding one up to her mother, a full moon in her hands, 'can't be damaged or broken.'

Ruth could feel the Persian rug against the backs of her legs, cool and silky. A woman's voice emerged from the speakers.

'Lie on the floor with your arms by your sides,' said the voice. 'Now close your eyes and take four deep breaths, letting any tension in your body flow away with each outward breath. Good,' she said, as if she were in the room and watching. 'Now I want you to think of a place you find relaxing. It might be a real place, or somewhere you've visited only in your imagination. It might be a meadow, a deserted beach, or a garden. Perhaps it's a peaceful room. Once you've visualised your place, I want you to imagine you are there.'

Ruth didn't choose an outdoor location; the only ones she could see were the icy landscapes in Malcolm's photographs. No, she wanted to be inside. And she was, she was inside their old house, in the lounge, and everything was the way it had been when Laura was still there.

'What can you see around you?' said the voice. 'What can you smell? What sounds can you hear?'

The sound Ruth heard was a knock at the door, twelve years earlier. It was a sound she'd been hearing for days, ever since Laura had been in the news. For a moment she didn't move from her armchair. The house had been occupied by visitors all morning, most of whom, it seemed, had come only to tell her how awful she looked, what a terrible time she must be having, how they wished there was something they could do. Malcolm was still out searching. It was an arrangement they'd come to wordlessly: while he checked rivers, beaches, pockets of bush, she waited for news. Ruth didn't mind being the one to wait. She knew that Malcolm needed to get his hands dirty, to turn over every log, lift every stone, find something that had been missed. But she also knew that someone needed to be at home. 'In case there are any important phone calls,' she explained to visitors, but meant something else. If Laura arrived home and found nobody there, who would wipe her face, run her a bath, apply sticking plaster?

There was another knock at the door.

'Mrs Pearse?' called a voice. 'Anybody home?'

Ruth stubbed out her cigarette. Malcolm hated her smoking; she'd stopped for him, just after they met. She knew he could smell the smoke in the house now, when he came home each day, but he hadn't said anything.

'Mrs Pearse, are you there?'

She stood, smoothed her hair. She'd spoken to Joshua on the phone a couple of times since Laura had disappeared, but only to ask if he knew anything, whether Laura had contacted him. He hadn't been round to the house at all.

'I've got some of Laura's CDs,' he said. 'I thought you might want them. I thought you might want to put them back in her room.'

'Thank you,' said Ruth. There was a moment's awkwardness,

the two of them hesitating on the threshold as if on a first date.

'Would you like a coffee?' she said. 'It'll have to be black—' She trailed off, flicked through the handful of CDs. She recognised one of them from Laura's last birthday, a present from Joshua. Bon Jovi's *Slippery When Wet.* 'Hardly appropriate,' Malcolm had remarked. Laura had played it over and over.

Ruth put the CDs on the hall table. That was where she put all of Laura's things; she'd stopped tidying her room months ago, when Laura had accused her of going through her desk.

'How's school?'

'It's okay,' said Joshua, looking round the lounge at the flowers, the newspapers, the cards and letters, looking anywhere but at Ruth.

'So you haven't heard from—'

'No,' he said, 'there's nothing to report.' He stole a glance at Ruth. 'You look,' he said, and stopped. 'You look—'

'I know. Tired. Drained. Old.'

'You look like her. I never noticed before.'

When he was gone Ruth took a CD from its case and turned it over and over. It flashed in the late sun, covered the ceiling with rainbows. And then Malcolm came in and stood in front of the window and soaked up all the sun. There was no news, he said, and the rainbows disappeared.

Even though there was nothing to tell them, still the visitors came.

'You look awful,' they said. 'All washed out and haggard. You look like you haven't slept for weeks.' They leaned in close, took Ruth's chin in their hands, squinted at her. 'You're not yourself.'

This was something she didn't need to be told. She knew that Ruth Pearse was neat, washed her hair, didn't smoke, kept her nails tidy. Ruth Pearse's cupboards were stocked, her washing folded. Her house was dust-free. She had been known to iron underwear. No, she was not herself. She was a nothing, an absence. She was her daughter.

'We've examined the Mini,' said the detective inspector, 'but there's very little to go on. Usually there's a hair or two, some footprints. All we have is the blood, I'm afraid.'

'The blood,' said Malcolm, 'yes.'

'We're testing it. We're doing all we can, I assure you.'

Malcolm had always been a little mystified by his daughter. She hadn't been a teary infant, prone to crying fits the way some babies were, but neither had she been very affectionate. Sometimes, when he'd held her, she'd gone completely still. She'd stared at him as if expecting him to entertain her, to inform her about the world. He tried jangling the car keys, offering her his little finger, nuzzling her cheek with a soft toy, but nothing he did made her smile. She just watched him, becoming more and more still, it seemed, the more he struggled to amuse her. And as she grew older, her stillness grew too.

'Look, darling,' he'd said once on a picnic, 'a buttercup. Shall we see if you like butter?' He held the glossy flower under her seven-year-old chin. 'Hmm,' he said as a cloud crept across the sun, 'you don't like it much at all.'

'Yes I do,' said Laura, frowning and scratching at her neck where a careless streak of pollen had tickled her. 'Mummy puts it in my sandwiches every day. Don't you know anything?' And she'd turned back to her book, her fingertips imprinting the story with buttery dust.

Malcolm wondered if there would still be pollen between the pages. Laura's old books were stored in the ceiling somewhere, along with everything else Ruth was keeping for the grandchildren. There were rows and rows of boxes stacked on the roof beams, straddling pockets of glass-fibre insulation which looked like candy-floss but which could cause great irritation to the skin and eyes.

'You should never go up there without a mask on,' Ruth warned when Malcolm mentioned Laura's books, 'and even then it's risky. And it's so dusty, you'll just make a mess.'

'Don't worry,' he said, 'I'm not going up.' It was a ridiculous idea, he was aware of that. He wouldn't know where to start looking, and he had no idea which book to examine if he did find the right box; at the picnic Laura had remained silent when he'd asked what she was reading. And she was still as incommunicative now, providing no clues to her whereabouts.

'We think she was just in the wrong place at the wrong time,' he told the many acquaintances who rang or visited looking for news, wanting some scrap of information that wasn't on television or in the papers.

'Our forensics team is running some more tests on the Mini,' said the detective inspector, 'and we'll let you know if they come up with anything. They're a pretty thorough bunch of guys, don't you worry. You'd be lucky to get much past them.'

Malcolm didn't like to think of these people, these strangers, combing and re-combing Laura's car for evidence. The way the officer described them made him think of a sports team, dressed in spotless uniforms and playing silently in her car, passing clues to one another, making secret signals, establishing a strategy. Each player would have certain abilities: there would be a gun man, a knife man, a glass man, a blood man. Malcolm wanted to talk to this forensics team. He wanted to ask them what they were looking for, what their tests had shown so far. He'd been doing some homework. He had researched their tricks, keeping from Ruth the fact that he was doing so.

Every contact leaves a trace, he read; that was the basis of forensic science. People leave behind evidence of themselves when they walk through a room, sit in a chair, brush against a wall. Malcolm could picture Laura doing all those things: strolling through the lounge Ruth had decorated with marble, glass, chrome; running a finger over the glossy leaves of the rubber plant; sprawling in an armchair with her Walkman on, the music leaking from the headset and jarring Ruth's cool surfaces. Laura, Malcolm learned, would have deposited hair, flakes of skin, droplets of saliva, fingerprints, fibres, footprints.

And the person she met that day, whoever he was, would have done the same. It was very difficult—virtually impossible—to leave no sign of one's presence. And often, when a person tried to cover his tracks, he left more clues than ever.

'Have you used Luminol on the car?' he asked, watching the inspector's face. 'I understand,' he said, 'that Luminol glows in the presence of blood, even after rain.'

The inspector raised his eyebrows for just a moment, then smiled and said they would be sure to let him know if they found anything.

'It's not your daughter's blood in the car, Mr Pearse,' he told him the next day. 'We don't know who it belongs to yet, but it lets us rule out any existing suspects.'

'You don't have any suspects,' said Malcolm.

'It's something, though,' said the inspector. 'It's still a very significant lead.' He was smiling again, wanting Malcolm to be pleased. And in a way, Malcolm was. But not because they now had the DNA profile of a stranger. He was pleased because it meant, perhaps, that Laura had put up a fight, had drawn blood.

Sunday 13 March 1988
Dear Mr and Mrs Pearse,
We feel for you at this difficult time. Words can't express how dearly we, and the entire country, hope that Laura will be found. She is such a beautiful girl in her photos, so vivacious and friendly. She is the last person who deserves to find herself in such a situation. We pray she is returned to you soon.

March 15 1988
Dear Mr and Mrs Pearse,
I wanted to let you know that I understand what you're going through, and that Laura's disappearance has taught my toddler a valuable lesson. I hope this will be a small comfort to you both.
Only last week Benny was separated from me at the Downtown

Mall, and was missing for over an hour. It turned out he had wandered into the McDonald's playground and hidden himself behind Hamburglar, but those sixty-five minutes were the most terrifying of my life. When we got home I showed him your daughter's picture in the paper and told him that if he wasn't more careful, he might go missing like poor Laura has. Since then Benny has been very well behaved.

22 March, 1988
Dear Malcolm and Ruth,
    I see Laura near water. There are rocks surrounding her, and a broken fence. Her hair and clothes are wet. In the background there is a hill, or perhaps sand dunes. I have a very strong feeling that you must look in rocky places if you want to find Laura. I could give you clearer information if you let me have some personal object of hers. Clothing that has been worn recently and next to the skin is best.

6 April 1988
To Ruth & Malcolm Pearse,
    You said all you wanted now was Lauras body. Have you tried looking for clusters of gulls. If a bodys ended up in the sea or if its washed up on a beach somewhere therell be gulls circling above it.

Monday, April 11, 1988
Mr and Mrs Pearse.
    My wife and I have heard a lot about what a wonderful daughter you had. Every time we pick up a paper or listen to the news we are treated to fresh reports about what a saint she was. It is amazing to us how many of her teachers, relatives, neighbours and friends are prepared to come forward with their glowing opinions, not to mention your own frequent comments. We find this quite tiring. Yes, it is a shame that she's gone, but please, spare a thought for the rest of us. Your daughter was not a saint.

Malcolm stored the letters in an old suitcase. It had belonged to his mother originally, and had accompanied her on countless family holidays to beaches, camping grounds, rough coastlines, areas of bush. He suspected there might still be dark sand lodged in its crevices, perhaps a sliver of dried grass, a leaf's spine. The residues of summer.

The case hadn't been anywhere for a long time, not since he was a boy. Ruth had kept recipe clippings in it for a while, when she and Malcolm were first married, always intending to paste them into scrapbooks. When the letters started mounting up, Malcolm retrieved it from the garage.

'Are these any good now?' he said, bringing Ruth a thick sample of recipes which, he knew, she had never cooked. She looked at them—chocolate soufflé, lamb casserole, beef Wellington—and finally shook her head.

'No,' she said. 'No, I'll never use those.'

So Malcolm discarded them. He emptied the case of profiterole diagrams, Hearty Stews, Soups Your Family Will Love, and re-placed them with letters from strangers. He and Ruth did as they were told and kept every piece of correspondence, even the un-pleasant ones, except for a few the police took and examined and finally discounted.

Malcolm buckled the straps tight each time he closed the case, as if to prevent the letters from bursting out like bad seeds, letting loose papery theories, accusations, condolences. The smell of the leather reminded him of summer, and he shivered.

There were phone calls as well. One man said they would find Laura if they went to church.

'Why?' said Malcolm, his voice too loud. 'Is she hiding in one of the pews?'

Another caller, after asking if Laura had a dog and expressing delight at the fact that it was a labrador, suggested taking it to the wind turbine.

'Animals—especially dogs—have a sixth sense about these

things,' said the woman. 'He may well lead you to his mistress. My own dog Truffles has a remarkable psychic ability. He always knows when I'm leaving for work.'

One night the phone rang about eleven o'clock.

'Hi Dad, it's Laura,' said a voice. 'Can you come and get me now?'

And then there was scuffling and giggling in the background, and the line went dead.

'If the car was found so close, she could still be round here somewhere,' said Malcolm's colleague Phil. 'She might have been dazed and wandered off.'

'Maybe she left the car there on purpose and hitched a lift. She could be at the other end of the island by now.'

'Or she could have jumped on a train. How much money did she have on her?'

Malcolm's friends presented their theories as if discussing a football match or predicting the outcome of an election. He knew it was their way of offering him hope, of refusing to voice the probability that Laura was dead.

'An attractive girl like that,' said Phil, 'she'd have no worries getting a ride.'

Malcolm said nothing. The only information he had was that there was no information, and there was no point in telling them that. It would only elicit more guesswork, allow the construction of further improbable scenarios. He had trusted that science would find his daughter, and he knew that in so many other cases science had proved the only reliable witness. Where people failed, or provided half-truths, or were simply wrong, science was exact. It was like accounting; there was only one right answer. But it was a month since Laura's disappearance, and the police seemed no closer to finding her than they had been on day one. He knew that this wasn't what his friends wanted to hear. It made them uncomfortable, made them regret their polite inquiries.

'They've done more forensic tests on the car,' he mumbled. This piece of information stopped even the most persistent questions. Everyone knew what forensics meant, what it meant for an investigation to have reached that stage. Blood was involved, seminal fluid, saliva. The unmentionable secretions of the body, its liquid secrets. Malcolm's friends nodded grimly, and bought him another Scotch.

There were ways of telling. There were ways of reconstructing an event from one or two muddy footprints, or carelessly placed fibres, or pieces of glass. The shattered window on Laura's car, for instance, could tell a story. Malcolm hugged this possibility to himself, did not mention it to Ruth or to anyone. He went to the library and found more books, ones detailing the properties of glass, and at night, after Ruth had taken her sleeping pill, he examined them. He pored over sketches showing the various compositions of glass, the many different ways in which it could break. The pieces illustrated were not real, of course; they were hypothetical breakages, shattering which demonstrated rules. In actual investigations, the books warned, the evidence would never be so clear-cut, but Malcolm understood that there had to be a benchmark, a perfect, laboratory specimen. It was the only way of judging the real world, with all its wildcard quirks.

He inspected the pictures through a magnifying glass. He turned them sideways and upside-down, held them under the glow of the bedside lamp. Every now and then he looked over at Ruth, watched her face for signs of waking, but she never stirred. She hardly changed position all night, it seemed. Malcolm took notes from the glass books, made his own sketches of damage. *Figure one,* he wrote in careful italics. *The flat-backed pig. Figure two. The beading of glass exposed to extreme heat.* It gave him a sense of satisfaction, this precision. Labelling his sketches gave them dignity, scientific value. He added a little more detail to his drawing of Laura's car window, and tried to think of a suitable label. The shattering, however, was not as simple as the single shards illustrated in the books. Was it one piece of glass containing many fractures, or many pieces of glass held together like a jigsaw? He turned this question over and over in his mind, and could not fall asleep. Even with his eyes closed he saw the radiating lines he had sketched. They extended out and out, past the edges of the paper and over the bed, and at the centre was a dark mass, the point of impact made solid, a stone thrown into still water.

When the detective inspector came downstairs for breakfast he found his wife crying.

'What is it, what's wrong?' he asked, but received no answer. 'Tell me what's the matter, sweetheart, there's a good girl.' He crouched on the floor in front of her armchair and she cried even harder. 'Is it me, is it something I've done? Can I get you a cup of tea?' His voice was growing anxious, but still she said nothing. He looked at his watch. 'I hate to leave you,' he said. 'I hate leaving you so upset, but I really do need to get going.' His wife waved him away with a damp hand. 'Are you sure?' he said. She waved at him again, as if he were an insect.

She heard his car backing down the drive, waiting for a hole in the morning traffic. As the sound of the engine grew distant and faded, she stopped crying. She sat very still in the gold velour armchair, the morning paper resting on her lap. The pages were damp from her crying, wrinkled and puckered like shrunk washing. The girl's picture was distorted, ugly, and the detective inspector's wife was glad. She had taken over their lives, this girl. She had captivated her husband, made him passionate. He'd never been so passionate.

On the way to her aquarobics class she glanced at the warrant of fitness sticker on her windscreen. It had expired well over a month ago, and she laughed. The wife of a senior police officer, she thought, driving round without a warrant of fitness. Her husband called them wofs. He liked to talk in initials, and where possible would run them together to make one word, rather than pronouncing each letter separately. This had endeared him to her at first.

On the other side of town, the man upended a cornflakes box. A small, dusty pile pattered on to his plate, barely covering the seashell design. Fuck, he thought. He shoved the box and the plate to the floor. Broken china skittered across the vinyl. More mess to clean up.

As she drove to the pool, the detective inspector's wife turned on the radio. To put herself in the right mood, she always listened to music before aquarobics. She had so many tapes that they spilled across the floor of her car, rattling in their cases when she drove too fast. She was about to press play when the morning bird call sounded through the speakers: the bellbird. It made her think of the tramping holidays she'd taken with her husband, before they were married. It made her remember nights in dank cabins, tree ferns brushing the windows, her sleeping bag a soft sarcophagus. And then the bellbird was drowned by the electric pips signalling nine o'clock, and all of a sudden the car was filled with the missing girl's name, and then with her husband's voice, and all he talked about was the girl. The detective inspector's wife didn't stop at the pool. She kept driving and driving in her wof-less car until she was on the other side of the city, until she was, she considered, about as far away from home as she could be without actually leaving town. And it was at this point she realised she was hungry. Starving.

She steered the trolley from one aisle to another, gripping the cool handle. She avoided the precarious displays of tins and boxes, the young woman giving away Instant Cheesecake samples, the harassed mothers. She was glad she had no children. She didn't know where anything was in this out-of-the-way store, but she was in no hurry. She perused every aisle, selecting products she never usually bought, items for which she had no use. Luxury items. Pâté, scented toilet paper, gourmet dog food. It was as if she were shopping for someone else, someone with a different life.

In front of her at the checkout, a young man was piling box after box of Cornflakes on to the counter. As she reached for her purse, her overloaded trolley nudged his hip.

'Watch out,' he said, glaring at her.

Patrick's mother had a huge crystal vase which she filled with flowers from her garden.

'White carnations for truth,' she'd say, pushing a stem of blooms into the water. 'Striped carnations for refusal, ambrosia for love returned, ivy for fidelity.' She always added sugar, stirring until, like magic, it disappeared. 'Invisible food,' she said. 'Flowers need to eat too.'

It seemed as if she were talking more to herself than to Patrick, but he stood watching anyway, transfixed by her agile fingers twisting the flowers into a bright globe, sweet violet for modesty, azaleas for temperance, white daisies for innocence, sweet pea for delicate pleasure and departure. The scent was heavy and delicious, like warm honey. Then Mr Morrin died.

'He fell down dead at the bus stop,' said Patrick's mother. 'He was on his way to visit his sister,' she added, as if his death would have been explicable had his destination been more outlandish.

Patrick wasn't allowed to attend the funeral, but through the venetian blinds he watched the mourners arrive at the Morrins' house for morning tea. In they marched, black-clad clusters of twos and threes, worker ants bearing shortbread and sandwiches and Swiss rolls, making their way to Mrs Morrin who sat huge and terrible in her front room. And there were his parents, filing in with the others in their dark finery. He rarely saw them so dressed up, and as they passed he wondered if they really were his parents at all, or just actors pretending to be the Morrins' neighbours. His mother was wearing her cornflower eyeshadow and had a gauzy veil covering her eyes, and his father had his hat positioned low on his head like a film-star spy. For a moment Patrick wanted to tap on the window to them, but then they were inside and the street was empty.

They were gone for a long time. Patrick made himself some toast and a boiled egg around one o'clock, and some tea a couple of hours later. He cut himself two large wedges of sultana cake, too, hoping his mother wouldn't notice how much had been eaten, and was just settling into a third slice when she appeared at the front door. She stumbled slightly over the mat and leaned on the hall table.

'Patrick sweetheart,' she said, 'get the crystal vase for your mother would you, there's a good boy. Mrs Morrin has so many flowers and nowhere to put them all.'

When Patrick returned she was examining herself in the mirror, turning her head this way and that.

'Do you think this hairstyle makes me look frumpy?'

'I think you look like a film star,' said Patrick. 'In a spy film.'

His mother laughed and took the vase from him. Her breath smelled stale and sweet at the same time, like the sugar water smelled after the flowers had started to turn slimy. 'Poor Mr Morrin,' she sighed, reapplying her lipstick. 'Fell down dead at the bus stop.'

Patrick watched her teeter down the drive and up to Mrs Morrin's front door, and decided that she didn't look like a film star at all any more. She was back to being an ant.

Mrs Morrin took her time returning the vase. After a fortnight or so, when Patrick's mother was gazing out the sitting-room window at her beds of chrysanthemums, their heads heavy with the weight of petals, she said, 'I must get my vase back.' A week more went by, and she said, 'Surely all her bouquets have died by now, the shop-bought ones never last.' After another week she said, 'I hope she doesn't think it was a present.'

'Why don't you just ask her for it?' said Patrick's father, stoking the fire with dry pine logs. 'I will if you don't.'

'I need it back,' said Patrick's mother. 'All my chrysanthemums are going to waste, it's a crime.' She stared through the glass at them, and as the new logs caught and flared behind her, the flower beds seemed to burst into flame.

Patrick and his parents spent their evenings in the sitting room, his mother knitting, his father reading the paper. Sometimes Patrick read, and sometimes he drew pictures of the Meccano constructions he and Andrew made, and sometimes he just sat and listened to the flames hissing and spitting in the grate like a nest of bright snakes. The fire was kept in check by his father, who stood every half hour to feed it careful logs. If no wood was required, he still made a point of inspecting it, neatening it with the brass poker. Patrick wasn't allowed to touch it.

'I once saw a man with third-degree burns over ninety per cent of his body,' his father said. 'He looked like a plum that had burst its skin.'

Only when the grate needed cleaning was anyone else permitted access. Patrick's mother took over then, dabbing the cold bars with black, wrapping dead cinders in paper and sprinkling them on the garden like a witch.

It was Andrew who showed Patrick how to make his own fire. At school, in the lunch-hour, they positioned a pocket magnifying glass to catch the sun.

'Watch,' said Andrew, and held an ant still with a pin. Patrick concentrated on the insect, watched its tiny legs squirm, and the sounds of the playground retreated and the sun beat down on Patrick's neck and the backs of his legs, and he concentrated and the ant's feelers fluttered and suddenly it was alight, and for a moment Patrick believed he had made it happen by the power of thought. Then Andrew explained how it worked, how the sun could be magnified, the light bent, and it was so easy it scared Patrick a little. He thought about Christmas, when he'd stayed at Aunt Joyce's and slept in the room made of glass, and how he'd seen Faye flitting past in her nightdress. Andrew let him borrow the magnifying glass, just for one day, and he sat on the back porch and burned holes in dry leaves, paper, scraps of cloth from the dresses his mother had made.

The fire was nobody's fault. Patrick's mother said that over and over, as if trying to convince herself of it. Because what everybody knew, but what nobody said, was that Patrick was responsible.

'The main thing is, we're all fine,' she said. 'We can replace furniture and curtains and books. We can't replace people.'

They stayed with her sister while the new house was built on the foundations of the old one. At Joyce's suggestion they began making a list of everything they'd lost, for insurance. The bigger items—tables, beds, the hall stand, the stove—were easy to recall, as were things used every day: crockery, hairbrushes, slippers, pots. Things that were seldom needed, though, things that had been packed away in drawers or trunks or cupboards, were harder to remember. Patrick's father kept a notebook by his bed, and each morning the list had grown, an inventory compiled, it seemed, as he slept. For the first few weeks he and his wife conducted strange conversations as, little by little, they recalled their possessions.

He said, 'The boxes in the scullery.'

She said, 'My blue ball-gown.'

He said, 'The gardening books.'

She said, 'Your leather gloves.'

It made Patrick think of the party game where a selection of things was placed on a tray, displayed for a few minutes and covered again. He'd always been hopeless at that game. His memory wasn't methodical; he mixed things up, confused colours and names, got the order wrong.

Faye was away at boarding school so Patrick was allowed to sleep in her room again. At night he explored it, picking up china ballerinas and books and lengths of ribbon. He discovered a small wooden box containing hair clips, combs, a few fine brown hairs. In a drawer was an old pair of tights with holes in the heels and the knees. Sometimes he could hear Aunt Joyce and Ronnie giggling through the wall. Sometimes, too, he could hear his parents arguing in the guest suite, and now and again he heard his own name.

'Accident?' his father yelled one night. '*Accident?*'

Things were different by day. His mother flitted about like a new bride, poring over furnishing catalogues and visiting shop after shop. When she returned to Joyce's each afternoon her handbag was swollen with samples of fabric and wallpaper and carpet. She tracked down replicas of their furniture, happily announcing that she'd found a kitchen table just like the old one, a sofa covered in the same material, a rocking chair that was almost exactly the same.

'Look at these,' she said, arranging her swatches in various combinations for her husband's approval.

Graham liked all of them.

'But you must have a favourite,' she said. 'If you had to decide between the primrose and the marigold, say, which one would you prefer?'

'I'm happy with whichever one you like best,' was all he would say.

Patrick waited to be asked what he thought, but his mother pressed her lips tight and continued arranging the samples in silence, as if playing Patience. After a while she said, 'Yes, there we are,' and Patrick looked up from his book to see the colours of their old house spread on the table. He opened his mouth to speak, but already his mother was collecting up the reject samples for disposal. He felt as if he were looking through his kaleidoscope—which he'd lost in the fire—and no matter how he turned and turned it the pieces of glass fell the same way. Their new house was to be a recreation of their old one.

Patrick's father spent his weekends there. He'd decided he needed a garden shed, and he wanted to build it himself. He was putting it right down the end of the garden, past the plum tree, he told his son, out of harm's way. For emergencies, a torch would be kept in the workbench drawer, but no matches.

Everybody was nice to Patrick at school. The other boys gave him toy cars and aeroplanes and books to replace the ones he'd lost, and the masters took an extra interest in him, constantly asking if he was all right, if he needed anything. Mr Ross gave him a whole new set of pencils and pens, including a sleek green fountain pen in its own case.

'Make sure you don't lend it to anyone,' he said. 'Fountain pens mould to the shape of your hand, and someone else can put it off balance completely.'

Patrick wrote a few lines with the fountain pen every day so that it would take on the contours of his hand. He didn't show it to his parents. He kept it hidden in Faye's hair-clip box.

'Now you're not messing up any of Faye's things, are you?' his mother asked from time to time. 'We can't have her arriving home for her holidays to find everything in the wrong place.'

His father took no notice of the gifts Patrick received at school, until he came home with a Meccano set from Andrew.

'The No. 2 Outfit,' said Graham. 'Not particularly comprehensive, but a good basic selection of parts.'

'I'm not sure I want you accepting things from that boy,' said his mother. 'It was Andrew who lent him the magnifying glass,' she told Joyce. 'Of course, the main thing is, we're all fine.'

'I've been doing a spot of research,' said Graham, 'and it seems Meccano might be a good investment. The special Outfits that were made before the war, in particular, are highly sought-after. The trick is knowing what to buy.'

From then on, when other fathers came home with sweets in their pockets and coins in their fists, six o'clock heroes cold from the street, Patrick's father unpacked Meccano brochures and issues of *Meccano Magazine*. He studied them at great length, ticking certain pages, ringing certain pictures, noting down details from the collectors' private advertisements.

The Meccano Magazine, read Patrick, *published in the interests of boys, contains splendid articles on such subjects as Famous Engineers and Inventors, Electricity, Bridges, Cranes, Railways, Wonderful*

Machinery, Aeroplanes, Latest Patents, Nature Study, Stamps, Photography and Books—in fact it deals with those subjects in which all healthy boys are interested. New Meccano models and new parts are announced from time to time; interesting competitions are arranged for Meccano boys, and there are special articles for owners of Hornby Trains. The Meccano Magazine has a larger circulation than any similar boys' magazine, and is read in every civilised country in the world.

'Did you know,' he said to his father, 'that you can make a real loom from Meccano?'

His mother looked up from her knitting.

'You can weave real hatbands and neckties,' he said.

'After careful consideration,' said Graham, 'I've decided to start with a No. 115 Shipbuilding Outfit. They were faithful reproductions, Doreen, made exactly to scale. I've found one for a reasonable price.'

On the day they moved into their new house, Joyce insisted on accompanying them. She brought Ronnie with her, and Ronnie brought his camera. Patrick soon saw why: a wide red ribbon hung across the front door.

'If you'll do the honours, Graham,' she said, handing Patrick's father her dressmaking scissors.

That was the first photo from after the fire: Patrick and his parents and their new front door, which was almost indistinguishable from their old front door. Patrick's father was bent over the ribbon, the scissors poised like the silver hands of a clock. Another minute and the three of them would be inside, and their new life would have begun.

Patrick was uncomfortable in the new house. Every day there were sombre looks from his father, and his mother spent the house-keeping money on frivolous things like lace handkerchiefs and hair slides. Patrick learned to be very quiet, to make himself transparent, as insubstantial as a puff of smoke. And it seemed to work, because when he did speak—may I have a piece of sultana cake or may I go and play at Andrew's—his mother would start, and look up from her knitting as if she had forgotten he was there. Knitting took up all her spare time. She made ill-fitting jumpers for Patrick and his father. She made cardigans, socks, sometimes a waistcoat or a tie. She made more than they needed; it kept her hands busy.

'Thank you, Doreen, just the thing,' Graham would boom. 'You'll wear them and you'll like them,' he'd say when she was out of earshot, so Patrick had no choice but to inhabit these outfits, these lumpy costumes, and play at being a good, quiet boy.

The house, too, had an artificial feel, as if rebuilt by someone unfamiliar with the old place. There was a greyish blue sofa under the sitting-room window, exactly where the old one had stood, but the shade chosen was too dark, the fabric too slippery. It was like trying to sit on water. The rocking chair swung back too far, the wallpaper was too green. And the dialogues were unnatural, over-rehearsed. The more Patrick's father chatted on about the weather, local news, the meal they were eating, the more Doreen retreated into silence. Patrick kept expecting to open the front door one day and find nothing behind it but arms of wood propping up a façade, and, smiling in the ruins, cardboard cut-outs of his parents.

One evening his father arrived home from work beaming, carrying a heavy parcel.

'Open it,' he said to Doreen. Inside, after she'd removed a layer of newspaper, was a dinner plate, and beneath it another layer of newspaper and another plate, and she kept unwrapping plate after plate until a complete dinner set covered the table as if for an impromptu banquet. And it was exactly the same as their old set: a rim of gold around the edge, a border of ivy leaves, and a single leaf in the centre.

Each day the Mercers ate their meals off the new plates, just as they had before the fire. Patrick watched his father cutting tidy portions of food, efficiently and sensibly pressing peas and carrots and meat into forkfuls of mashed potatoes. Each night Patrick dried the dishes, taking the wet plates from his mother one by one and moving the tea-towel across the rings of ivy, back and forth, while his father read the paper in the sitting room. Patrick focused on the leaves, drawn into the dark clusters until the kitchen receded and he was encircled by ivy, by green stars. And then his mother let the water out of the sink, and the drain sucked and coughed, and then she filled the kettle, and everything was as it had been, or close enough for the differences not to matter.

When he arrived home from school one day he found her in his room. She was sipping an amber liquid, the colour of tea without milk.

'I've put your socks in with your underpants,' she said, 'so you've got a drawer free.' She gestured at a mound of his belongings in the centre of the room: a messy pyre of comics, writing paper, odd pieces of Meccano. 'I'm very tired of stepping over all of this, Patrick. Just very tired.'

And she did look tired. Her eyes were bloodshot, her words ran into each other. She took another sip of her tea-coloured drink.

'I liked them where they were,' said Patrick in a small voice. 'I knew where everything was.'

'They were all over the floor. It was dangerous.'

'It was deliberate,' he said, but couldn't explain that as long as he hadn't found a place for everything in his new room, it was as if he hadn't moved in at all. As if, at any time, he could leave this new, skewed place, where things were the same but not the same.

'What's this?' said his mother. She was fingering the green fountain pen, opening and shutting its slim black case.

'A present.'

'Who's been giving you presents? It's not your birthday.'

'Mr Ross gave it to me.'

'Ah, Mr Ross.' She pursed her lips. 'It's far too good for you to take to school,' she said, and snapped the case shut. 'We'll put it away somewhere safe.' And the green pen was locked away in the new sitting-room cabinet, where she'd filed the receipts for all the other new things, including the one for the cabinet. Sometimes he saw her using it to sign cheques or write letters, moulding it to the shape of her thin hand, her little fingers. He kept hoping Mr Ross wouldn't ask where it was. When he mentioned the pen to his father, Graham told him not to bother Doreen about it, as she was very tired.

'You can use it when you're older,' he told Patrick. 'You've had quite enough new things lately.' But Patrick knew that the pen would never fit his hand now.

At night, after he'd gone to bed, Patrick could hear his mother's knitting needles clicking. Some nights she knitted in his dreams, and he saw not sleeves and heels and cardigan halves growing beneath her needles but pieces of their old lives. They were lumpy in places, and there were inconsistencies, and holes, and sometimes they came undone. And sometimes, if the tension was too great, they buckled.

It didn't seem odd to Patrick that Aunt Joyce should come and stay.

'Your mother's going away for a little while, to have a rest,' his father told him. 'Aunt Joyce is going to look after us.'

Like the blue sofa, the rocking chair, the wallpaper, Aunt Joyce was a replacement. She looked very similar to her sister; people had always said so. In fact, the match was so close Patrick hardly missed his mother, hardly noticed she was gone.

'I have something for you,' Aunt Joyce said, 'from Faye.' She produced a small volume bound in red from her suitcase. '*A Book of Golden Deeds*,' she said. 'It's one of Faye's favourites, but I'm sure she won't mind you having it, under the circumstances.'

'That's very kind,' said Patrick's father. 'We lost all our books, of course. Very thoughtful, isn't it, Patrick? What do you say?'

'Thank you, Aunt Joyce.'

'You're sure Faye won't mind?'

'Not at all. She has too many others she never even looks at. Ronnie keeps buying them for her.'

That night Patrick began to read. *A Golden Deed*, wrote Charlotte M. Yonge, *must be something more than mere display of fearlessness. Grave and resolute fulfilment of duty is required to give it the true weight. Such duty kept the sentinel at his post at the gate of Pompeii, even when the stifling dust of ashes came thicker and thicker from the volcano, and the liquid mud streamed down, and the people fled and struggled on, and still the sentry stood at his post, unflinching, till death had stiffened his limbs; and his bones, in their helmet and breastplate, with the hand still raised to keep the suffocating dust from mouth and nose, have remained even till our own times to show how a Roman soldier did his duty.*

Patrick kept turning the pages until he couldn't stay awake. He read of the Constant Prince, who offered himself as a prisoner so that the town of Ceuta could be freed; the Heroes of the Plague, who ministered to the stricken despite the danger of infection; the Shepherd Girl of Nanterre, who protected Paris from the murderous Franks and Huns; the Faithful Slaves of Haiti, who saved their white masters from massacre; and the Children in the Wood of the Far South, who were lost in the Australian bush for more than a week, the youngest surviving only because his sister gave him her dress for warmth. There was mention, too, of heroic canines such as Delta, who saved his master from the sea, from robbers and from wolves; a Newfoundland dog who won a silver collar by saving first a postman and then his bag of letters from a swelled ford; and the dog who daily carried bread to a shepherd's child lost in a cave behind a waterfall. *And oh, young readers,* said Charlotte M. Yonge, *if your hearts burn within you as you read of these various forms of the truest and deepest glory, and you long for time and place to act in the like devoted way, bethink yourselves that the alloy of such actions is to be constantly worked away in daily life; and that if ever it be your lot to do a Golden Deed, it will probably be in unconsciousness that you do anything extraordinary, and that the whole impulse will consist in the having absolutely forgotten self.*

Before he went to sleep Patrick looked again at the name inked inside the cover: Faye Elizabeth Stratford, written in small, careful letters.

'I wish they'd bring back summer time,' said Aunt Joyce. She shook out Patrick's jacket and held it open for him. 'Daylight saving. We could do with some extra daylight. It'll be chilly coming home from Ronnie's.'

Patrick nodded. Aunt Joyce was always offering him portions of information: it was going to rain, there was fish pie for dinner, his father would be home late, Ronnie was coming to lunch. It was her way of keeping him informed, of ensuring he wasn't upset by anything unexpected. He was not to be upset. He'd overheard his father saying so the first night Aunt Joyce stayed.

'We were on summer time throughout the war, do you remember, Patrick?' she said. 'Even in winter. And then we had double summer time in summer. It was strange, the way it stayed light till so late, but I loved it.'

'Why did they call it daylight saving?' said Patrick. 'If we lost an hour?'

Aunt Joyce sighed. 'You got it back again, at the end of summer.'

'What did they do with it that whole time? Did they keep it somewhere?' Patrick had a sudden image of nationwide frenzy, concerned citizens rushing outside and collecting the daylight in buckets, bowls, wine goblets, putting it aside for leaner times. He wondered how it might be stored, how long it kept. Could it be frozen? What was the shelf-life of daylight?

'Patrick,' said Aunt Joyce. 'For goodness' sake. Your other arm.' She held out the stiff jacket and pulled his hand through the hole as if threading a giant needle. 'And this,' she said, stretching a knitted hat down almost over his eyes. 'It might be nearly summer but it's still cool in the evenings. We can't be having you catch cold, now can we?'

As they walked to Ronnie's, Patrick began sweating under all the layers, but he didn't say anything. Aunt Joyce held his hand, and whenever he looked up he could see fibres of wool; a haze of red, as if the clouds had changed colour, as if the sky were on fire.

'You must be missing your mother,' said Aunt Joyce, and Patrick, inhaling her perfume and wondering whether Faye smelled like that too, said yes.

When Doreen came home from her rest, she didn't look rested at all. She moved slowly and spoke slowly and she'd turned grey. Her hair was brittle and stuck out around her face at odd angles, and her skin was very soft, as frail as ashes. And then Patrick realised. Along with his clothes and his books and the beds and tables and photographs and dinner plates, along with the blue sofa and the velvet curtains and the mirror in the hall, he'd also lost his mother in the fire.

Mrs Morrin came to visit her, a tin of biscuits under one arm and the crystal vase under the other.

'So awful for you, Doreen dear,' she said. 'But haven't you made a great effort with the house?' She scanned the sitting room, ran one gloved hand over the sofa as if smoothing the folds of a dress.

'The main thing is, we're all fine,' said Patrick's mother, her hand shaking a little as she poured the tea.

Mrs Morrin handed her the vase. 'I'd been meaning to get this back to you ages ago,' she said, 'but you know how the days just disappear. It was lucky I hung on to it in the end, wasn't it?'

Patrick's mother held the vase on her lap as she and Mrs Morrin sipped their tea.

'I couldn't believe how quickly they rebuilt,' said Mrs Morrin, her chained reading glasses resting on her chest. 'Mind you, they were here morning, noon and night, mixing the concrete and crashing about, weren't they?'

Patrick's mother smiled and sipped her tea, and rubbed her fingers back and forth across the ridges of crystal. 'It's lovely of you to return this,' she said.

In the new house, though, there were no more flowers. Instead, Patrick's mother placed the vase in the bathroom, on the marble cabinet. Sometimes, if she'd just had a bath, there would be talcum powder everywhere, resting on the cold linoleum, the edge of the bath, the chrome taps. It was like very fine, scented ash, and if Patrick lifted the vase he could see the flower-shaped base in negative, picked out in relief on the dark marble.

Slowly, month by month, Doreen began filling it with guest soaps, fancy coloured gobbets the size of small stones. Sometimes they were pale pink, like the inside of a shell, or sometimes violet, or the same shade of lemon as her fragile tea set. They came wrapped in translucent paper, as fine as a butterfly's wing, which held the scent of the soaps even after it had been smoothed and placed flat in a drawer for safekeeping. She said the paper was useful for wrapping small gifts, but she rarely gave gifts, unless you counted the socks and ties and jumpers she knitted for Patrick and his father—and one did not wrap such masculine items in flimsy, scented paper. Every few weeks she would bring home another guest soap with her shopping, unwrap it and place it in the vase. But there were never any guests.

Then Ronnie took Aunt Joyce on a cruise, and Faye came to stay during the Christmas holidays. Patrick slept in the sitting room, and Faye had his room, and his mother left a small pile of fluffy towels and flannels on the end of the bed. On top of them, like an ornament, she placed one of her guest soaps: a pale green mermaid, one of a pair.

'I'm sorry the towels don't quite match, Faye,' she said. 'I do love matching towels. I had seven beautiful sets, wedding presents mostly. I had some mauve ones from Faye's mother, actually, didn't I, darling?' She looked at Graham. 'Joyce has always had such good taste.'

'I'm sure these will be lovely,' said Faye. 'Patrick really doesn't have to sleep in the sitting room, I'd be fine on the sofa.'

'Nonsense,' said Doreen. 'It's cold in the sitting room in winter. We might not have the space your mother does, but we still know how to treat a guest.'

'I think the new house is very nice.'

Doreen piled another biscuit on to her niece's plate. 'Eat up, I made them specially,' she said. She dabbed at the crumbs on her own plate with a moistened finger. 'We did lose a few things, of course. We've been able to replace most of them, not all. But the main thing is, we're all fine.'

When Patrick lay down on the sofa that night he found that he couldn't stretch out. His legs were too long, or his body was, or perhaps even his neck. He didn't take much notice of these changes from day to day, but here everything felt out of proportion, growing all at once. His arm trailed on the carpet, his fingers locating gritty crumbs. Under his hipbone the sofa was hard, packed solid with horsehair.

As he was falling asleep he saw himself on a huge greyish blue horse which shook him to his bones as it cantered along a beach. Sand sprayed up around him, caught in his nostrils, his hair, worked itself under his fingernails and his clothes. He felt like one of the heroes from his *Book of Golden Deeds*. The sea became a blur, and Patrick began to think the horse would run right into the water. Sand blasted his skin, and the horse bucked, and Patrick was thrown through the air. Instead of landing with a sting the way he did when he bellyflopped at the baths, though, he came to rest very gently in shallow water. He felt the waves sidling up his long arms, his legs. He imagined he could stay like that forever, and underneath him the sand moulded to the shape of his body, and he was not too gangly or out of proportion. Someone spoke his name, and the waves were lapping at him, stroking his hair. *Patrick*, said the voice again, *Patrick*.

Faye had slipped under the covers and was lying on her side, balancing on the hard edge of the sofa. Her hair was wet, and a strand of it slid across Patrick's cheek. He could feel the line it left, like a snail's silvery track.

'I just had a bath,' she whispered, 'and I was so cold when I got out.' She draped Patrick's arm around her shoulder and shivered. His hand extended out past the edge of the sofa and hung in mid-air. 'Don't you want to kiss me?' said Faye after a moment.

Patrick remembered what his mother had said: 'You must be on your best behaviour when your cousin's here. We don't want any bad manners.' He gave Faye a quick peck on the cheek.

'I'm not your aunt,' she laughed, and dived under the eiderdown. 'You're such a lucky boy,' she said, or perhaps it was, 'You're such a naughty boy.' Patrick couldn't tell; the covers muffled her voice. And then she stopped talking altogether, and Patrick felt her mouth seal around him. Lucky, he thought. She must have said lucky.

He was woken by his mother pulling back the sitting-room curtains.

'Go and call Faye, there's a good boy,' she said. 'We're having breakfast at the table today.' She took a lacy tablecloth from the dresser and unfolded it with a flourish. She was wearing her good dressing-gown—quilted velvet piped with satin at the cuffs, hem and collar. Her hair was pinned into a sleek roll and it appeared she was wearing make-up. She seemed taller, too, and when Patrick looked at her feet he saw she was wearing high-heeled slippers trimmed with fur.

'Are they new?' he said.

'Do you like them? My blue ones are looking scruffy already.' She hurried through to the dining room and placed four fringed mats around the table. In the middle she arranged a silver tray spread with a selection of small crystal dishes, each one containing a different type of jam or jelly or marmalade or honey. A silver bowl held tiny servings of butter, each one a perfect yellow curl.

'It's a lovely spot here in the morning,' said Doreen, looking round at her husband and Patrick and Faye and beaming, as if eating breakfast at the table was the most normal thing in the world. Faye was buttoned up to the neck in a pink candlewick robe. A flannelette collar, also buttoned, was just visible. She did not meet Patrick's eye.

'It gets the sun until midday in the winter. Just what you need to wake you up.' Patrick's mother ruffled his hair. 'Not as cosy as your mother's breakfast nook, of course, Faye. She always likes telling us about her breakfast nook.'

'Mum never bothers with breakfast. She's too busy in the morning, getting dressed. Ronnie likes her to look smart.'

'But breakfast is the most important meal of the day! She can't go without her breakfast. Imagine, Graham!'

Patrick's father sliced into a grilled tomato. 'A cruise,' he said. 'That must be setting Ronnie back a fair bit.'

'He doesn't mind spending money,' said Faye, smoothing her napkin carefully across her lap. 'You can't take it with you, he says.'

'I've always wanted to go on a cruise,' said Doreen. 'So romantic, sailing the seas.'

'I don't think I'd like it,' said Faye. 'Being surrounded by all that water, and nowhere to escape to.'

'Escape?' said Doreen. 'You wouldn't need to escape. Everything's right there, on board the ship. Everything you could ever need.'

'Well,' said Faye, 'maybe Uncle Graham can take you on a cruise some time.'

'Yes,' said Doreen, 'maybe. Now, dear, what will you have?'

Faye waved away rashers of bacon, fried eggs. 'No thank you,' she said. 'I'll just have a piece of toast. I'm watching my weight.'

'Nonsense,' said Doreen.

'When you're dieting you never have breakfast either,' said Patrick's father. 'Or lunch, some days.'

Patrick's mother giggled. 'Poor Graham! He thinks women are such picky creatures, Faye. Patrick, eat your egg.'

'Faye said Aunt Joyce lives on coffee and cigarettes,' said Patrick. 'That's how she keeps her weight down.'

'Oh dear, I've forgotten the butter knife,' said Doreen. 'Would you just run and get it for us, Patrick, there's a good boy. We can't have Faye thinking we're uncouth, can we?' And she laughed her tinkly laugh.

'Where is it?' said Patrick.

'Pardon, dear?'

'The butter knife. Where's it kept?'

'Oh, you are a cheeky boy,' laughed his mother, 'you know perfectly well it's in the dresser drawer.'

From the sitting room Patrick could hear her questioning Faye about boarding school. He couldn't hear Faye's replies, but his mother's voice became more and more shrill as she insisted that Faye have a sausage, some more toast.

'You must never have the chance to eat a proper breakfast, you poor love,' she said. 'Go on, have some bacon, that's what I bought it for.'

Patrick couldn't find a butter knife anywhere, so he took another ordinary knife from the kitchen. All over the bench were the sticky jars he helped himself to each morning with his toast. He usually left crumbs and streaks of butter in each one, but the jars were all empty now. In the sink there were scrapings of reject jam, jelly, marmalade; the vestiges of previous breakfasts. The lids were scattered across the bench like dropped coins. *Black currant*, they said, *strawberry, cherry, bitter orange.*

After Faye left, Patrick moved back into his bedroom. He'd expected to find some trace of her there, a sock under the bed, a flimsy handkerchief, perhaps just a perfume lingering in the air. There was nothing. He'd been hoping his mother wouldn't have changed the sheets, but of course she had. His bed was made up stiff and new, as tight as a closed book.

It wasn't until the next morning that he found the mermaid soap. It must have fallen down the side of the bed at some stage, and Faye had never used it. Perhaps, Patrick thought, it had slipped under the covers; perhaps Faye's body had warmed it in the dark. It had left a green smear on the floral wallpaper, as if an extra, blurry leaf had sprouted overnight. Patrick cupped it in his hand. It fitted there perfectly, the mermaid's curling tail almost reaching the base of his thumb, and if he closed his fist it was completely hidden, and nobody else would know it was there.

'Don't use all the hot water,' said his mother. 'I've got a lot to get through today.' She brushed past Patrick with an armload of dirty sheets and towels. She was back to wearing her blue slippers, he noticed, and hadn't bothered to pin her hair up.

Only when he was in the bath did he unclench his fist. The green mermaid floated in his palm, moving slightly with the currents when he shifted his arms, his legs. He rubbed the soap over his skin and watched foam appear. The mermaid slipped and slid from his grasp like a tiny fish, and he had to keep snatching her back from the warm water, trying to make her last as long as possible.

When he got out of the bath he dressed for school. He studied himself in his mirror, and found he looked the same as ever. The same clothes, the same fine hair. He smelled different, though; every now and then, as he moved, he caught the scent of the mermaid soap on his skin. He scanned his bookcase for something to read on the bus. There was a space on the shelf. One of his books was missing.

'Mum,' he called. 'Mum!'

He found her in the garden, hanging out a load of washing.

'Have you seen my *Book of Golden Deeds?*' His breath pushed behind his words in clouds; there had been a heavy frost in the night and the grass was still white with it.

'What book? What are you talking about?' she mumbled, her mouth full of pegs. He was about to answer her. Then he saw the dress.

It hung on the line like a frozen flower. The skirt was stiff and cold, the folds set solid by frost, rows of lace encrusted with silver. It reminded Patrick of a cake his mother had once made: she had iced it to look like an ornate wedding dress, and in the middle she had positioned a kewpie doll which she'd covered with a modest icing bodice. Patrick didn't recall what the occasion had been, but he remembered thinking that his mother's creation was all out of proportion; the kewpie doll's legs couldn't possibly be long enough to reach to the bottom of the huge cake dress. He also remembered his mother cutting wedges out of it with a bone-handled knife, and seeing her afterwards in the kitchen, licking the bodice off the kewpie doll, whose legs, he was shocked to see, had been amputated for the occasion.

'What book?' she said again. She was pegging towels and sheets at the other end of the line, her movements sending shock-waves down the thin cord, making the dress shiver and glitter. Patrick touched it, lifted the icy hem. It was a party dress, he thought, a little girl's dress, too young for Faye. The fabric was heavy and fragile at the same time, and for a moment he thought a piece might break off, just come away in his hands.

'Nothing. It doesn't matter.'

'She forgot to bring it in last night,' said his mother through her mouthful of pegs. 'Goodness knows how much it'll cost to post to her at school.'

When Patrick came home that afternoon the dress was hanging in the scullery. It had thawed out and was almost dry, although on the floor there was a small patch of water. He decided not to ask his mother about his *Book of Golden Deeds* again. Perhaps it had been missing for a while and he had never noticed, or perhaps he had lent it to someone at school and they had both forgotten about it. It was so easy to mislay things if you weren't careful.

He used the mermaid soap each time he had a bath. He kept her in a box under his bed, and every day she grew smaller and smaller, her scales rubbed smooth, her eyes disappearing. Soon she would break in two.

At the cemetery there were angels, anchors, stars. Colette weaved her way through the plots, *Ethel Ruby, Doris Ada, We sleep into everlasting waking, Beloved husband.* She didn't stop to read any inscriptions in detail; she was looking for a place to sit. She could feel the letter in her jeans pocket, bending to the shape of her body, the sheets of paper slowly reaching blood temperature. *Father in thy gracious keeping, George Arthur, How sweet to rest, Esteemed— beloved—lamented.* She was in the old part of the cemetery, where hardly anyone came to visit, and many of the plots were in a state of neglect. Stone wreaths and urns and ornate crosses had been toppled from their bases by wind or gravity, lettering had been eaten by rain. A few graves were covered with black-and-white china tiles. They made Colette think of chessboards, and she imagined pieces assembled for a mossy game: pebbles, carved bone, perhaps tiny figures woven from grass. *Winifred Myrtle, Whoso' walketh uprightly, The deep blue sea hath won.* Bees meandered from stone to stone, and high in the macrocarpas a tui preened its parson's heart. The sun caught on something white nestled in the grass just ahead. When Colette got closer she saw it was a stone dove, marble probably, carrying a laurel wreath in its beak. She sat down.

It didn't look as if the bird had fallen from any of the surrounding monuments; here there was only a cluster of dark obelisques, the occasional severe cross. Colette stroked the bird's outstretched wings, its cold belly. Far too heavy to fly. The point at which it had broken off its marble base was rough, covered with tiny facets like the crystals she had grown when she was a child. She remembered stirring salt and water together in a jar, then lowering a string into the liquid and waiting. Every morning she checked it, and every afternoon when she came home from school. It was like magic when the crystals started to grow, even though, as her *Hey Kids—Science is Fun!* book explained, there was a perfectly good explanation for it.

'Why does Colette get all the good presents?' Dominic had whined when the book arrived. Aunt Pam had sent it from the United States, where she and her American husband and Nina ate out at restaurants and went skiing and took cruises. The gifts she sent Colette—gauzy scarves, earrings, beaded shoulder bags—suggested a magical, glamorous creature, someone Colette might turn into one day.

'Your aunt's sent you a parcel, has she,' her mother had said. 'I thought she was too busy buying new cars and having her hair coloured.' She never called Pam by her name, and used a particular emphasis when talking about her: it was always your *aunt*, or my *sister*. 'Doesn't she know you've got piles of books you've never even opened?'

Inside the cover was written *To darling Colette, with all our love, Pam, Rick and Nina.* There were three kisses, and underneath, in different handwriting—Rick's, presumably—were the words *Have a wild one!* Colette wasn't quite sure what this meant, but she took to saying it whenever possible.

'And not *Aunty* Pam and *Uncle* Rick,' she pointed out at school. 'They're more like friends, really.'

The book described how to insert a boiled egg into a narrow-necked bottle, how to write letters in code and how to construct pinhole cameras that captured light in a box. Some of the activities called for equipment Colette had never heard of, like dimes or Pop-Tart boxes.

'We can't do those ones,' her mother told her. 'You can only get those in America.' And the way she said America, it was as if she'd been asked to swallow vinegar.

The crystals were a great success. One of them was huge, as big as Colette's thumbnail, and she made a ring out of it. She twisted an Easter-egg wrapper into a silvery rope, then glued the crystal to it.

She wore it on the way to school, intending to show it to her classmates, perhaps hint at a boyfriend or a wealthy, offshore father, but it had started to rain and the crystal grew smaller and smaller and by the time she reached school it had melted away.

She slipped the letter out of her pocket.

31 March 2000
Dear Colette,

Patrick has been making excellent progress and the doctors are confident he will make a complete recovery. This does not mean, however, that he is any less in need of your visits, phone calls and letters. Perhaps now more than ever your support is vital, so we hope you will continue to help with his recovery in any way you can.

Patrick is learning to speak all over again, and is doing very well. Every day he rediscovers new words, which is exciting for all of us. 'Extinguish' is his favourite at the moment. We're hoping it won't be too long before he can write a note to you himself. The doctors think this should only be a matter of time.

At the bottom of the page there was a handwritten note. *Just thought you would like to know he has been repeating your name quite frequently. He says 'Colette' almost every day. One of the Friends suggested it is simply a good name for practising consonants, but he said it before he came round, too. I'm aware that you and he were once close. I'm sure he'd love to hear from you.*

As Colette picked her way back down the path, a skateboarder whizzed by, nearly knocking her over.

'Hey!' she shouted, 'don't you know where you are?'

He didn't say anything, or even look at her. His jeans were so baggy she wondered how they stayed up, and his striped shirt and hat suggested a make-believe creature, a pixie or a gnome. Patrick would not be a slave to such ridiculous fashions. Patrick would have a wardrobe full of sleek suits and immaculate shirts, pressed and ready for him to slide into again, still faintly scented, perhaps, with Fahrenheit or Boss. None of this CK1 rubbish. He would be tall, she decided, and on the weekends, when visiting his country home, say, he would wear simple but elegant clothes: well-cut khaki trousers, black polo-neck jumpers. She fingered the envelope, ran her thumb-nail under the stamp of the Queen in profile. Perhaps, she thought, she should visit him. See whether his face rang a bell, or whether hers did. She could afford to take some time off from her studies of New Zealand's past in order to investigate her own, and she wanted to do some more travelling anyway. She'd been saving her money from minding Daniel and her father had sent his usual Christmas cheque, as well as a decent amount for her twenty-first birthday, so there was nearly enough for a ticket. And the letters did keep asking for visitors. She must have read them a dozen times by now, but still they made no sense. She'd searched every page for clues, for something that would tell her how he fitted into her life. She thought of the lemon-juice letters she and Nina had exchanged, of how simple it had been to decode them once she knew the trick.

She must have met Patrick when she was travelling. It was a long time ago, long enough to forget people she'd met along the way. She counted back in her mind, and realised it was two years since she'd been overseas. Two years since she'd left Justin, whom she barely thought about now.

'I speak French,' he said, 'we'll be fine.'

Colette studied the phrasebook anyway, practising her questions during the bus ride from Frankfurt. Across the aisle from them sat a very fat girl of about twenty.

'I learn too,' she said, holding up a German/French phrasebook. 'Do you know the word for fax machine? I must fax my mother when I arrive.'

Colette shook her head. She didn't want to encourage a conversation, and the girl seemed eager. Her fat face puckered when she smiled, and there was a thick black hair growing from a mole on her chin. Her ugliness offended Colette. Had she been feeling less tired, she told herself, she might have made an effort with the girl. But she muttered, 'I don't know,' and turned back to Justin. 'Will we arrive on time?' she asked him in French. 'Do I have to change?'

'For someone with a French name,' said Justin, 'your accent is hopeless.'

'It's not my fault they called me Colette. My mother just liked the name, she said.'

'You have to exaggerate your vowels more,' said Justin. 'Use your cheek muscles.' He pinched at Colette's face.

'The engine is overheating,' she said. 'What time do you close?'

'Colette. Is your jaw wired together?'

'No.'

'Move it, then. Pretend you're singing.'

'I can't sing, I've got a terrible voice. You told me so.'

Justin sighed. 'You don't actually have to sing, just move your face as if you are. Here, look.' He flipped through the phrasebook. 'Where does it hurt?' he said. 'It is nothing serious.'

'I thought you spoke French.'

'I do.'

'Why do you need the phrasebook, then?'

Justin dropped it back in Colette's lap. 'Fine. If you don't want my help, that's fine. We'll just see how you get on when you have to ask for directions.' And he closed his eyes, reclined his seat.

'We have reservations,' said Colette.

She flipped to the list of useful words: post office, exchange rate, doctor, chemist. Chemist. Her pill. She'd forgotten to take her pill the previous night. She'd had too much to drink—it's our last night in Germany, Justin had said—and they'd stumbled back to the hotel and had quick, slurred sex without even thinking about it. She yanked her day pack from beneath Justin's feet and rummaged through it, shaking out brochures, riffling the pages of her address book, unzipping every hidden pocket. Then she remembered. She'd put her pills in her sponge bag, and her sponge bag was in her full-sized pack, and that was in the luggage hold.

'Justin,' she whispered, 'my pills are in my other bag. I forgot to take one yesterday.'

He opened his eyes and stared blankly at her. Across the aisle she could see the fat German girl cocking her head, listening.

'My *pills*. You know.'

'Just take it when we get there. It'll be fine.'

He closed his eyes again. The fat German girl grinned at Colette. Colette closed her eyes too, and leaned against Justin. The fibres of his jersey scratched her cheek.

She couldn't sleep on the bus, even when they put the lights out. By the time they were in Paris, she calculated, she'd have missed two pills. She imagined a tiny creature forming inside her, its cells replicating and dividing and grouping themselves into a human shape as she and Justin climbed the Eiffel Tower, strolled along the Champs-Elysées. It would be minuscule, no bigger than the forgotten pill itself, so small it couldn't be felt, but growing. Justin leaned against her in his sleep, heavy, possessive.

It was early when they reached Paris, about seven a.m. Colette must have fallen asleep after all, because she jolted awake at the sound of the crackling microphone.

'We can't check into the hotel until nine,' said the guide, 'so you can either do the special orientation tour with us, or take the chance to look around on your own.'

Most of the travellers, too tired to get out of the bus, agreed by default to do the tour—which, the guide added with a smile, cost thirty francs.

'Come on,' said Justin, 'they've got enough out of us already.'

Outside the snow crunched underfoot, and the air was icy.

'I should see if I can get to my pack,' said Colette, but the bus had already started its engine, and the doors were hissing shut, and Justin was taking her arm and saying look, there's Sacré-Coeur.

The steps were wide, and so shallow Colette hardly realised she was climbing at all until she turned and there was the city stretching out at her feet. Justin put his arm around her, and for a moment everything was all right.

In the cramped hotel foyer, room keys were distributed. One by one groups of two and three, sometimes four, hauled luggage up the narrow staircase. Justin was leaning against the counter, flicking through some sightseeing leaflets, unworried. They were distributing the keys alphabetically, Colette realised, and Justin had booked the tour under his name. Warwick. She glared at him. She was being unreasonable, she knew. This was not a good way to start a holiday in Paris. She yanked open her pack. Clothes burst from it: jeans, sweatshirts, her slinky cream nightdress. It had straps that cut into her shoulders and made her feel cold, but Justin had insisted she bring it along. He would, he said, buy her another one in Paris that was even better. Her hand closed around the sheet of pills. The metallic covering was cold from its journey in the belly of the bus. She split open the foil, swallowed one pill and then another without water. The fat German girl watched her.

'This is going to be great,' said Justin, and took her hand and led her underground. 'There are entrances to the catacombs all over Paris, but most of them are sealed and you can't even tell where they are. If you know the right people, though, you can get into the illegal New Year's parties they have down here.' He did a Dracula laugh.

That's Transylvania, thought Colette, but she didn't say anything.

They passed under an archway carved with a French inscription.

'You are now entering the realm of death,' read Justin. 'Take a photo of me.'

There was a line of people behind them and Colette fumbled for her camera.

'Okay, now one of you,' said Justin, but Colette said no, there were people waiting to get through, and she could get one on the way back.

'We won't be coming through that door again,' said Justin, and although Colette knew there was no reason to be frightened, she pulled her coat tighter around her.

Along the passageways, dozens of skulls were set into the walls, formed into patterns which reminded Colette of weaving. Every now and then there was a cross made of skulls. They looked artificial, she thought, like something off a film set.

'Get a shot of this,' said Justin, and squatted in front of a cross. As Colette clicked the camera the film began to rewind. The sound was huge against the stone walls. It echoed off the bones, was amplified inside each hollow skull and thrown back louder than ever.

'I need some fresh air,' she said. She rushed on ahead, bending and curling through bone-lined passages that seemed to become tighter and tighter. She could hear laughter echoing through the tangle of pathways, snatches of many foreign tongues. Somewhere behind her was Justin, trying to keep up, pushing past tourists and woven bones. She didn't wait for him. When she reached the exit she ran up the steps, hungry for daylight.

'But this isn't where we came in,' she said, looking round at a street she'd never seen before. 'Where's the ticket office gone? Where's the Metro station?'

'I told you we wouldn't be coming through the entrance-way again,' said Justin.

'I think I need to sit down,' she said. She felt dizzy, as if she'd just climbed off a merry-go-round and her mother wasn't standing where she should be. She leaned against a building and closed her eyes.

'Are you okay?'

'I just wish you'd told me. I don't like surprises. You should have told me.'

'But it said in the guide book. You read the guide book, didn't you?' Justin rummaged in his bag, anxious to locate the relevant material, to prove himself right.

'I have no idea where we are,' said Colette quietly, but Justin said, 'It's all under control,' and unfolded the flimsy map. It rippled and snapped like a flag and Colette thought for a moment the wind would snatch it away, and they would never find their way back.

'You won't be able to fold that away again properly,' she said.

Justin seemed not to hear her. 'It's this way,' he said. 'The Metro's just round that corner.'

Colette didn't know whether to believe him or not.

That night she went walking through underground passages. Unlike the catacombs, though, the walls were not stone. They were white, almost transparent in some places, and very smooth. They were made entirely of bone. As Colette walked on, they thickened and closed like diseased arteries so that she had to stoop, crouch, and finally crawl. When she breathed on them, she found that they melted, and so she concentrated on one patch and breathed and breathed until the passageway rang with her own sighs. And eventually the bone melted away, and behind it was a door.

She felt unwell the next morning, but Justin insisted they rise early to visit Versailles. A proper visit wasn't included in the bus tour, he reminded her, so if they wanted to explore it thoroughly they would have to go that day. After nine a.m. the queues were impossible. He'd read that in the guide book.

They arrived just on nine, and already a line of people stretched down to the palace gates. Hundreds of feet had cleared a path in the snow from which nobody deviated; the expanses of white on either side were untouched. Just in front of them in the queue was the fat German girl. She was holding hands with a man Colette didn't remember from the bus. When the girl turned, Colette saw that her lips were so chapped they were dark with dry blood.

After waiting for more than an hour, the tour was over very quickly. Colette would have liked more time to admire the spindly furniture, to imagine herself sleeping in the high, curtained bed, writing at the inlaid desk with its many secret compartments.

'Moving on, moving on,' the tour guide kept saying.

Justin was reprimanded for taking a photograph; others were asked not to touch chairs, not to lean against walls. One of the last rooms they visited was the Galerie des Glaces. Its wall of mirrors was designed to throw sunlight back outside, to remind visitors to Louis XIV's garden that this was the residence of the Sun himself. Colette watched herself passing the icy wall. And then Justin came up behind her and took her hand, but she didn't see the real Justin, only many different reflections of him, and her own hand being taken again and again.

One Sunday after the fire, so he didn't have to spend time at home, Patrick went to the museum. He wandered from room to room, past glass cases filled with dead birds, butterflies, shards of porcelain, past mannequins dressed in antique clothes and positioned in antique bedrooms and parlours, past swordfish and suits of armour, masks and maps and bones. In his pocket was the silver disc from the cloakroom, and every few minutes he made sure it was still there. Without it the women behind the counter might not believe he was himself, and he wouldn't be able to retrieve his bag with his name written inside, or his coat with the label saying *Mercer* sewn to the lining.

In the Egyptian room he saw golden fingertips which ensured dexterity in the afterlife. He saw golden eyes and a golden tongue, and fragments of flowers buried with a princess. He also saw a mummified cat; like an awkwardly shaped gift, its wrappings betrayed their contents at a glance. Displayed around it were the embalmer's tools: bandages, stoppered vials and jars, beeswax, resin, moss, thin hooks as long as knitting needles. In a neighbouring case lay a much smaller creature, its contours suggesting a pine-cone or an egg, perhaps a fish. *Mummified falcon*, read the plaque. *For the Egyptians, falcons embodied Re, the sun-god.* Patrick imagined it inside the bandages, wings folded against its soft body, feet tucked away. All these years later, the plaque told him, it would still be preserved.

At one end of the Egyptian room was a door Patrick hadn't noticed at first. Everybody else was passing it as if it didn't exist, and for a moment Patrick thought it must be closed to the public. When he got closer, though, there was no sign denying him entry, so he turned the handle.

The first thing that struck him was the fragrance. The air was close and sweet, like skin dusted with powder after a bath. Very little light entered through the high, tight windows.

'Can I help you?' said a voice, and Patrick jumped.

'I'm sorry,' he said, 'I was just, I'm sorry—'

A man appeared from the shadows. He was about the same age as Patrick's father and he smiled and said, 'I don't get many visitors.'

He motioned to Patrick to follow him, and as they made their way through the gloom they passed rows and rows of books.

'What would you like to see?' said the man. 'Did you have anything particular in mind?'

'I don't know,' said Patrick, his eyes slowly adjusting to the light. 'I'm not sure.'

'This one, then,' said the man, stopping and selecting a thick volume. 'Here might be a good place to start.' He unfastened two gold clasps, laid the book on a sloping oak stand and opened it. 'A psalter,' he said. 'A book of psalms, made six hundred years ago.'

Patrick had never seen anything so beautiful. Framing two columns of text was a border alive with beasts and birds and curious figures: there was a mermaid, a man with bird's feet, a woman playing a tambourine, another with a unicorn in her lap. There were herons and stags, peacocks and rams. There were ivy leaves and centaurs, a hunter with a crossbow, a man blowing a horn, a woodsman swinging an axe. In a large initial D, a robed man poured oil on the head of a boy while angels watched. Scattered through the text, wherever there was space at the end of a line, were winged serpents, dogs' heads, lizards with leaves in place of tails. And, dotted across the page, filling the background inside the D, speckling the border, was gold.

'It's all written by hand,' said the man. 'Every letter. Can you imagine?'

Patrick shook his head. He tried to make out some of the words: *Dominus illuminatio mea—*

'It was saved from destruction in 1573,' said the man. 'There was a fire in the cathedral where it was kept, and the entire building would have burned to the ground had it not been for the wolf.'

Patrick looked up. 'The wolf?'

'The fire was discovered because a wolf rang the cathedral bell.'

'Oh,' said Patrick, and returned to the saved book. As he turned the pages the dots of gold sparkled and danced.

'It's parchment,' said the man. 'It's skin.' And he told Patrick how an animal pelt—usually calf, sheep or goat—was soaked in lime for days on end, how the hair and fat and shreds of flesh were scraped away, how the sharp paring knife could make holes if pushed too hard. Sometimes, he said, damaged skin was used anyway, particularly in monasteries, where the monks couldn't afford perfection, and he could show Patrick a page of text with a hole in it, a space like an egg or a white eye, and the words, he said, had simply been written around it. He told Patrick how the skin was rinsed in water for two more days to remove the caustic lime, how pebbles were twisted into the edges to form a sort of button, how the buttons were tied to a frame and the skin stretched taut. Then, he said, it was scraped again, the lunellum—the crescent-shaped knife—peeling away layer after layer. When the skin was dry it was scraped yet again until the parchment was fine enough, and the surface suitable for writing.

'Look closely at the page,' he said, handing Patrick a magnifying glass. 'Do you see the tiny dark dots?'

Patrick nodded.

'Now turn it over. Any there?'

'No,' said Patrick.

'The flesh side is always the finest,' said the man. 'It's whiter and softer, it's easier to write on and it naturally curls away. It's the side that once faced the animal's flesh, the underneath part of the skin. The hair or grain side, on the other hand,' and he turned the page back again, 'is darker. The tiny dots are the traces of follicles, from the animal's hair.'

As the man continued talking, Patrick ran his fingers across the page. It was thin and soft and velvety, slightly furred, like the skin of an apricot. The dots of gold felt like Braille to the touch, the larger strips like raised veins. This was the source of the sweet smell; it was coming from the pages themselves. He had a sudden memory of Faye curled into him on the blue sofa, her skin soft from the bath. He continued turning the pages while the man told him about the tree-like vein marks which were sometimes visible, and which were the result of blood in the skin when the animal died. Sometimes, too, on larger pages, dense ridges could be made out; vestiges of the point at which the backbone transected the skin. And very occasionally, on one edge, a scalloped curve could be detected. That, said the man, indicated the animal's neck.

'That's horrible,' said Patrick.

'Well,' said the man, 'why do you think books are shaped the way they are?'

Patrick shrugged.

'Think about the shape of a calf, or a goat, or a sheep. Think about the shape of the pelts from those animals. They're always going to be roughly oblong, aren't they? Always higher than they are wide.'

Patrick nodded.

'That's why manuscripts are rectangular. And modern, printed books preserve the form. They echo the dimensions of a skin.'

On the way home, Patrick could still smell the pages on his fingers.

'Where have you been all afternoon?' said his mother. 'It's getting dark, you know.' She placed her glass of sherry very carefully on the new table and hugged Patrick, her breath hot and cloying. 'Your father's been out too. You are a naughty thing, leaving your mother alone all afternoon.'

Patrick went back to the manuscripts room every weekend after that, and the curator always had something new for him to look at, something new that was hundreds of years old. Sometimes he showed him lives. They were usually brief, jumping from birth to death in less than a page, the illustrations showing men pierced with arrows, swallowed by lions and dragons, women broken on wheels, beheaded, burned. There was Saint Luke the Younger, who levitated during prayer; Saint Bee, who was fed by gulls and who received a bracelet from an angel; Saint Alexis, whose corpse exuded a fragrance so powerful that his tomb was believed filled with perfumes; Saint Juliana, who was put in a tub of molten lead which became a cool bath around her. There was Saint Columba, who copied Saint Finnian's valuable psalter in secret, and whose fingers shone when it grew too dark for him to see. Of course, said the curator, Patrick mustn't believe a word. The lives were as untrustworthy as fairy tales. They were mongrel blends of hearsay, fact and plain fabrication; they were Chinese whispers written down. Often the text had been copied and recopied, each author making alterations, adding embellishments in order to preach to the faithful, convert the wicked, or simply tell a good story. One miracle was interchangeable with another; the same visions surfaced over and over like recurring dreams. And they were all written by hand. Had Patrick ever tried to copy something word for word? Had he made mistakes, misread certain sentences, skipped lines? He should remember Saint Columba, the one with the glowing fingers. The bible copier. Who was to say that his replica was exact? Who was to say that Finnian's was? How could we ever know the true story, when even the word of God might contain errors?

Patrick didn't mind. True or false, the manuscripts were beautiful things. They had lasted hundreds of years. They had survived floods and silverfish, lootings and rodents, moths and mould and fire.

After finishing with a book the cover was closed tight, the clasps secured. Parchment needed to be kept under slight pressure, said the curator. Without clasps to hold them firm, the pages would cockle. They would return to the original shape of the animal.

Losing a child was the fear of every parent. It was planted in the heart's warm chambers when the creature was still boneless and unborn, when it was without a name, without fingerprints or gender. It was fear that accounted for a parent's many crimes: the laundering of favoured toys, the disposal of sweets and bus tickets found on the street, the confiscation of sharp things. The rationing of television, the curfews, the unreasonable judgement of friends, the banning of particular movies, certain parties; all such actions were motivated by fear of loss. Ruth had done those things, had made an enemy of her daughter because of it, and still it hadn't been enough. She wished she had imposed far greater limits. Other parents, she knew, while they didn't say as much, believed that there must have been some negligence involved in Laura's disappearance, some moment of carelessness on Ruth's part. Over their coffees and hot chocolates and herbal teas, she imagined, they congratulated themselves on their own caution. She wished she had permitted Laura no driving lessons, no outings alone. No interaction with others. She wished she had kept her inside forever.

Before she started taking the sleeping pills, in those first few wretched days, Ruth jolted awake several times a night. She had always been a deep sleeper, but now any creaking of the house, any click from the contracting metal roof was enough to rouse her. The hours of darkness were broken into many fragments, abbreviated nights lasting a few minutes, an hour at most. It was like the day Laura disappeared, she thought, when there had been a three-minute night in the morning, and all of nature was thrown off balance.

The strange thing was, Ruth always heard the clicks and creaks a split second after she felt herself jump. There was a snatch of panic as she wondered what had woken her, why she was poised for flight, and then the sound came. And although these moments startled her, she took comfort in them. They reminded her of the body's instinctive abilities, its ways of recognising possible danger and responding, keeping itself safe. During the day, as she waited outside on the porch, the door open so she could hear the phone, she watched goosebumps appear on her forearm. She saw the tiny hairs rise and trap a layer of warm air about her, a shield to protect her from freezing. She had not willed this; her own body knew what was necessary, and provided it. We are all much more hardy than we believe, she told herself. She thought of documentaries she had seen that showed the formidable strength humans could exert in emergencies. Cars could be lifted, fallen trees thrown aside. Nights could be spent in the snow, incredible distances covered on foot. Even newborn babies were much stronger than they appeared. Young fathers often had to be told that they needn't hold their infants like bone china cups, that the child who survives birth can survive being hugged, and swung in the air, and cuddled, and loved. Perhaps, she thought, even if Laura had no one to help her, her body would keep her safe.

As a child, Laura had always been alert, rushing to answer the telephone before anyone else heard it, often spying coins on the street. She had never been interested in team sports; all those pushy netballers thundering about the place bored her stupid, she said. On the tennis court, though, she shone, anticipating the moves of her opponents as if reading their minds.

'How do you do that?' Ruth asked her once. 'How do you know where they'll hit the ball before it's even reached them?'

Laura laughed and said it was all done with mirrors, and really she wasn't clever at all, just good at physics.

'But you hate physics,' Ruth said, frowning.

Laura laughed again, so Ruth dropped the subject. She resented her daughter's evasiveness, the private jokes she suspected were often at her expense, but pushing her for information only made her angry.

Ruth hadn't known about the diary—or rather, she hadn't known

Laura had kept it. She remembered Malcolm's mother sending it for Christmas, but she also remembered Laura tossing it into her pile of unwanted presents.

'Grandma means well,' Ruth had said, and Malcolm had slipped his new home-knitted socks over his hands like gloves, although the morning was humid, and said, 'Good old Mum, another set of elbow-warmers,' and he and Laura had laughed. The diary had fallen open among the boxed handkerchiefs and the garish scarf and the little-girl hair clips, its pages bright white in the sun and fluttering every now and then in the breeze from the garden. A blank year.

'People who keep a diary must be the most tedious creatures on the planet,' Laura said. Beyond the open window the cabbage butterflies were devouring the garden, their papery wings opening and closing. Ruth watched them eating holes in the lettuce, turning the leaves of the runner beans into dark lace. They only lived for a day, but a lot of damage could be done in a short space of time.

'We must spray the garden,' she said.

The police found the diary in Laura's shelves, neatly wedged in as if it were a normal book, one of the horsy novels she still read now and then, or a high-school romance.

'We'll need to borrow it for a while,' they said, and took it away just like that.

Ruth waited a few days but it wasn't returned. When she rang she was casual, gripping the edge of the table to keep her voice slow. She was just wondering, she thought she might just check, she didn't suppose there was anything—

'It's not quite what we were expecting, Mrs Pearse,' the detective inspector said, 'but there might be something useful in it. We'll need to keep it for a while.'

Ruth hated to think of the officers handling Laura's diary, dissecting it word by word. Perhaps, she thought, they talked about it over lunch, passed it to interested colleagues like a cheap romance. Perhaps that was how they dealt with the unpleasant nature of their work; perhaps it was a way of forgetting. She couldn't bear the thought of official hands all over it, her daughter's life read aloud in the tearoom, her Laura—it was unthinkable—fuelling the fantasies of middle-aged men.

'I'd like a photocopy,' she said. 'Every page. I realise you need to hang on to it for a while, but I'd like my own copy.'

They hadn't pressed hard enough on the spine. There was shadowing down the middle of each page where Laura's writing grew darker, rose with the pull of the binding and tumbled into black. Ruth had to lean in close to make out the words.

4 January 1988
I met him today. He is the most beautiful man you could imagine— wavy black hair, green eyes, olive skin. He's quite a bit taller than I am, but I like that, because when we kiss I can feel him pushing my neck right back and I think of Vivien Leigh on the posters for Gone with the Wind, where her neck's almost horizontal with the weight of Clark Gable's kiss, and that's how I see myself too, and if I were to open my eyes I would be looking straight into the blue sky or the stars.

8 January 1988
I have a present for him, a real present, not socks or writing paper or hankies. I've wrapped it in shiny silver paper, so he'll see himself as he opens it, and me looking over his shoulder.

9 January 1988
He was very happy with his present, and said it would make him think of me. To say thank-you, he took me to lunch at Lorenzo's, and I had venison with a rich berry sauce. After that we fed each other chocolate soufflé, which was so light I could hardly feel it on my tongue, but the icing sugar made me sneeze and he laughed and said I was so unspoiled, and that was why he loved me.

12 January 1988
We went ice skating today. The lake was frozen over, for the first time
ever, and it was very beautiful in the late afternoon. The sun was
hanging so low I thought I could touch it. He held me around the
waist as we glided across the frozen water, and in some places we
could see right through to where there were leaves and sticks suspended
in the ice, and one silvery fish.

Children had found the Mini first.
    'Look,' said the boy, 'a tennis racket.'
    The girl peered in the back window. 'There's some CDs too.'
    They tried the doors and windows but the car was sealed tight.
    'I know,' said the boy, and he ran to the river's edge, where the
willow trees made green caves. The stone he chose was smooth and
heavy, as big as two fists. He struck the passenger window. The glass
cracked, but it wouldn't break.

20 January 1988
Although I've only known him for a short time, I know we're meant
to be together. He's asked me to go skiing with him, and says he'll
teach me how. We're going to stay in a cabin owned by his family. I've
never been up the mountain. I've never even seen snow before.

26 January 1988
I didn't want to come home. Up there it felt like there was nobody else
but us alive, and the white went on forever. When we skied downhill
I thought I might fly off the edge of the mountain.

27 January 1988
I bought a new dress today, especially for him. It has a deep cut at the
back and is very fitting. I think it makes me look older. I'm going to
wear my hair up so I can feel the air on my skin. He likes my hair up,
he says it gives him easy access to my neck.

30 January 1988
When we went out last night he said he had a present for me. Lying
at the bottom of my wine glass was a key, and he held his hands over
my eyes and led me outside. Parked there on the street was a silver car,
and when I tried the key in the ignition it sounded just like Smoky
does when she's purring, and I nearly said so but I'm glad I didn't
because it would have sounded so babyish. We drove and drove, and I
could feel the leather seat against my bare back, and when we reached
a quiet spot on the waterfront we stopped.

Ruth didn't show the photocopied diary to Malcolm. It would only
upset him, she told herself, to read the romantic fantasies of his
little girl. And they were fantasies, that was obvious. Laura had never
been wooed by a rich man, she'd never owned a silver car or been
skiing or skating on a lake. No lakes froze this far north, Ruth knew.
It wasn't cold enough in winter, let alone in January. Every word
was untrue, but still she read on, upsetting herself page by page,
unable to stop. On 6 March Laura didn't mention the eclipse. She
didn't say how she'd had breakfast with Ruth, how she'd dripped her
blackberry toast on the tablecloth and had then driven in her rusting
Mini to the wind turbine. Instead, she described a moonlit walk on
a beach, tender words, a kiss. It could have come straight from a
hackneyed movie, or one of Laura's romance novels. And then Ruth
saw that it wasn't the last entry. Every page had been filled, every
day of the year described. And although she knew it was ridiculous,
she couldn't stop thinking that perhaps these things really had
happened, that perhaps this dream life described where Laura was
now.

The police returned the original diary to Ruth seven years later,
when Laura was officially dead. The pages had been tested for clues;
they were smudged with purple and still smelled faintly of chemicals.

Malcolm had always been fond of gardening, and after Laura
disappeared it occupied more and more of his time. He gave up

landscape photography. There seemed little point in taking pictures of ice, snow, water. He wanted to make things look nice, he said, to create his own living, growing landscape, and he spent hours weeding, digging, scattering the soil with blood and bone. He familiarised himself with the phases of the moon, with the different varieties of iris and how they ranged from white to deepest purple. He learned to distinguish between jonquils and split-cupped daffodils. He understood words like *Chrysanthemum morifolium, Pyrostegia venusta, Aquilegia caerulea.* His garden was a machine, an engine; if one part malfunctioned then everything was thrown out of balance. He worked on it with the devotion other men lavished on cars. Sometimes he had the odd sensation that the roots were humming beneath his feet, knitting together, eating up the earth.

In summertime, the garden shook with flowers. Tea roses and clematis hid the back fence, delphiniums grew waist-high. At work, Phil teased him about it, asking in a lisping falsetto how the pansies were coming along, whether Malcolm had seen any fairies. 'And he bakes bread, too,' he told the rest of the office.

'I don't know what to do with all the flowers. I wish I had somewhere to take them,' Malcolm said to Ruth, who didn't understand.

'But you take a bunch to Mum every week,' she said. 'She loves them.'

Malcolm preferred the garden in winter. He relished the emptiness of it, the sense of waiting, the ribs of the fig tree bare and clean, the daphne filling cold days with perfume. He liked to dig the vegetable patch, to turn the black soil over clod by clod. Sometimes he found things: pieces of fat green glass, broken plates and teacups, coins, jars. Once he found the leg of a porcelain doll with a tiny shoe painted on its foot, and once a thick old bottle with a marble trapped in its neck. He kept all the pieces he dug up. He rinsed them off and displayed them on the bottom shelf of Ruth's china cabinet. She didn't like him digging too much; she said it worried her.

'You never know what you'll hit,' she told him. 'You can't just go digging haphazardly, it's dangerous.'

Sometimes she stood at the front door and called him for lunch or a cup of tea. 'Malcolm?' she said. 'Malcolm?' As if his name was a question, although she could see him from the porch.

Malcolm knew he wouldn't hit anything. He was too careful, and besides, there was nothing dangerous buried in their garden— he knew the location of every power cable, every water pipe. Sometimes, as he dug, he thought about the wind turbine turning its white arms on top of the hill. It was noisy up close; on blustery days the blades swooped and whistled, and you had to shout to be heard. On still days, though, they barely moved, floating against the blue sky like fingers in water. The turbine provided enough electricity for seventy average households, Malcolm recalled. He wondered which seventy, whether their house was powered by wind.

There wasn't a big garden at the new place; the back yard had been almost entirely paved. Malcolm was disappointed when they first looked at the property, but Ruth seemed to love it.

'Imagine all the extra time you'll have,' she said. And when she was arranging the lounge furniture, stacking her teacups and teapots and cake plates in the china cabinet, she filled every shelf. 'Much better,' she said, 'don't you think?'

Ruth was glad to be rid of Malcolm's bits and pieces. She didn't like having them in the house; they made her uneasy, so many broken things. She couldn't help wondering what had happened to the remaining parts; whether, for instance, there was a doll's hollow head still underground, its glass eyes stopped with earth. Malcolm gave the garden at the old house one final dig before they moved, to tidy it up for the tenants, he said. She watched him from the window. He sliced the soil, pushing the spade in with his heel as if stamping out a fire, then turning it. He never broke his rhythm. Daniel played in the puddles at the edge of the garden, examining worms, slaters, ants. He was covered in mud, but Ruth didn't mind. At least he was showing an interest in the natural world, in things living. When she came out with a jug of iced water, Malcolm was holding two shards of porcelain on his dirty palm.

'Do you think these were part of the same plate?' he said.

The surface of the china was crazed, and it reminded Ruth of the brittle toffee made for school fairs or during school holidays, as a treat. She didn't know why pieces of china made her think of toffee; she hadn't made any in years. But it could be sharp like broken china, she remembered. It could shatter on the tongue, and the only way to avoid jabbing the soft walls of the mouth was to wait until the pieces melted, disappeared into nothing. She wished Malcolm could get some time off work, come away on a holiday. They hadn't been on holiday since Bali, and that was four years ago.

'Daniel was a baby then,' he'd said when she suggested a break. 'It's different now, it would be too hard. It wouldn't be a holiday at all.'

Ruth poured two glasses of water, but Malcolm didn't drink his. He trickled it over the porcelain shards, rubbing them clean until they shone like bones. She wondered what he thought about as he worked; if he thought about anything at all. It was unhealthy, all that digging.

The man had been thrilled with his idea. He was dying to tell someone about it, but he stopped himself each time he felt the words welling up. It wasn't the girl he wanted to talk about. She was gone and forgotten; that had been easy. There was no drama, just a few kicks and scratches, a bleeding nose. No, the idea was the clever part. The plan. He was so proud of it, he could hardly sleep. He wondered what his mother would say if he told her; whether it would shut her up for a minute or two, make her look at him through new eyes. He would love to see the expression on her face.

He didn't know how he'd come up with the idea. Once, at school, he'd got a perfect score on his maths test and the teacher had asked him to stay behind after class.

'How did this happen?' she'd asked. 'How did you do this?' And he said he didn't know, he'd figured out the right answers, he supposed.

'I see,' she said. She'd be watching him closely, she said. She was most interested to see if he could repeat his extraordinary performance the next time. He couldn't.

The man's idea had come out of nowhere just like his good mark had. It was better than good, it was brilliant. It was so brilliant he was a little afraid of it.

Nobody noticed that Walter Hicks's grave had been disturbed. He'd only been in there a day, the soil above him still a swollen mound, filled with pockets of air. That first night, as his children and his grandchildren drank to him, as his wife Edna read cards and watered vases of flowers and froze leftover cakes and savouries, the man began digging. Quickly, quietly, the loose soil was removed and then, just as quickly, replaced and smoothed over so that in a week's time, when Walter's headstone was laid and his family brought flowers, nobody noticed a thing.

'Poor old Walt,' his grandchildren said at Christmas, or on Anzac Day, or over a pint of beer. They continued to bring flowers to his grave a couple of times a year, skinny bunches of carnations which they bought at the dairy and which were always too tall. At the cemetery they lifted the squat concrete vases from either side of Walter's headstone, removed the old, slimy stems and added fresh water. Then they poked the flowers in, arranged them as best they could, replaced the vases and left. They didn't linger the way other mourners did. They didn't talk to Walter, jab plastic windmills into his grave, picnic on top of it. They didn't attach photographs sealed in plastic bags. They were dignified and quick, and went home feeling pleased with themselves.

Walter's widow Edna wouldn't visit the cemetery. She preferred, she said, to remember Walt as he was. Slowly, the soil settled.

'The No. 115 Shipbuilding Outfit has arrived!' yelled Patrick, running to the front door as soon as he heard his father's key, hugging the parcel to his chest.

'Now then, now then,' said Graham, removing his hat and coat, uncoiling his scarf from about his neck. 'Bring me my knife.'

He pushed out the blade and screwed it into place, inspecting its edge under the reading lamp. He turned the parcel this way and that as if looking for a secret catch, his own name and address revolving in his hands. The contents made no sound. He sliced the string, then ran his knife under the paper, where the folds were so he didn't damage the box. 'The No. 115,' he said, clearing the severed wrappings—suddenly of no interest—away from the box. 'A very limited edition, made exactly to scale. This'll be worth a lot in a few years' time.' He lifted open the box and checked each part. 'Good,' he said, 'very good. Mint condition. I've managed to track down an Aeroplane Constructor Outfit too, Doreen, did I tell you? And I've ordered another No. 7 Outfit.'

The unassembled ship sat on the sideboard for the rest of the evening, on display alongside the meat platter and the gravy boat from the new dinner set. Patrick kept glancing at it, but it wasn't mentioned. The next day was Saturday, though, and his father would have some free time. Perhaps he was saving it until then.

Patrick could hardly sleep that night. He kept thinking about the ship, about how magnificent it would look when assembled. He hoped his father would let him do the funnel. His toes tingled and he gripped the sheet with his fists. It felt like the night before his birthday.

In the morning, the Shipbuilding Outfit was gone.

'Dad's put it away for safekeeping,' said Patrick's mother. 'He didn't want it to get damaged.'

'What could happen to it?' said Patrick. 'It hasn't even been taken out of its box.'

Patrick's mother bit her bottom lip. 'I'm not sure he wants to unpack it. I think he might want to keep it nice and new. As an investment.'

'But it's not new,' said Patrick. 'And it's meant to be put together.'

He gulped a mouthful of green beans.

'Combine, son, combine,' barked his father. 'It aids the digestion.'

Patrick eyed the space on the sideboard where the shipbuilding box had stood. 'Andrew and his brother got a No. 4 Outfit for Christmas and they've just made a mechanical crossbow,' he said. 'It's not as good as the Shipbuilding Outfit though.'

'It looked like a complicated one, Graham,' said Patrick's mother. 'How many hours does it take to put together?'

'The labour's not the point with a model like that, Doreen,' said Patrick's father. He pushed a piece of sausage, a slice of carrot, some mashed potato and a bean on to his fork, and waved the laden utensil at his wife like a stern finger. 'I have no intention of assembling the Shipbuilding Outfit,' he said. 'The reward is in the knowledge that such a construction is possible. It's not necessary to put it all together.'

'Oh,' said Patrick's mother. She ate a single sliver of carrot. 'Do you remember, years ago, Graham, before Patrick was born, there was that pantomime with the giant Meccano models?'

'Pantomime?' said Patrick's father. 'Why would I remember a pantomime?'

'It was *The Sleeping Beauty*. Prince Florizel passes through a land where everything is made of Meccano. They used special parts eight times the usual size, do you remember, Graham, and there was a giant arch bridge spanning the stage and glittering under the lights, and they had a windmill, and cranes, and a ferris wheel, and all sorts of other giant models. And Prince Florizel builds a Meccano aeroplane, and flies away to the turret chamber of the witch's tower and rescues Sleeping Beauty.'

'Ridiculous,' said Patrick's father.

'Could you go up on the stage?' said Patrick. 'Did they let you touch the models?'

'Oh, we didn't see the play,' said his mother. 'Did we, Graham.'

After dinner she found the brown paper the Outfit had been wrapped in and she smoothed it out. 'There are some good stamps on here, Patrick,' she said. 'You could soak them off for your collection.'

Patrick dropped the scraps of paper into a dish of water. Slowly the stamps came away, floating like flimsy life rafts. When he fished them out the gum on the back was slippery, and he placed them to dry face-down on a clean handkerchief.

The next morning they were all curled up, and they felt grainy and brittle, like dead leaves. He went to the museum.

'We have some new acquisitions,' said the curator. 'Would you like to earn some pocket money?'

All Patrick had to do was insert a filmy piece of tissue between the pages of each manuscript, to prevent ghosting. The curator showed him a miniature, 'The Lover Admitted into the Garden'. It had been imprinted with text from the opposite page; backwards writing surrounded the garden and the lover like shadows. And the miniature had left traces, too: superimposed on the text was a backwards lover, a mirror garden.

As Patrick covered up pictures and words, the curator talked. Didn't the manuscripts look as if they were painted yesterday? Weren't the colours still luminous, untouched by time?

'Stale urine,' he said. 'They added it to the pigment. Or egg white, or gum, sometimes honey. Or crushed egg shell, glue made from the bladder of the sturgeon,' he scratched his ear, 'or ear wax.' He listed ingredients as if reciting a spell. Red, he said, was made with cinnabar, commonly found in Spain, or with brazilwood, or madder root. Dragonsblood red was made with the sap of the shrub *Pterocarpus draco*, although some medieval recipes called for blood from elephants and dragons which had killed each other in battle. Vermilion was produced by heating mercury with sulphur, then collecting and grinding the deposited vapour. Licking a vermilion paintbrush, he said, was unwise; the pigment was poisonous. White came from white lead, green from malachite or verdigris, yellow from volcanic earth or saffron. Blue came from azurite, a very hard stone which was slowly ground to powder. The seeds of the turnsole plant produced a more violet shade, but ultramarine was the blue most highly prized and most costly. Made from lapis lazuli brought from beyond the sea—*ultra mare*—a 1403 inventory of the Duc de Berry's possessions listed two pots of ultramarine among his riches.

Patrick peered at a page. 'What about the gold?' he said. 'What was that made from?'

Gold was made from gold, said the curator, and he described how the metal was hammered until it was tissue-thin, how gold-beaters could produce one hundred and forty-five leaves from one ducat. Gold leaf had virtually no weight. If rubbed between the fingers it disappeared, if dropped, it hardly seemed to fall. It could be unwrinkled with one gentle breath; it could be eaten. It was best applied in wet weather, or in the early morning, and it would never tarnish.

'And the dots?' said Patrick, gently touching a beaded, glittering border.

'The design,' said the curator, 'was picked out in gesso—plaster or chalk mixed with glue—and allowed to dry. The illuminator then breathed on it to make it sticky—' he exhaled, as if trying to fog a window pane '—and laid the gold leaf on top. It adheres very easily,' he said. 'It almost seems to jump into place.' He opened a drawer and withdrew an instrument: a long handle mounted with a stone. 'Agate,' he said, 'for burnishing the gold. Dogs' teeth were also recommended, or teeth from any carnivore—lions, wolves, wild boars.'

Patrick ran his finger over the agate. It felt smooth, just like a tooth.

Malcolm looked out at their new, paved back yard. A garden without grass, without flowers.

'Phil's passing through next week,' he said, 'on his way to a big conference down south. I've asked him to stay for a couple of days.'

'Oh,' said Ruth. 'Oh. I suppose so.'

'I haven't seen him for years, you know.'

'No.'

The last time had been at a staff Christmas party, right before Phil moved to the Sydney office.

'Congratulations, mate,' Malcolm had said several times during the evening, slapping Phil on the shoulder, the back, shaking his hand. 'You deserve it, mate, you really really deserve it.'

That was their first Christmas without Laura. Ruth hadn't come to the party, so Malcolm spent the night telling people he was drinking for two. He couldn't remember much more than that, but he did remember Ruth's white face at the window when he arrived home.

'I was worried, I didn't know where you were, I was so worried,' she said.

Phil had left for Australia a few days later, to take up the job Malcolm had wanted and probably would have got if it hadn't been for Laura.

'He'll only stay for a couple of nights,' said Malcolm. 'It'll be fun, you know what Phil's like.'

'Yes, I do,' said Ruth.

He hadn't changed much in twelve years.

'Ruth,' he said, enveloping her in a bear hug, 'still as lovely as ever.'

After dinner they drove out to the beach. In the back seat Daniel giggled as Phil tickled him and told him jokes.

'Does your dad still grow flowers?' he said. 'Does he still bake bread?'

Daniel laughed and laughed.

Malcolm parked the car as close to the water as possible and they began walking, past the silky mudflats, past the knotted, twisting mangroves to the sea.

'I need to go to the toilet,' said Daniel.

'Come on then,' said Ruth, but Daniel said no, he wanted Malcolm to take him.

Ruth and Phil continued along the beach. In the gathering dark the sand was almost black. Phil lit a cigarette and the smoke drifted past Ruth's face and out to the wide water.

'Can I have one?' she said, and he lit it for her. 'Don't tell Malcolm, he hates it.'

She watched the white hook of moon on the horizon and waited for Phil to speak. She wondered whether he would suggest a swim; it was warm enough. In a way she longed for the water, its salty grip, the danger of stingrays and sharks, perhaps, and jellyfish which numbed careless swimmers. Ruth remembered reading that drowning was peaceful. There was a romance about it, a sallow glamour. Limbs were made graceful by water; a wrist curved like a dancer's, hair ribboned out in slow motion, wreathing the silent face. At certain stages of development, Ruth recalled, a human foetus has gills, a vestigial tail. It lives in fluid for nine months. If Laura had drowned, if this was the wrong place and she'd come to at the wrong time, perhaps it had been as easy as swimming.

At the pub the next night Phil ordered round after round, refusing to let Malcolm pay.

'Hey Mal,' he said, 'whatever happened to old Joanna? You ever hear of her these days?'

'Who? Joanna?'

'You remember her—big girl, sweated a lot. Worked in admin.'

'I'm afraid I don't know who you mean,' said Malcolm.

'Joanna. Fat Jo. The office bike.' Phil was becoming impatient.

'No,' said Malcolm, 'I don't remember any Joanna.'

Phil took a long sip of beer, head back, throat open, his eyes on Malcolm the whole time. 'Okay,' he said, wiping his mouth, 'all right.'

Joanna had been wearing tinsel round her head at the Christmas party. As the night wore on she added extra decorations: a star in her hair, a bell looped over her wrist, a plastic snowflake on each breast. Malcolm avoided her; he disliked her over-friendly way with all the male staff. Didn't she realise that they were revolted by her? That they called her Pig and Buttockface? At some stage he stumbled to his office to phone Ruth and tell her not to keep dinner for him. And Joanna must have seen him leave the party, because suddenly she was in his office too, and he didn't phone home, and then she had her hands down his trousers and he was fumbling to undo her bra and his hands were full of her, and she was pulling him down to the floor and at one point, when he looked up, he thought he saw Phil watching from the corridor, but he couldn't be sure.

Every now and then, if Ruth was silent too long, Phil touched her on the arm and asked about her job, or about Daniel.

'He's a good kid,' he said, 'once you get to know him. And your babysitter's so great with him. She's not much more than a kid herself.'

'She's twenty-one,' said Ruth, gulping wine so she didn't have to talk.

'You'll have to come over to Sydney again,' said Phil. 'And make sure you get in touch this time. We've got plenty of room, Daniel would love it.'

And Malcolm said Ruth had been pestering him for a holiday for ages, and Phil should watch out, because they might just take up the offer.

On one of Phil's many trips to the bar, Ruth saw an attractive young woman approach him and chat for a few minutes before he returned. The next time he went to get drinks the young woman engaged him in conversation again, and Phil brought her back to the table with him.

'This is Paula,' he said. 'Paula, Ruth, Malcolm.'

Paula smoked long, thin cigarettes and wore a charm bracelet which tinkled each time she moved. She was a pharmacy assistant, she said, but really she wanted to go to medical school. She was going to apply next year, when she'd saved a bit of money. In between mouthfuls of wine, Ruth watched the charms on Paula's wrist. There was a rocking chair, a pair of tiny silver shoes, an alligator jointed at the legs and jaws which writhed as Paula moved her hand. There was a heart, a ship, a crown, a key. Ruth could picture her working in a pharmacy, her neat, polished fingers gift-wrapping soap, perfume, bubble bath for men to take home to their wives. She would tie each parcel with ribbon, using scissors to curl the ends until they spiralled like ringlets.

When Phil next patted Ruth's shoulder and said, 'So, you've got the new house looking really great,' she shook him away.

'Don't touch me please,' she said, and Paula stopped talking and laughing and flicking her hair and stared at Ruth, and Malcolm and Phil stared too, and Ruth said nothing. She couldn't explain what was wrong, that it was this bland, inoffensive girl who'd upset her. She couldn't say that she remembered the way her daughter had been around Phil, that he was the type of man Laura fantasised about in her diary. And that here Paula was, hanging on his every word, applauding his clumsy games of pool, sipping with freshly painted lips the drinks he bought. She didn't know a thing about him, this girl. He could have been anyone at all.

'Just calm yourself down,' said Malcolm, moving Ruth's glass from the edge of the table.

'Perhaps we should take her home,' said Phil, reaching down and attempting to retrieve Ruth's bag.

'Leave my things alone,' she said in a low, steady voice.

'But you're all hooked up here, Ruth. If we can just get you to move your chair a bit—'

'In Sydney they snatch your bag right out from under you, don't they?' she said. 'I had my bag snatched in Sydney the second day we were there, didn't I? Remember that?'

Malcolm nodded, his hand on his wife's elbow, trying to pull her to her feet.

'The policemen were so nice. They didn't find my bag for me, but they told me what to do in future. You have to be cunning, you see, Paula. You have to be sneakier than the bag-snatchers.' And she tilted the chair forward on two legs and unhooked her bag. 'It's not possible for us to visit you in Sydney, Phil,' she said. 'Malcolm doesn't have time for holidays now.'

Nobody talked about Laura any more. Nobody had mentioned her for what seemed like years. It was as if she had never existed, and Ruth understood that now, for most people, she hadn't. If a person could disappear without trace, then perhaps they had only ever existed in the imagination of someone else.

Except Laura had left traces of herself, things useless to all intents and purposes, and of no interest to the police or to the careful searchers. She'd left her tennis rackets, her hair clips, her little bottles of nail polish stored in the fridge to keep them liquid. She'd left earrings, school blouses, half a bag of toffees, three rented movies. They'd been hopelessly overdue by the time Ruth returned them. The boy behind the counter started to tell her how much she owed when he stopped short and peered at her and then said, 'That's okay, Mrs Pearse, you've got a lot on your mind.' Ruth wanted to tell him that she hadn't forgotten about the tapes. On the contrary, she'd kept them stacked on top of the television, in full view, for when Laura returned home and flopped into her armchair and aimed the remote control.

'Don't you find it strange there are so few clues?' Ruth asked the detective inspector. 'Perhaps there's something you've missed, someone you could speak to again?'

He tapped a sheaf of papers into alignment. 'There is always the possibility,' he said, 'that Laura doesn't wish to be found.'

Ruth liked to imagine her daughter as a star. Laura, she decided sometimes, had run away with the circus and was performing to adoring, foreign audiences. She was as strong and graceful as a diving bird, her costumes stitched with jewels, sleek plumage glinting in the spotlights. On the trapeze she slipped through the air as if it were water. Her judgement was perfect; she was always in the right place at the right time, always met her partner mid-air. Laura would understand that one split second could upset everything, could mean tragedy. And she would understand, too, that this was what thrilled the crowds: the knowledge that, because of a fraction of a second, her partner could turn to catch her and find his hands meeting with nothing but air. But Laura never fell.

In more sensible moments, Ruth knew her circus imaginings to be nothing more than a dream, her own silly fantasy of years before. Her mother had sent her to gym classes, and while other girls had flipped and arched and made bridges and pyramids of their bodies, Ruth puzzled over what to do with her head during a forward roll.

'Come along,' urged the instructor, 'surely you can manage one?'

Ruth watched her classmates tumble across the sticky red mats one after the other, a blur of red leotards and pointed toes. They tucked their sleek, braided heads into their bodies, formed themselves into tight coils. Any daughter of hers, she'd decided, would be graceful.

The problem she always encountered, though, the thing that hit her in the face, was that she had no idea what Laura would look like. It had been twelve years; she would be twenty-seven by now. When Prince Charles had married Diana, a women's magazine had featured an artist's impression of their offspring. Ruth remembered studying the sketches of golden, toothy pre-adolescents. She'd thought that they looked artificial, lifeless, like identikit pictures rather than princes and princesses. She wondered what the artist would make of a grown-up Laura, which features would be more pronounced, how her hair would be cut, where wrinkles would fall. When she tried to picture her now, all she could see were photographs. The images she summoned were static and clouded, as if seen through the translucent leaves of a photo album. Ruth had such an album. The pages separating the photos, protecting one moment in time from another, were patterned with cobwebs.

'Nobody's irreplaceable,' said Jan. 'And it's Easter coming up. We can cope without you for a week or two, don't worry.'

Ruth didn't pack much. She'd been monitoring the weather reports and was confident it would be warm up there. It was closer to the equator, as close as you could get without leaving the country. She tucked a note inside an envelope and left it propped against the electric jug.

Two American women reached the check-in counter just before she did. They were twins, she realised, and she looked from one to the other without trying to hide her curiosity. From the way they were dressed, it was obvious they enjoyed the attention, and Ruth could see the man at the counter—Dennis, according to his name tag—staring too. Both women were dressed in track suits, one pink and one yellow. They had the same haircut, the same sunglasses, the same black money belts locked to their stomachs.

Before Dennis could smile and ask how they were today the pink twin said, 'We'd like 5a and 5b.' She presented him with their tickets. 'They're the ones by the emergency exit.'

'Not that we think there'll be a crash,' said the yellow twin, 'but there's more leg room there.'

'No, we're sure it won't crash, it's the leg room, that's all.'

The yellow twin heaved a suitcase on to the scales. It was made of thick brocade, like a lounge suite, and was secured with a tiny gold padlock. She wore a black ribbon around her neck. Ruth suspected that hanging from it, nestled in her wrinkled cleavage, was a tiny gold key. The needle swung wildly as Dennis positioned the case, and Ruth was pleased to see that here they still used manual scales. Like a one-handed clock, she thought. She disliked the electronic ones, with their digital panels set into the counter top so that the exact weight of a holiday was displayed. On the way back from Bali, her case had weighed twenty-five kilos. A third of a person, she'd thought as she read the glowing panel, she was carrying a good third of an adult. Or half a child. It was Malcolm's masks that had weighed her down; he'd bought seven or eight of the things, each one carved from thick teak. He thought they'd look good hanging in the bedroom, but they didn't.

As she waited to board the plane she sat opposite the twins and a young couple. On their honeymoon, perhaps. The woman read the paper while the man held the latest copy of *Woman's Day*. *Fergie's Fab New Figure*, read the cover, the elaborate pink letters curling and creeping between his fingers. Next to him the yellow twin took a lipstick from her money belt and began applying it.

'No, Lois,' she said as her sister reached for the tube, 'you know this colour doesn't suit you.'

Ruth had never been on such a small plane. Out on the runway it looked like one of Daniel's toys, like a model pieced together by a schoolboy. There was no handrail, just a thin blue cord that indicated the edge of the stairs, the point at which they fell away to nothing. The pilot stood on the tarmac, his shirt whiter than the billows of cumulus piling overhead. He took Ruth's boarding pass and, like a cinema usher, tore off the stub. As she moved up the stairs he said, 'I hope you enjoy your flight.' A gust of wind buffeted her and she grasped at the blue cord, which felt like string in her palm.

There were only two seats in each row, with the aisle running between them. Behind Ruth the American twins were settling in, arranging their legs around their hand luggage.

The pink twin smiled and said, 'Isn't it nice, we all get a window seat.'

The walls of the plane were covered with cream vinyl, like the interior of an old car. Laura's car. It even smelled the same. Ruth closed her eyes.

'Well what am I going to read then?'

'I don't know. The emergency procedures card.'

The young man and woman from the terminal were taking the seats in front of Ruth. The woman rolled and punched her anorak, squashed the air out of it.

'You hate *Woman's Day*,' she said. 'You think it degrades women and insults their intelligence, remember?'

'It does. That's why you should read something else.'

'Such as?' The woman rammed her anorak under the seat.

'You should have brought the newspaper with you.'

'It belonged to the café, it wasn't mine to bring.'

The man riffled through pages of fashion, beauty tips, recipes. 'That's your problem then, isn't it?'

The pilot grasped the blue cord and pulled the door shut—as if hauling in a net, thought Ruth—and in a moment they were rushing along the runway and everything was blurring and then they were climbing above the clouds.

The air conditioning came on when they had completed their ascent. A vent above Ruth began to breathe out a stream of mist. She could see it forming clouds above her head, like unspoken words on a cold day. The young woman was watching it with some alarm.

'Simon, what's that?' she whispered, but he didn't hear her.

Ruth hadn't realised how quickly home could be left behind. Before long the captain was announcing their descent, and as they approached the airstrip, she watched the shadow of the plane moving along the land like a ghostly fish.

'What are you doing?' Patrick's father stood in the doorway, his lean silhouette breaking the light from the hall. 'I hope I won't find any of the packaging damaged.' He picked up each Meccano box and scrutinised it. 'Mmhmm,' he said, and, 'Aha, aha.'

Patrick wondered if he should say something, but his father seemed so absorbed in his inspection he thought it best not to interrupt. Finally Graham let out a sigh and looked at Patrick.

'These are not toys,' he said, holding a No. 5 Outfit as if it were made of glass. 'They are an investment. We have to think about the future.'

Patrick nodded. He studied the pictures on the boxes and the instruction manuals and the advertising brochures, the colours so vivid they hurt his eyes. *The World's Greatest Toy*, read one cover. *Meccano Hours are Happy Hours*. A train rushed towards his foot, all red metal and silvery steam; the Quebec Bridge spanned a bright blue river; a pipe-smoking father watched two boys working on the Giant Block-setting Crane; a group of boys on a palm-fringed island unpacked Meccano from treasure chests.

'We can never know what the future holds for us,' his father continued. 'It's important to plan. To have something put aside for emergencies. I might not always be earning what I am now.'

Patrick traced the palm leaves with his eye. In the distance was a sailing ship, and beside it, waving to one of the marooned boys, were tiny figures on a life raft. *Toys of Quality*, read the lettering on the brochure. Beside the boys was an unfurled treasure map. Patrick nudged a box with his toe, hoping for a faint chime, the sound of metal on metal, but there was nothing. His father never talked about money, unless it was to complain about the cost of steak or petrol or Patrick's school uniform. He certainly never acknowledged the fact that he earned a salary, and that it was reasonable. Patrick eyed the velvet curtains, the fringed cushions his mother arranged on the bed every morning and removed every night. He felt the thick carpet under his knees. Could it be that his parents were well off despite the fire? *With my Meccano Outfit in front of me I am the keenest, brightest, and happiest boy living,* he read. *It's fine to be a Meccano boy, and that's why I want to tell you here about Meccano—the jolliest, manliest game ever.*

'Choose one,' said his father. 'You can choose one set, to keep for yourself.'

'The No. 115 Shipbuilding Outfit,' said Patrick. 'Please.'

His father nodded and placed it on the dressing-table. Patrick looked at the backwards writing in the mirror: OᴎAƆƆ3M. It looked like a Russian word, a message in code from one of his spy novels.

'Your mother can take you to the bank tomorrow,' said Graham. 'I'll pay for the safety deposit box.' And he smiled, as if he'd just promised Patrick a treat.

'Aren't you a lucky thing,' said Doreen. 'You know how your father prizes his collection.'

The bus rumbled and bumped, and in Patrick's lap the unassembled ship felt heavy as a brick. It lurched forwards as they turned a corner and his mother grabbed at it.

'Do take care, Patrick,' she said. 'We need to look after it, it'll be worth a lot of money one day.'

Outside, above the thundering of the bus's engine and the cars whizzing past and the passengers discussing the coolness of the evenings now, the criminal price of ham on the bone, Moira somebody's wedding, Patrick heard a clock strike a quarter past the hour. The quarter-past chime always annoyed him. It sounded so incomplete.

At the bank they were greeted by a dark-suited man.

'We'll parcel it up in tissue paper first,' he told them, taking the

Shipbuilding Outfit from Patrick and placing it neatly on the desk.

For some reason Patrick thought he was going to produce scented pastel sheets, like the ones saved from the guest soaps, but the man in the suit spread two pieces of dark blue paper on the desk.

'It keeps out the light,' he said. 'It'll protect the box. Did you know, Mrs Mercer, that ordinary white paper lets in the light?'

Doreen admitted she did not.

'It leaches the colour out bit by bit,' said the man.

'But it'll be dark in the safety deposit box, won't it?' said Patrick.

'I like to use the blue paper,' said the man, 'as a backup. A safety net. One can never be too careful with one's valuables. Wedding dresses, for instance, should always be stored in blue.' He looked at Patrick's mother, waited.

Patrick thought of all the parchment manuscripts in the museum, all the books made of skin rather than paper: the bibles and breviaries and books of hours and herbals, the romances and bestiaries, the psalters, the passionales. He wondered what would happen if every one was unclasped and left to revert to its animal form. He imagined painted goats springing from the shelves; rustling, reconstituted sheep wandering the manuscripts room; deer and calves and squirrels and hares filling the museum corridors.

'My wedding dress is in a special cotton cover,' said his mother, and the man nodded.

'Cotton is also acceptable.'

The dress had been wrapped in an old blanket, Patrick knew, but he didn't say anything.

The dark-suited man wrapped the No. 115 Shipbuilding Outfit in brown paper, coarse and murky-coloured, like very fine sand. It gave nothing away; the package could have contained meat, or books, or it could have been a box filled with earth. Patrick recalled the mummified falcon at the museum, the cat wrapped for centuries. He watched the man folding precise corners, creating paper seams as neat as any tailor might. His hands were small but very broad, with short white fingers and carefully trimmed nails. On one little finger he wore a gold ring in the shape of a shield with a tangle of initials engraved on it. He tucked and pleated the thick paper. He had done this before. He had sealed up hundreds of treasures in nondescript brown. Patrick pictured all the different parcels stored in their safety deposit boxes, nestled in the dark. There must be walls filled with them: papery brown cocoons.

When the man had sealed the box completely he asked Patrick's mother to sign her name over the joins.

'Here,' he said, motioning with his little shielded finger, 'and here—and here.'

Patrick thought of the parcel one day being opened, and every version of his mother's name being split in two. He wondered whether the dark-suited man would still be there, whether he would be the one to undo it. His mother signed slowly, making sure that every signature looked real.

Colette reached inside the mailbox. The electricity bill, a few thin, garish catalogues, a letter for Nathan from his family—and, right at the bottom, two letters addressed to Colette, from overseas, and forwarded north by her mother. But they weren't from Patrick.

Dear Colette,

Just a note to let you know that I'm coming to New Zealand! I decided it was time I had a look at the place, and Mom said she'd pay for my ticket, so I'll be there next month. I want to visit your mother for a few days and then I thought I'd head north and see you and Dominic. I'm guessing you will be on Easter break then, and am hoping you might have some free time to spend with your old pen-pal! It will be great to finally meet you in person.

Lots of love, Nina

Dear Colette,

Although I haven't had any contact with you for a couple of years, I've been thinking a lot recently and decided it was time to write.

When I first met you, obviously I found you attractive, and I thought you were a lot like me. We had the same sense of humour, we liked each other's friends and you said you wanted to travel too. It took me a long time to realise how different we are. Sometimes I think the only reason you were interested in me was because I was doing a law degree—because I would earn a lot. You used to joke about wanting to marry well, but now I think you were serious. I think you saw me as the golden goose—someone who would buy you your big, well-situated house and your trips overseas and your overpriced antiques. But I have no regrets about dropping law—in fact, it was the best move I ever made. I certainly don't miss New Zealand. Have you done any more travel, Colette? I suspect not. I suspect you haven't left the country since you got back from our 'round-the-world trip'. For someone so tight with her money, that was a real waste, wasn't it?

Your basic problem, Colette, is that you are too cautious. You don't like taking risks. What this means for anyone involved with you is that they have to bow to your will, and if they don't, you show a very hard, ugly side of your character. You become ruthless in the pursuit of your own goals and have little consideration for how that might affect others. Take, for example, Venice. You knew I wanted to see the Doge's Palace—the prisons, in particular—but you insisted on a ridiculous gondola ride. Then there was your attitude in Paris. It was obvious you didn't want to be there. Every café I chose was too smoky, you refused to come on the perfume-factory tour, the Mona Lisa was too small for you. I could go on. Why, Colette, did you even bother to leave your tiny little island at the arse-end of nowhere? Perhaps you've changed since I last saw you, but I doubt it. You care about one person only, and that's Colette Hawkins. I hope whichever poor bastard you're with now won't take as long as I did to come to his senses.

Justin Warwick

'Anything for me?' said Nathan.

Colette handed him the letter from his family and burst into tears.

'What is it? Bad news?'

'It seems I have a very hard side to me. I'm ruthless, apparently.' Even as she said the words, she regretted it. Nathan was watching her, murmuring sympathies, but she knew he was also assessing her character, trying to fit Justin's description to the person he knew.

'Unbelievable,' he said, and took the letter from her. And although he snorted and was indignant on Colette's behalf and muttered, 'Lies. All lies,' and, 'You can't say that,' disagreeing with

Justin as if they were in the same room, he read the whole document very closely.

'His handwriting is terrible,' he said finally.

'He was probably drunk when he wrote it.'

'Well then,' said Nathan, still reading, 'you can't believe a word, can you? Just ignore it.' He screwed up the letter and dropped it in the bin. 'There now. It's gone. Let's have a drink.'

But it wasn't gone. As they sat on the couch sipping wine, Colette could hear the crushed pages rustling, slowly unfurling themselves, demanding attention.

'He's right, you know,' she said. 'I am unadventurous. I paid for a round-the-world trip and I came back early.'

'I'm not surprised, if you were travelling with him.'

'I've never even been to Australia,' she said, 'and my dad lives there. I'm specialising in New Zealand history, for God's sake.'

Nathan opened another bottle of wine. 'The Australians do good reds,' he said, inspecting the label.

'I've flown over Australia,' said Colette, 'on the way back from my aborted round-the-world trip, the summer before last. We were meant to have a week there, but I only saw it from the air.'

'I'd like to see the outback,' said Nathan. 'Hire a car, travel at my own pace. Get a feel for the country.'

'My cousin's coming to visit over Easter, by the way,' said Colette, stumbling over her words, 'from America. We used to write to each other in lemon juice.' She laughed and refilled her glass, and kept refilling it until she couldn't hear the letter in the bin any more, until all she could hear was Nathan telling her she was beautiful.

She frowned. The tree outside her window was in the wrong place, and for one bleary moment she wondered if it had moved in the night, uprooted itself and turned to face the ocean. Or, perhaps, the whole house had shifted, pivoted on its axis in the dark. And then she realised it wasn't her window at all. It was Nathan's.

'I love this room in the mornings,' he said, placing a breakfast tray on the bed. He pulled back the rest of the curtains so that light poured in every side of the turret. 'These were built so wives could watch for their husbands returning from sea.'

Colette tried to nod, but her head hurt too much. 'My cousin's coming to New Zealand,' she said, closing her eyes. 'From America. Is it okay with you if she stays? She can sleep in the lounge.'

'Is she gorgeous?' said Nathan.

'Oh yes.'

'Then it's fine,' he laughed.

In 1973, the very first time they went out to dinner, Rosemary asked Patrick what made him choose museum work.

'Such dusty places,' she said. 'And don't you get tired of having to be quiet?' She clasped her hands together and tilted her head on one side, waiting for his answer, never taking her eyes off him. Patrick pressed the softened wax on one of the candles. He could feel the heat from the base of the flame, the hot blue diamond almost touching his thumb. Today was a special day. He had just purchased a manuscript he had wanted for a long time, not for the museum but for himself. It was an instruction book, written for medieval scribes and illuminators, and although it was relatively unadorned he liked to think of it as a template for far more lavish works. A starting point, the beauty of which was in the words themselves. He thought of the directions for making ink: *Cut for yourself wood of the thorn-trees in April or May, before they produce flowers or leaves, and collecting them in small bundles, allow them to lie in the shade for two, three, or four weeks, until they are somewhat dry. Then have wooden mallets, with which you beat these thorns upon another piece of hard wood, until you peel off the bark everywhere, which you immediately put into a barrelful of water.*

'Well, don't you?' said Rosemary.

The candles were lined up in threes on every table in the restaurant. It was an expensive place. He peered through the waxy bars at her, wished they would burn away.

'I suppose, I mean,' he said, 'I haven't really thought, it's something that's never—'

Rosemary smiled, waited.

Afterwards, thought Patrick, *put this water into a very clean pan, or into a cauldron, and fire being placed under it, boil it; from time to time, also, throw into the pan some of this bark, so that whatever sap may remain in it may be boiled out. When you have cooked it a little, throw it out, and again put in more; which done, boil down the remaining water unto a third part, and then, pouring it out of this pan, put it into one smaller, and cook it until it grows black and begins to thicken.*

'Do you know the derivation of the word ink?' he said. 'It comes from the Latin *encaustum*, meaning burnt in, because it eats into the page.' He could see Rosemary frowning. 'Later medieval ink was made from gall nuts. The swellings that grow on oak trees when a gall wasp lays eggs in the bud.'

'Oh,' said Rosemary, and began playing with her salad.

'The gall nuts were crushed and infused in rainwater in the sun, or by the fire, and—'

'What about the baby wasps?' said Rosemary. 'What happened to them?'

'The baby wasps?'

'In the bud.'

'They bored holes,' said Patrick. 'When they hatched, they drilled through the gall nut and flew away.'

'Before crushing?'

'Oh yes, well before crushing.' Patrick stopped. 'What did you ask me?'

'About the baby wasps.'

'No, before that.'

'Ah. Museum work.' Rosemary had resumed playing with her salad.

'When I was a boy,' said Patrick, aware he was talking too much, 'I used to go to the museum every weekend. The manuscripts curator was very kind to me.' Rosemary slid a tomato wedge back and forth. Patrick wished she would eat it; the meal would cost a lot. 'It was the need to preserve the past,' he said, and suddenly he wanted to tell her about the fire. He wanted her to sit watching his lips, his tongue, while he told her how he'd destroyed everything his family had owned.

'Patrick,' she said, 'are you always so serious?' She laughed and brushed his cheek with her fingertips, and he laughed with her, and caught her hand before it crept back through the candles to cradle her wine glass. And he kept the fire to himself.

Patrick disliked visiting his mother. He put off taking Rosemary to meet her until embarrassment over the delay outweighed embarrassment over Doreen herself. She'd been an old woman for years; ever since he left home she'd been wearing brown tights and cardigans and floral blouses buttoned to the neck. She drank tea, sucked boiled sweets. And she knitted, more than she ever had, even though Patrick bought his own clothes now and Graham was seven years dead, felled by a stroke while wearing a Fair Isle jumper. Whenever Patrick came to see Doreen she sat in her chair, woollen garments growing from her hands, the steel needles clicking like bones.

'I've been seeing someone for a couple of years now,' he said. 'I thought I might bring her round next time I come.'

'Your ship,' said his mother, 'is still in the bank.'

'Mum,' he said, 'I'm seeing someone. Rosemary. She wants to meet you.'

'Don't you want to assemble it? Aren't the parts made exactly to scale?'

'We could go out somewhere, if you like. The three of us. We could go to lunch in town, how about that?'

'It's a faithful reproduction,' said Doreen. 'An exact replica. It was very expensive.' She sighed. 'Lucky old Joyce, going on a cruise. I always wanted to go on a cruise. So romantic, sailing the seas.'

'Tell you what, Mum,' said Patrick, 'I'll get the Shipbuilding Outfit from the bank and we'll sell it. We'll put it together with all of Dad's other sets and sell them to a collector or a dealer, whoever offers the best price, and then you can buy yourself a few treats. Take a holiday, perhaps.'

Doreen fixed him with a stare. 'Don't be ridiculous, I could never sell Graham's collection,' she said. 'It's worth too much.'

When Patrick did bring Rosemary round, Doreen kept calling her Faye and telling her how much better she was looking.

'You've really filled out again,' she said. 'Of course, I always thought you had a lovely figure.'

'Mum, this is Rosemary,' said Patrick. 'Faye's still in hospital. She's still very sick.'

'I don't know why you thought you needed to lose weight, dear,' said Doreen. 'Your mother's fairly well padded, and she never had any trouble getting boyfriends.'

She watched him from the bed, her eyes taking up too much of her face.

'Hello, Faye,' said Patrick. 'Aunt Joyce thought you might like a visitor. How are you feeling? Have they said when you can go home?'

Faye turned her head and stared out the window. 'I don't want to go home.' The voice was scratched, barely more than a whisper.

'The food's that good, is it?' said Patrick, and bit his tongue. His eyes travelled from Faye's concave cheeks to the crook of her elbow, where a needle was taped. Above the bed a bottle filled with a colourless solution hung like a hurricane lantern.

Faye followed his gaze. 'They told me everything I need is in there,' she said. 'It could be water, for all I know. Do you think it's water?'

'Aunt Joyce is very worried about you. She wants you to get better and come home.'

Faye sighed and laced her fingers together. Her arms were so thin that her hands appeared enormous, like adult hands on a child. And the identity bracelet encircling her wrist would have fitted a child; her name, written in black ink capitals, met its own beginning. If she lost any more weight, Patrick thought, her name would start shrinking, disappearing letter by letter.

'I don't want to see my mother. She fusses too much. And Ronnie's always there. Always.'

'Is there someone else who can look after you, though? What will you do when they let you out?'

'Nothing,' said Faye. 'I don't want to *do* anything.'

'Well, you'll need to rest for a while of course—'

'Sometimes I used to stand at my dressing-table wondering what to wear. How do you know, in the morning, what the rest of the day will be like? How do you even know what it'll be like across town? And will it rain? And if it's cool now will it get warmer later? If I wear cotton will I freeze?'

She took a gasp of air. Patrick watched her collarbone moving up and down like gaunt wings and thought of the little-girl dress she'd left at his parents' house once, of how it had hung outside overnight and frozen on the washing line.

'I need someone to tell me things,' she said. 'There are so many decisions to be made in a day. I wander around at the grocer's sometimes, not even taking anything from the shelves. Why are there three brands of butter? Are red apples better than green ones?'

Patrick studied the pattern in the linoleum.

'I just want someone to take over,' Faye said, her too-large eyes on Patrick now, eating him up. 'I want someone else to make the decisions. I want someone to tell me what to eat and what to wear, and what I should read and which songs I should enjoy. Is that so bad?'

'I need to get going now,' said Patrick, and he bent over and kissed Faye on the cheek. Her skin felt like paper money, and he could smell the hospital bedclothes, her acetone breath. 'I'll come again soon,' he said. 'As soon as I can manage.'

When he was in bed with Rosemary that night, watching her fingers move over his skin, he thought of Faye's hands. He saw them locked behind her back, a ball of knuckles, and his own arms attached to her body, performing every task for her, making the decisions. He would look after her when she came out of hospital. Rosemary would just have to put up with it. Faye was family.

'It seems ridiculous,' said Rosemary, 'that she can't stay with her mother. They have that huge house, while we're cramped in here like sardines.'

'I don't think it's healthy for her there,' said Patrick. 'I don't think she'll get better, with Joyce breathing down her neck. And Ronnie.' He dried a crystal glass—a wedding present from his mother—and filled it with orange juice. Then he placed it on a tray, beside a plate of soft scrambled eggs. 'The museum wants me to go on a buying trip. They want me to look at some manuscripts that have come up for sale in Italy and Turkey, a couple in Australia.'

'Australia?' said Rosemary.

'It's an island continent in the south Pacific.'

'I had a great-uncle who emigrated to Australia. My mother said he went opal mining.'

'Tell you what,' said Patrick, gathering up the tray, 'Faye should be better by then, why don't you come with me? We could see New Zealand too, while we're down there.'

Rosemary peered at her reflection in the kitchen window. 'Do you think these trousers make me look fat?' she said. 'The sales girl told me black was very slimming, but then, she was thin as a rake.'

In the end, Patrick went travelling on his own.

'It's not that I don't want to come,' said Rosemary. 'I'm just so tired. It's been very tiring, having a house guest in such a small house. We have so little room.'

'Watch out for pick-pockets,' said his mother, who had never been abroad. 'Don't carry bags for strangers. And mind the sun, it's very strong. Mind your moles.'

'I'll be fine,' said Rosemary. 'You deserve a break, looking after your cousin all this time. It's been months and months. Make it a bit of a holiday. Go.'

He climbed from the water and let the sun dry his skin.

'This is the end of the world,' she said, and splashed his back with drops of ocean. She was golden from the sun, not like the women at home. Not like Rosemary, or pale Faye. And she smelled different, too. Her skin was muskier, tinged with the outdoors. Every manuscript had its own particular scent, he recalled. He traced a message on her back with his fingertip, scrolled letters across her shoulder-blades, down her spine. Under his touch, tiny hairs raised.

'After this, there's only ice,' she said. He looked out to the horizon, and it was true, there was no other land in sight. She rolled over. Grains of black sand clung to her shoulder, her back. 'How much longer do you have?'

'Two days.' He thought of the purchases he'd made, the fragile manuscripts that would follow him home, packed and sealed to withstand motion, insured against disaster. The museum would be pleased. 'I'll keep in touch,' he said, brushing away the black sand. 'We can exchange addresses.' He thought of Rosemary, waiting for him to return. She would be planning his homecoming meal, selecting flowers from the garden, making the bed with clean sheets. He thought of a recipe for ink: *Add one third part of pure wine, and putting it into two or three new pots, cook it until you see a sort of skin show itself on the surface; then taking these pots from the fire, place them in the sun until the black ink purifies itself from the red dregs. Temper it with wine over the fire, and, adding a little vitriol, write.* 'In Indonesia,' he said, already rehearsing what he'd tell Rosemary, his colleagues, Faye, 'I saw a puppet show made of shadows.' Sand collected under his fingernails.

'You can never contact me here,' she said, writing herself into his book, 'but take it anyway. In case things change.' She was silent after that, and wouldn't name the things that might or mightn't change. The sun poured and poured.

'I think I'm burning,' he said.

When Colette brought Daniel home she found Malcolm sitting alone in the lounge.

'Sorry we're a bit late,' she said. 'We were at the park and we missed our bus back.'

'Have you seen Ruth?'

Colette shook her head. 'Why?'

'She's never this late. I rang periodicals and there was no answer, everyone's long gone. She's never been this late before.'

'Daniel,' said Colette, 'why don't you go put your bag away and wash your hands?'

'If she was going to be late, she would have phoned.'

'I'm sure there's nothing to worry about,' said Colette, but Malcolm wasn't listening. He was staring past her, to the sideboard, she realised, to the cluster of photographs. 'I'll make some tea,' she said.

The envelope wasn't sealed. It was propped against the electric jug, an unobtrusive cream rectangle. It wasn't even addressed to anyone. Whoever had left it there had been in a hurry to leave. Colette didn't open it.

'I found this in the kitchen,' she said. As Malcolm read the note, she watched his face for clues. She wasn't expecting him to laugh.

'She's gone on holiday,' he said. 'Just like that.' He laughed again.

'Where is she?'

'I've absolutely no idea.'

Colette looked at the photo of Laura. 'It must be hard for her, not knowing,' she said. 'Even all this time later, it must be very hard.'

'I used to do a lot of photography,' said Malcolm. 'Landscapes, mainly. Mountains, frost. I was never very good at people.'

'Does she say when she'll be back?'

Malcolm scanned the single creamy page again and shook his head.

'It's just that my cousin's coming to stay over Easter, from America, and I wondered if I could have some time off. We've never met.'

'Where's Mummy?' said Daniel, appearing at the door. 'I can't find her.'

'She's having a holiday,' said Colette. 'She'll be back soon, there's nothing to worry about.'

'Hol-i-day, hol-i-day,' sang Daniel. He sat on the Persian rug and examined a woven flower.

'I wouldn't ask,' said Colette, 'it's just that we've never met. We used to be pen-pals.'

Malcolm folded the note back into its blank envelope. 'I'm sure we can cope,' he said.

While Ruth was away, Malcolm took up the paving stones in the back yard and dug a garden. He planted seedling lettuces, beans, roses. He sowed a row of carrots, a row of snow peas. One corner he reserved for a patch of herbs: mint, rosemary, parsley, coriander, sweet basil. Normally he wouldn't have planted at that time of year— summer was over, daylight saving had finished—but there was a chance, he told himself, that things would grow.

He left the back door open when he worked outside in the evenings, so he could hear Daniel or the telephone. He was surprised how placid his son was without Ruth there. He didn't even ask where she'd gone, or when she was coming back, but simply accepted Malcolm's explanation that she was having a little holiday on her own. He brushed his teeth without being asked, and put away his toys each day so nobody would break their neck.

Malcolm closed his office door and rang the periodicals department again.

'She didn't mention where she was going,' said Jan. 'I think it was a last-minute decision. Why, is something wrong?'

'No,' said Malcolm, 'no, of course not.'

'But she didn't leave you an address, or a phone number?'

'I'm sure everything's fine,' he said. 'She just needed a break, that's all. She's been wanting a holiday for ages.'

'Well, let me know if you hear from her, won't you?' Jan hesitated. 'She's seemed a bit distant lately. A bit sad.'

That night Malcolm worked in the garden until late. He erected pyramid-shaped frames for the beans to climb, so they would form a leafy wigwam. The space inside, he thought as he secured twine to the bars, would accommodate a child. He tried to picture what Ruth might be doing: relaxing in a spa pool, watching television, sipping a cocktail. Washing up, removing her make-up, dancing, sleeping. Flirting with rich tourists. Smoking. Gambling, perhaps. He thought about the note she'd left. *Don't worry about me. It's not your fault. Nothing is wrong.* It was, though. People didn't disappear unless something was wrong. And Ruth, he realised, had been disappearing for years, becoming more and more distant from him and Daniel, trickling away from them one grain at a time. When she came back, he decided, he would make a real fuss of her. He would do all the cooking, surprise her with gifts, take her out to dinner. He would stop reading the newspaper in bed, he would send flowers to her at the library. He would make sure she knew she was wanted, loved. He would make her feel so wanted that she would never go away again.

When he finished with the bean frames he made his way to the back porch. The door was shut. He turned the handle quietly, careful not to wake Daniel, but it wouldn't open. Someone had locked it from the inside. Malcolm felt in his pocket for his keys, his fingers searching for the plastic disc containing Laura, but they were in the house. He'd left them on the kitchen table the way he did each night when he returned home.

'Daniel,' he called, knocking on the door, 'Daniel, can you come and let Daddy in?' The outdoor light shone on the neat new garden. There was no sound from inside. 'Daniel? Can you hear me?' Malcolm walked round the side of the house and rapped on his son's window. Daniel peeped out between the curtains, stared at his father for a moment and disappeared again, and no matter how hard Malcolm knocked or how loudly he called, he wouldn't come back.

As he waited on the neighbours' front doorstep, Malcolm tried to brush the worst of the dirt from his hands. 'I'm so sorry to trouble you this late,' he said when the door opened, 'but I'm locked out. Would it be possible to use your phone?'

He didn't even know the woman's name, he realised as he padded down her hall in his gardening socks. He wondered whether he should introduce himself, but decided it was too late; they'd been living side by side for months now.

'Hello, Nathan speaking.'

'Nathan, Malcolm Pearse here. I wonder, would Colette be there at the moment?'

'Sorry, she's out with her cousin. I don't know what time she'll be back.'

'Right,' said Malcolm, 'it's just I wanted to use her key. My key, to our house. I'm locked out.'

'Sorry,' said Nathan again.

Back in the garden, Malcolm removed his sweatshirt and wrapped one of the uprooted paving stones inside it. Then he swung it at the back door, and some of the frosted glass shattered over his feet, and some of it fell inside.

At lunchtime he took his key to have a copy made.

'We had a bit of excitement last night,' he told the man at the Mister Minit stand. 'I was locked out.'

Mister Minit nodded. 'You wouldn't believe the number of people who don't have a spare. They never think about it till it's too late.'

Malcolm forced the key-ring apart with his thumbnail.

'That's okay,' said Mister Minit. 'You don't have to take it off.'

'No trouble,' said Malcolm as the sharp end of the ring dug into his thumb. 'Here we are.' And he shut the picture of Laura in his palm.

He watched as Mister Minit selected an uncut key from one of the many hooks. There were rows and rows of them, toothless things, blank tongues of metal. He thought about how he'd broken the glass in the door, how he'd walked over the shards in his gardening shoes and headed for Daniel's room. Daniel was sitting up in bed, wide awake. Above his bed hung the silhouette of Laura, a hole in the white wall.

'Hello,' said Daniel.

'That was very naughty,' said Malcolm. 'Daddy had to break the glass in the back door.'

Daniel didn't answer.

'There's a big mess in the porch and it's very dangerous and you mustn't go there or you'll cut your feet. It'll be very expensive to fix.' He stared at his son, who remained silent. 'We'll have to leave it open all night. I'll have to cover it with paper. It's very dangerous.'

Daniel lay down, his head dark against the white pillowcase. 'Good night,' he said.

'Do you really do them in a minute?' said Malcolm. Mister Minit nodded. There was a squealing sound as he traced the machine round Malcolm's key, and it was done.

A postcard was waiting for him when he got home. Colette had left it bundled up with all the other mail, but Malcolm had the distinct feeling it had been read. He didn't care. He was relieved. People didn't put bad news on postcards; they sealed it in envelopes, surrounded it with other information. They cushioned it with roomy details of good health, new babies, pleasing exam results. He looked at the picture, which gave nothing away. It wasn't a landscape or a building but a single paua shell, available throughout the country. He tried to make out the postmark, but it was too faint.

Dear Malcolm and Daniel,
    I'm having a lovely relaxing time and hope you are too. I've been going swimming a lot and am getting so brown you might not recognise me! There is a gallery here where you can see glass-blowers at work—I could watch them for hours. I should be back some time next week. Say hi to Colette, lots of love, Mummy

Malcolm wrapped the new key in plastic and sealed it inside a film canister, then buried it in the garden. He chose a spot beside the Italian parsley, because of its key-shaped leaves, and he made sure that the hole was shallow. In an emergency, it would be easy to find the key again, and there would be no shouting, and no broken glass.

Ruth watched the woman at the furnace door twirling the pipe. When she withdrew it, the bulb on the end was red-hot. She rolled it on a metal slab, then placed her mouth to the cool end and blew, and the glass stretched and swelled, as pliable as hot toffee. It was a versatile material, the woman said, turning and shaping the glowing bubble, flattening the base with a spatula, defining the neck with narrow tongs. Glass was made of melted sand, and sometimes formed naturally when lightning struck a beach. When it was hot enough to be poured, it coiled like a snake. Flat panes, she said, nodding towards the window, were made by drawing a ribbon of molten glass across liquid tin. If an object—a vase, a goblet—cooled too quickly, it was pushed back into the furnace through a space called the glory hole. Glass even made it possible to take pictures inside the human body.

    Ruth went to the gallery every day and looked at the perfume bottles, the vases, the bowls and goblets that were for sale. There was always a small crowd watching the glass-blowers. One day she saw the young couple from the plane there. They left with their little fingers linked.

The motel unit was like a miniature home. It had tiny soaps and tiny bottles of shampoo, and in the kitchen there were tiny sachets of sugar and jam and coffee. There was a little oven and a little fridge containing a carton of milk and blocks of butter suitable for a doll's kitchen. Even the television was small, the actors' faces illegible. Ruth gave up trying to improve the reception; she couldn't get rid of the ghosts. On the bedroom wall hung a round mirror. Sometimes, if she woke at night, she thought the moon had come inside.

She went to the beach most days and swam and read frivolous magazines, the sort frowned upon by the periodicals department. Her skin darkened more each time, which made her feel healthy. Some of the beauty articles she skimmed warned that any tanning indicated damage, but others insisted that a little exposure afforded protection from the sun. Both couldn't be right, Ruth knew, so she believed those that suited her and discounted the others, left them face-down in the sand and headed for the tepid water.

In the gift shop she fingered postcards glossy with sun. She was reluctant to send a mountain, a beach, a particular church; unwilling to choose a scene that pinpointed her location. There was always the chance, of course, that the postmark would give her away, but often the ink was blurred, indistinct. She would take her chances. She chose a card shaped like a shell, an oval paua. It was blue, green, turquoise, teal, all the colours of the sea and sky mixed together. They were making paua pearls now, the man at the counter told her, and he showed her necklaces and bracelets and rings. They were big business. The pearls didn't occur naturally, of course, but were cultivated from a grain of sand inserted into the soft mollusc body.

At night it was too hot.

'It's fine to leave the doors and windows open,' said the motel owner. 'Just hook the fly-screens shut.'

When Ruth looked through the fine metal gauze to the bush, the water, the shimmering sky, the view was blurred, broken into thousands of tiny dots like a newsprint picture. The screens were very fine, she thought; anybody could break them with a fist. Still, she needed to let her miniature home cool down. She needed to let the air circulate. And, even though there was only gauze between her and the night, something not much stronger than paper, she slept soundly.

She cut her knee on the fourth day.

'It was silly of me,' she said. 'I slipped when I was getting out of the shower.'

The motel owner produced some plasters from a first aid kit. 'It doesn't look too deep,' he said. 'It won't take long to heal.'

He was right. It soon ceased to sting, although for the next few days Ruth was careful when she moved around her compact unit, her toy house. She stepped gingerly, protecting herself from knocks and bumps, avoiding the low couch, the sharp-edged coffee table. Her progress made her think of a game Laura had played as a child, where the idea wasn't to avoid the furniture but to cling to it, to move from room to room without ever touching the floor. Laura amused herself for hours by skipping over chairs and foot-stools and tables, moving them if necessary, taking the most circuitous path possible. Once she had a new route memorised, she flew through the house, breathless, the floor a blur beneath her.

'You'll break something,' Ruth always warned. 'You'll hurt yourself.'

But Laura never did.

When she next went swimming, Ruth pulled the plaster from her knee and examined the cut. It had a smooth, glazed surface. It was a chink of glass, a window into herself. She lay on the beach and read a magazine article on iron deficiency which was, apparently, epidemic among young western women. Blood, it said, was renewed every three years. Ruth thought of the cathedrals Colette had told her about, the ones she'd seen when travelling in Europe. More often than not, they were swathed in scaffolding. It was necessary, Colette explained, for ongoing maintenance. As the stones deteriorated, they were replaced with new ones cut to the exact size of the hole. So eventually, Ruth said, there would be nothing left of the original walls? One by one, stone by stone, entire cathedrals would be replaced? Colette had laughed and said she hadn't thought of it like that, but Ruth had been unsettled by the thought of such trickery, such sleight-of-hand right under the noses of the faithful. She ran across the hot sand to the water, her feet moving so fast they hardly seemed to touch the ground.

The day she returned home, she stopped in at the gallery and bought a glass vase which was flecked and dappled like the breast of a thrush. She was looking forward to having flowers in the house again. She held it on her lap all the way back.

Colette could see Nina eyeing the factory yards, the enormous oil reservoirs that stretched to the water's edge.

'It's not like this further round,' she assured her cousin. 'It's really very beautiful.'

Gradually the industrial landscape gave way to gorsy hillside, rocks, grey beaches. At the side of the road a sign read *Little Blue Penguins crossing at night.*

'Blue penguins?' said Nina. 'I thought they were black-and-white.'

'They're a bluish black, I imagine,' said Colette. 'You know how black can sometimes—'

'Maybe they're depressed penguins,' said Dominic. He began singing 'Don't It Make My Brown Eyes Blue'. 'Do you like country and western, Nina?'

They drove on through the bays. There was the occasional cluster of shops: arts and crafts, dairies, small cafés. Now and then they passed joggers, teenagers walking large dogs.

'Where are all the people?' said Nina.

'I think we've missed the crowds,' said Colette. 'And it's late in the season. You wouldn't want to be here in midsummer, it's overrun with tourists. Not that you're a tourist,' she added. She chewed the side of her mouth. 'Look, someone flying a kite.'

Nina peered out the window. 'I don't see it.'

'Over there, in front of that house with the brick fence. Oh— no, it's gone now.' The kite had plummeted from view like a bird felled by gunshot. Stupid country, stupid people, thought Colette. Couldn't get anything right.

Dominic saw the shop first, and he groaned and pulled into the curb.

'Antiques!' said Colette, throwing off her safety belt, and Dominic groaned again.

'We have to humour her,' he told Nina. 'She'll sulk for the rest of the day otherwise.'

'This is a bonus,' Colette was saying, already out of the car. 'I didn't know there was an antique shop round here.'

'She has a thing about old stuff. When we used to go on family holidays we'd take twice as long to get there as anyone else. She'd make Mum stop at every junk shop along the way.'

'Only at the antique places,' said Colette. 'Only at the good ones.'

She thought of the many shops she had dragged her mother and Dominic through. Shelves bowing with dinner sets and tea sets; glass cabinets holding letter openers, pen knives, hairbrushes with elaborate handles; the smell of beeswax and silver polish and golden linseed oil: these were the things she associated with picnics and barbecues and days at the beach.

'So you're a junkie, Colette,' said Nina.

Dominic laughed and said, 'Junkie! A junkie!' but Colette didn't hear. She was already inside the shop, scanning, assessing.

The quality was excellent. A lot of large pieces of furniture, some silver, a few elegant sets of glasses. Not much china, which was good. There was a beautiful octagonal lantern hanging in the window, made of bevelled glass and decorated with sharp brass leaves and flowers. *Spanish*, said the label. *Seven hundred and fifty dollars.* She examined an oak coffer, opened a writing desk.

'Lovely, isn't it?' said the woman, who sported the usual fob chain and lavishly sprayed hair. 'It's late Victorian.'

'A pity the inkwell's gone,' said Colette and turned away, smiling to herself. It was a game she liked to play in any new shop, a way of establishing her credentials.

'Why do you insist on proving yourself like that?' said Dominic when they were back in the car. 'It's embarrassing. She's been doing it since she was about ten, Nina.'

'They take one look at me and think they can sell me any old junk,' said Colette. 'You have to show them who's boss.'

'Er, wouldn't that be the owner of the shop?'

'Shut up.'

'Did you see that basket of tassels? Fifty bucks each. For a tassel.'

'They were handmade,' said Colette. 'That Spanish lantern was gorgeous.'

'Oh God, here we go,' said Dominic. 'You see, Nina, Colette fancies herself as a bit of a connoisseur. She does know her stuff, granted, but unfortunately she doesn't have the bank account to support her habit.'

'You'd love Mom and Dad's place,' said Nina. 'It's stuffed to the ceiling with antiques. They buy them up cheap on their trips to India and Turkey.'

'The thing with Colette,' persisted Dominic, 'is that she tends to fixate. She sees some hideous old piece of wood, usually way out of her price range and full of borer, and she talks about nothing else for weeks.'

'I do not.'

'She obsesses over them as if they're blokes she fancies. "I saw my Scotch chest again today, my Swedish dresser is hiding in the back showroom now, the hooks on my hall stand are all original—"'

Nina laughed, flashing her sharp, straightened teeth. Colette was glad she'd never had braces herself. She liked the gap between her front teeth; she decided it gave her face character. Her mother had told her it was a signal that wealth lay ahead.

'Of course, it never worked for your father,' she said.

'That's the other thing,' said Dominic. 'She talks about them as if she already owns them. "My hall stand, my inlaid tea caddy. Can you lend me a thousand dollars towards my lady's travelling case, Dominic." There was this blanket chest—'

233

'Give it a rest, Dominic.'

'There was this blanket chest she saw when she was about eight. Monstrous thing, painted with wonky birds and grapes and flowers and God knows what else. It was in one of the shops she forced us to stop at when we were going on holiday.'

'Dominic.'

'It was right at the turn-off to head north, one that's really easy to miss.'

Colette could remember their mother missing it once. The antique shop hadn't even been there then. They'd ended up on the wrong side of the island, staring up at the wrong mountain. The shop became something of a landmark when it appeared.

'Every year we'd have to stop and see if the chest was still there,' said Dominic, 'and of course it was, for ages, because it was so ugly nobody wanted to buy it. Then one year we went in and it was gone. You should have seen her. She cried for the next hour, until, to shut her up, Mum said something like you never know what's happened to it, it might still be around. Which was a huge mistake on Mum's part, because Colette took that to mean that she'd bought it for her, and it was somehow going to materialise under the tree on Christmas morning.'

'Oh dear,' said Nina, laughing.

'So when she got the My Little Pony stables, you can imagine the sort of scene we had on our hands. We had to stop at the antique shop on the way back and Colette marched in and asked the owner what had happened to the chest. And he said it hadn't been sold, it was out the back filled with bits and pieces that needed repairing.'

'So she bought it in the end?'

'Oh no. It wasn't for sale any more. That's the tragic part. It hadn't been sold, but it was unattainable. Colette was vile for months afterwards.'

They parked the car where the gates began. The beach was jagged here; no more smooth stretches of sand. *Rocks may fall,* warned a sign. Colette looked up at the cliffs—crumbling, toffee-coloured, dotted with gorse. Along the path were small heaps of rock, shattered and resting at the bottom of slips. Now and then large boulders blocked the way. Nina tiptoed around them as if they might explode.

'We're quite safe,' said Colette, glancing at her brother. 'Aren't we, Dominic.'

'Safe as houses,' he said, prodding a small slip with his toe. More toffee shards came scuttering down. 'In a few years the whole country will have crumbled away.' He laughed and tweaked the hood of Nina's jacket.

Colette wished her brother would stop making an idiot of himself. He was acting like an adolescent, all chummy slapping and energetic displays of how fast he could run, how much he could lift. Colette hated to think what Nina would tell her friends about them when she went home.

As they rounded a bend they came face to face with a sheep. It gave one loud bleat, then continued nibbling at the windswept grass. Colette scanned the hillside for others, trying to see where it had come from, but the gorse cover was too thick. The sheep turned its attention to a gorse bush, manoeuvring its lips around the thorns, coaxing the flowers off one by one.

'Do they bite?' said Nina.

Dominic smacked her on the arm. 'Don't be silly!'

'Maybe she's never seen one before,' said Colette.

'Of course I've seen sheep before,' said Nina, in a slow, bored way that Colette didn't like, 'just never up close.'

'Oh. Well. They don't bite, no.'

They continued in silence. A ship glided past, its destination a faint silhouette beyond miles of dark ocean. On days like this Colette found it easy to convince herself that no other land existed, that here was where the world ended.

'It's a bit cloudy today, I'm afraid,' she said, wishing she could stop apologising to Nina for her country's shortcomings. 'Are you near the beach at home?'

'It's California,' said Dominic. 'It's one big beach.'

Colette kicked a stone with her foot. Down on the shore, someone had pushed a row of sticks and driftwood into the sand. They formed a brief fence between Colette and the sea; a childish attempt to keep the water at bay. It would be washed away with the next high tide.

'So,' said Nina, 'what's your dad up to these days?'

'No idea,' said Dominic.

'He's still in Australia, of course,' said Colette, 'but we hear from him every now and then, don't we?'

Dominic didn't answer.

'You should come and stay some time,' said Nina. 'Mom would love to see you.'

'Colette's not known for successful overseas trips,' said Dominic.

'Well, we've got plenty of spare rooms. It'd be fun. I could show off my exotic cousins.'

'Actually,' said Colette, 'I've been thinking about doing some more travelling, maybe next month. I want to visit England.'

'Is that the lighthouse?' said Nina. In the distance was a tiny white column, almost luminous, a bleached bone nestled into rock.

'That's it,' said Colette, 'except that's the new one. I thought we'd climb up to the old original one.' All three pairs of eyes lifted to the cliff above. There was the older lighthouse, murky against the clouds, the ghostly sibling of the one on the beach.

'You and your bloody antiques,' said Dominic.

'The lighthouse-keeper's daughter's buried up there.'

'Do not collect shellfish past this point. Do not swim. Do not fish,' read Nina. 'This is a sewage outlet?'

'It's treated,' said Colette. 'You can't tell, apart from the sign.'

Nina just stared at her.

As they trekked around the coastline the lighthouses appeared and disappeared, sometimes straight ahead, sometimes obscured by curves of land. The gorse thinned and pasture took over, sheep negotiating the precipitous terrain like mountain goats. In some places the fence posts were almost horizontal.

'Why would you bother fencing that?' said Nina, but neither Colette nor Dominic knew.

As they arrived at the lower lighthouse there was a gust of wind from the south, and all three covered their mouths and noses against the stench.

Colette pointed to the track leading up the side of the hill. 'It'll be better once we're on higher ground.'

It was very steep, but none of them dawdled. Their feet sent stones and clods of earth tumbling down the track, over the edge of the hill to the beach. Alongside the crash and rumble of the sea Colette could hear Nina taking tiny gasps through her mouth, trying to inhale as little of the foul air as possible. Even Dominic was subdued.

They were puffing by the time they reached the top. There was a stile to cross, the wood grey with moisture. Dominic jumped over first, then took Nina's hand and helped her across. In front of them an expanse of green pasture sloped gently downhill, away from the sea, and as they descended the noise of the waves subsided. They could have been in the middle of the country. Sheep grazed quietly, untroubled by the arrival of three humans, and the air smelled clean and cold. Dominic led the way and they crossed the shallow dip of land, none of them saying a word until the path began to wind uphill again and the lighthouse loomed against the sky. Just below it was the grave, a modest plot about the size of a bed, fenced with white pickets.

'Let's have a look,' said Colette, but the others didn't follow so she picked her way alone around mounds of sheep droppings and uneven juttings of land, zigzagging back and forth so it wasn't too steep. The lighthouse-keeper's daughter would have been beautiful, she thought. Long hair, probably green eyes, slender wrists. Small, sharp teeth. Every day she would have swept the spiral staircase, polished the brass fittings, the scrolls and twists that evoked the shapes of shells, dusted the big glass bulb so it shone for miles across the sea. And every night she would have gone to sleep in her round bedroom, and listened to the sound of the waves below, and tried to make out what they were telling her, if it was the name of the man she would marry.

The grave was not what Colette imagined, not what she wanted. There were no grieving angels, no marble flowers. No stone at all, just a white wooden cross, and the words *Josephine Thomas, 30 March 1896, aged 6*. Another disappointment. The lighthouse-keeper's daughter was a child when she died.

On the way back to the track, Colette was so careful to avoid the piles of glossy black pellets that she almost stepped on an old white rag. When she bent closer, she saw four small hoofs among the folds. A dead lamb, or the skin of one. It was the sort of thing she would have shown Dominic once, when they were little. Now, however, she hugged the secret to herself, kept for herself the image of the lamb slipping out of its skin and dancing away naked. Besides, Dominic had already reached the lighthouse and was leaning into the wind, holding his jacket open like wings, and Nina was laughing.

It was growing dark very quickly as they climbed back over the stile. The sea faded, blurred. The ground was damp now and they made their way down the hillside slowly, knees bent, grasping at rocks and tufts of grass and bare clay banks. In the half light the sheep were woolly phantoms. Colette could feel their yellow eyes watching her descend and disappear, making sure she really did go. Dominic's and Nina's faces were indistinct, and Colette felt she could have been walking with anyone, with two strangers.

Dominic wiped the moisture off the windscreen. He let the engine run for a couple of minutes, trying to clear the back window. Colette watched the panels on the glass dispel the condensation, shrink the frosty bars to silvery, transparent lines.

'Maybe we'll see some penguins,' said Nina.

'You never know,' said Dominic. 'I'll stop if we do, and you can get out and have a look.' He spoke as if interesting wildlife crossed the road all the time, but Colette had never seen a penguin in her life, and was fairly certain her brother hadn't either.

They drove past the antique shop, and Colette looked for her Spanish lantern, but she couldn't see it in the window.

Her legs were aching by the time she arrived home, and she could barely climb the steps to the front door. She declined Dominic's invitation of getting a coffee with him and Nina. All she could think about was soaking in a hot bath and going to bed. Nathan was watching *Crimescene* on television; pictures of stolen cameras and watches and missing dogs filled the screen. Colette was glad Nina wasn't there. Even the crimes in this country were boring.

'What happened to you?' said Nathan.

'Lighthouse.'

'Want a cup of tea?'

'Bath. Bed.'

'Have you seen this man?' said the television. A blurry security-camera shot of someone presenting a stolen cheque appeared on the screen.

'That's what we need in the bathroom,' said Nathan. 'A good surveillance system. Nina's been nicking my shampoo, I'm positive.'

'I'll buy you some more shampoo, Nathan.'

'That's not the point though, is it?'

'No. The point is, you want to see naked women for free.'

'Where is she, anyway?'

'Out with Dominic. Having coffee.'

'Ah. Coffee, right.'

Colette dried between each toe, pushed the soft cuticles back with her thumbnail. There was a small chance, she thought, that the lantern had just been shifted. She would go in the next day and ask. It might still be there, in a side window, perhaps, tucked away behind a clock or a chandelier, its sharp leaves glinting in the dark.

She tried to read in bed, but couldn't keep her eyes open. Through the wall she could hear the television blaring away. There were crimes in the airwaves; houses across the country were filling with recreated robberies and rapes designed to jog the memory. *Do you recognise this car? Do you know this man?* She pulled the duvet right up to her ears, breathed in the muggy, sweet scent of inhabited sheets. She thought of the abandoned lamb's skin and shivered. *Have you seen this woman? Did you hear anything strange?* Perhaps, at night, the lighthouse-keeper's daughter rose from her picket-fenced grave, slipped inside the woolly pelt and went running across the hills, jumping and dancing in the moonlight.

'I was in your shop yesterday and there was a Spanish lantern hanging in the window.' Colette forced herself to sound relaxed. 'Is it still around?'

'I know the one you mean,' said the man. 'Lovely thing. Very unusual.'

'Yes,' said Colette.

'My wife picked it up on her last buying trip. She has such a good eye for these things. I'm more of a furniture man, myself.'

'Yes,' said Colette. 'Do you know if it's been sold?'

'Well now,' said the man, 'let's see. My wife's not in today, otherwise she could tell you straight off. She does Saturdays and I do Sundays, that's our arrangement.'

'It was hanging in that window,' said Colette. 'Just above the oak coffer.'

'One of my better finds,' said the man. 'I'm almost tempted not to sell it. I've got just the spot for it, in our hallway, but my wife says there's too much clutter in there already. She's a very strict woman.'

'Perhaps you could ring and ask her,' said Colette, trying not to shout.

'Oh, goodness me, no,' said the man. 'She's fed up with me pestering her about it. No, what I'm thinking of doing is getting it delivered to the house for her birthday. I've got a space all ready for it. I do love oak.'

'The lantern,' said Colette slowly. 'I was talking about the Spanish lantern.'

Some people had taken it home, it turned out. They wanted to try it in their conservatory before they bought it, to see how it looked. It was too ornate, though, and detracted from the orchids and the African violets, so they were going to return it and buy the French doll instead, the one with bisque hands, head and feet.

'I see,' said Colette on the phone, and, 'Yes,' and, 'French, how lovely.'

'My wife says the lantern will be back tomorrow, if you want to come and look at it,' said the man.

'Thank you,' said Colette. 'Tomorrow, yes.'

It was late by the time she rang Dominic.

'I was wondering if I could borrow a couple of hundred,' she said. She could hear someone laughing in the background, a deep, male laugh.

'Let me guess. Would a certain Mexican lamp be involved?'

'It'll only be till the end of the month, promise.'

'What about all your child-care money? And Dad's cheques, what's happened to them?'

'I'm saving for something important.'

'You still owe me for Mum's birthday, remember.'

'I know, you'll get that at the end of the month too. Please?' Again she heard laughter, and a man's voice. 'Have you got the TV on?' she said.

'Listen,' said Dominic, 'I'm cooking Nina dinner tomorrow night. Why don't you and Nathan come?'

'He's only my flatmate.'

'You slept with him.'

Colette lowered her voice. 'It's kind of sick, don't you think? Your little Nina obsession?'

'*Me* obsessed!'

'She's your first cousin, remember.'

'I'm just trying to make her feel welcome. Don't worry, she's not my type.' More distant laughter.

'She's gorgeous.'

'Colette, listen—'

'It's a lantern, by the way. And it's Spanish.'

When Colette returned to the antique shop, the lantern was hanging in the window. She browsed among the furniture for a minute or two, opening drawers, turning keys. Behind the counter, the woman flicked through a magazine, her husband nowhere in sight. Slowly Colette made her way to the lantern.

'You were in on the weekend, weren't you?'

Colette smiled, fingered a brass leaf. The lantern was smaller than she remembered, and as she examined it she noticed that one of the panes of glass was cracked, and three of the leaves damaged. The hinge, too, was bent out of shape.

'Ah,' said the woman. 'You're the girl who was interested in the lantern. My husband rang you about it.'

Colette looked through the cracked piece of glass and through the shop window to the beach. The sea was crooked, split in two.

'It's lovely, isn't it. I'll take a Polaroid photo of it for you if you like, so you'll remember it. It's hard to recall where you saw what when you're looking for something in particular.'

Now and then, in upmarket antique shops, Colette had seen Polaroids offered to well-to-do customers, but she had never been approached herself. The woman squeezed between a Scotch chest and a cabin trunk and pointed the camera and before Colette had time to move away she had taken the photo.

'There now,' she said. 'That'll help you remember.' She handed Colette a glossy grey square that looked like a picture of storm clouds.

'Thank you,' said Colette, 'but I didn't ask about it. It wasn't me.'

When she was outside she looked at the photo again. The grey was disappearing; in its place was a murky outline of the lantern and, to one side, herself. She looked disappointed, dissatisfied, and although the picture was still quite dark, it was growing clearer every second.

She'd wanted to wear it herself, but Colette ended up lending Nina her red dress.

'You look fantastic,' said Nathan. 'You too, Colette. What's the occasion?'

'Nothing special, just a family dinner. We won't be late back.'

Dominic kissed them both on the cheek. 'I thought you were bringing Nathan?'

'He's busy,' said Colette, avoiding Nina's glance. 'I'm thinking of moving, actually.'

'But it's a great place!'

'I don't know. It gives me the creeps sometimes.'

In the living room was a young man Colette hadn't seen before. He rose to his feet and shook hands.

'Colette, Nina, this is Brendan.'

While Dominic prepared dinner, Brendan poured drinks.

And how long are you over for, Nina?' he asked.

Nina crossed her legs, toyed with the buckle on her strappy sandals. She looked stunning in the red dress, better than Colette ever would. She laughed at all of Brendan's jokes, and when he laughed too Colette realised she'd heard him before. The previous night, when she'd rung Dominic so late. She stared at Brendan.

'Everything okay?' said Brendan.

'Yes,' said Colette, 'yes. Fine thanks.'

She watched Nina lean in close to him, pout, run her hands through her hair, and she smiled.

'Hey, I can lend you the money for the lantern,' Dominic said as they were leaving.

'Thanks,' said Colette, 'but I went and had a look at it again and it's not right. Tell you what, though,' she said, 'I could use a loan for my plane ticket.'

'Plane ticket? Are you going to visit Mum?'

'I'm going to England, next month. I want to finish my round-the-world trip, and visit a friend in hospital. A very good friend.'

'I'm surprised I've lasted as long as I have,' said the man's mother. 'Usually when one goes the other follows, but your dad's dead twenty years next week. It doesn't seem that long, does it, but it is. Nineteen seventy-six. I doubt I'll see the century out, mind. I doubt I've got a year left in me, let alone four.'

Here we go, thought the man, another one of her speeches. She always gave a speech on something when he visited. The danger of owning too big a dog, the rubbish on television these days, the trouble with people buying up fancy new apartments. It was during her speeches that he was tempted to tell her about his idea. He'd kept it to himself for eight years while she prattled on about how brainless he was. He'd sat on her couch and said nothing, even when, the previous year, he'd seen in her newspaper the picture of the girl playing tennis.

'I'd like to be cremated, not buried,' his mother went on in the background. 'Plots are so expensive these days, and it's not as if I can be put with your dad, unless you want to fly me there. I don't like the new cemeteries, anyway. They're all flat and there's no style to them. I like the big statues in the old ones, but the new ones all look the same. It's so the gardener can mow right over the top of them. They do that, you know, just mow right over the top in their big lawn-mowers, they look like tractors, those things. And they squeeze everyone in so when you go to visit the grave you're shoulder to shoulder with whoever happens to be visiting next door. No privacy. They don't even lay you side by side in double plots now, did you know that? They just plonk the husband in on top of the wife, or the other way round. It's indecent. And they don't mind charging you double. Oh no. They'll start charging for the water to fill up the vases soon, you wait and see. Are you listening to me? Have you heard a word I said? Sometimes I don't know why I bother with you, really I don't. You're useless.'

At the public library the man skimmed eight-year-old bundles of news. He knew what he was looking for and he couldn't sit still; his feet tapped, his lips twitched, his thumb flicked through the pages as quickly as if they were banknotes. And then he found them: the death notices. The names of all the people who had died at the start of March 1988. And his finger raced down the columns, over the As, the Bs, the Cs, and when he found the Hs he became completely still. He stared at the words, willing them to change, to erase themselves. *Walter Hicks, loved husband of Edna. Taken from us in his 80th year.*

He gulped down a can of beer as soon as he got home, the bubbles making his eyes water, filling him with air. Eighty years old. That meant Edna must be getting on too. She could go at any time. Perhaps, he thought for a moment, she had already died and was buried somewhere else entirely. Or perhaps she had remarried, and would eventually be buried with a different husband.

At the cemetery he found the place without any trouble. There was a headstone marking the grave, identifying the occupant as Walter Ian Hicks, stating in gold the date of his birth and his death. And, at the bottom, was a space for a second name.

The bitch, was all the man could think. The fat old stupid bitch. He didn't know if Edna was fat, or stupid for that matter, but those were the words that came naturally to him in moments of rage. Words like ugly, dumb, dirty, useless. There were too many people in the world, thought the man, too many stupid, boring people, and not even enough room to bury them all in separate plots. Everywhere you went people banged into you, rammed their shopping trolleys into you, jostled against you in the bus, almost ran you down in their cars. And most of the trouble-makers were female. Ancient old bitches who saw their husbands to early graves, little schoolgirl tarts who offered you a ride and then, once they'd made eyes at you, wouldn't follow through.

The man made reading the death notices part of his daily routine. He didn't know what he'd do when Edna Hicks died, he realised; his brilliant plan hadn't extended that far. At least, though, he would have some time. A day, maybe two. Enough time to pack a bag, go underground.

It was inconvenient for him, this daily checking of death. He couldn't get away from it; it came off on his fingertips and blackened his mood. Sometimes, if he'd had a few drinks, he considered it his punishment for inviting the girl to his flat and letting things get so out of hand, but mostly it was just another thing to be done, like emptying the rubbish. He didn't bother with the rest of the newspaper, just the death notices, but once in a while a missing child would loom from the front page and sometimes, somewhere down the bottom, there would be a photo of the girl.

As the years passed the man became accustomed to his task. He learned the language of the obituary, its special codes. *Passed away peacefully* meant the person had died of nothing in particular, just old age. Edna Hicks would probably pass away peacefully. The word *suddenly*, if a young person had died and there was no mention of an accident, usually meant a suicide. *In lieu of flowers, donations to* often indicated the cause of death: cancer, heart attack. *After a long battle* meant relatives would be speaking of thankful releases, blessings in disguise.

And, gradually, death lost its grasp on the man, and his bad dreams about the girl became harder and harder to recall, because people died every day, after all, columns of them, and they were just names, each one as unimportant as the last, and if he hadn't done it then it would have happened sooner or later anyway, because people were dropping off all the time, you just had to read the papers to see that.

The sheep and calves and goats on either side of the river had taken no notice as his car left the bridge and plummeted. The deer in the forest, the squirrels, the pigs and the hares all carried on as before.

The water was ice-cold when it met his skin, although it was a sunny day.

'Relax,' she said. 'You get used to it.'

She shone beside him. She moved so easily through the water he thought it might swallow her, that she might slip further and further away from him until she was gone. Her golden thighs shimmered and blurred and she swam ahead, her hair a billowing net. He felt water collecting on his skin like mercury.

'Hurry up,' she called. 'There's not much time.'

In his wake he could just see his gown, far behind them now and floating, a white jellyfish, the ties thin tentacles. He wanted to stay here.

But days had passed, and nights too, full of bad dreams and restlessness and lust and peace and sorrow, and there had been burglaries and New Year parties and snores and coughs and sighs of contentment, and frightening noises in gardens, and an entire winter, and he had forgotten how to speak and forgotten how to write and had learned all over again, and his cousin and his ex-wife had come and read to him, because they loved him or because he was family or perhaps both, and he had grown older.

He watched her swimming away and said, 'When am I allowed to go home?'

He'd been on his way to his mother's house, he knew that now. He'd given his first lecture and he'd been driving to his mother's house to sort through her things, but the sun had been too bright and he'd been rushing and had driven off the bridge and into the icy river. Faye and Rosemary had told him all this while they plumped his pillows and poured him water and told him how much better he was looking, how well he was doing, how pleased the physiotherapist and the speech therapist and the doctors were.

'There's still some glass inside you,' said Faye as she took him home. 'From the windscreen. Don't worry, you won't even know it's there. The main thing is, you're going to be fine.' She lifted Patrick's suitcase from the boot of her car and took it inside. 'Now, you're to stay as long as you like. I've got plenty of room, and Rosemary's coming every other day to give me a hand. We'll go to your place when you feel like it, and you can pick up some more things, whatever you need to make you feel at home.'

'What about my lectures? I'd prepared all the notes.'

'Yes, we found those,' said Faye. 'Not the ones from the first lecture, of course—they're somewhere in the river, or probably the sea by now—but we went through some things at your house, I hope you don't mind. We wanted to read you something familiar, that might bring you round.'

'Like Hilla's dialogues.'

'You heard us?'

'I think I must have.'

'Rosemary read you some bible passages too, but I couldn't be bothered with them. I made her stop.'

'Ah.'

'I did enjoy the dialogues. Rosemary always wanted to be God, of course, but I insisted we took turns.'

Patrick settled into Faye's guest room that night.

'This is where your parents stayed after the fire, isn't it?' she said.

It was the first time she'd mentioned it, and Patrick caught his breath. He hadn't thought about it for such a long time, it was as if it hadn't happened at all.

'I wanted you all to stay for good,' she said. 'I hated coming home in the holidays when just Mum and Ronnie were here. It felt so empty. Do you know, I could call out to her from my bedroom, and she'd never hear me.'

Patrick nodded.

'Ronnie did though.' Faye stopped, pressed her hands together. 'You were so kind to me when I was in hospital, and when I came home—'

'You were family, Faye, of course I was.'

She smiled. 'Well. Good night, Patrick. I'm just next door, if you need anything.'

Patrick examined the books shelved in the corner of the room, ran his finger along the spines. He thought of Saint Columba, who had copied Finnian's psalms illegally, his fingers shining as he wrote. That story ended badly. Finnian's messenger, sent to check on the precious manuscript, peered through the church keyhole and had his eyes wounded by Columba's pet crane. And the King ordered Columba to return the transcript to Finnian, declaring, 'To every cow her calf, and to every book its copy.'

Patrick knelt to read the spines on the bottom shelf. Right in the corner was a small red volume, its title faint from many handlings: *A Book of Golden Deeds*. He took it to bed and began at the beginning, with the author's 1864 preface. *The authorities have not been given,* said Charlotte M. Yonge, *as for the most part the narratives lie on the surface of history.* Patrick settled deeper into bed, folding the sheet over the woollen blankets so they wouldn't scratch his face. *There is a cloud of doubt resting on a few of the tales, which it may be honest to mention, though they were far too beautiful not to tell. But it was not possible to give up such stories as these, and the thread of truth there must be in them has developed into such a beautiful tissue, that even if unsubstantial when tested, it is surely delightful to contemplate.* Patrick listened to Faye turning on taps in the bathroom, splashing water, letting it drain away again. Charlotte M. Yonge, he read, had provided enough detail of surrounding historical events *to make the situation comprehensible, even without knowledge of the general history. This has been done in the hope that these extracts may serve as a mother's storehouse for reading aloud to her boys, or that they may be found useful for short readings to the intelligent, though uneducated classes.*

Before he turned the light out, Patrick read stories he still remembered. He read of valiant dogs and constant princes, faithful slaves and plague heroes, shepherd girls and lost children. His head felt as new as a baby's on the pillow; already his hair was growing back to hide the scars. Faye had lit a fire for him, and he got up and placed the guard around it, in case of sparks in the night, and then he went to sleep.

The fire was a real spectacle. People from up and down the street came to watch it and to look concerned. Some of them were so concerned that the firemen had to ask them to move along. Patrick saw one woman actually holding her hands out to the hot brick walls, as if she were cold, or wanted to touch them. The pale faces of his neighbours were illuminated by the flames, coloured with gold. He'd never realised how loud fire could be. It was never that loud when contained by a hearth, but his fire—for he had created it— was furious: wood cracking like bullets, sap boiling and whistling, paint sizzling. One by one the windows of the house smashed and flames whooshed through them like ragged curtains. Or was that his mother, hysterical, choking? He thought he saw her heaving with sobs, but her voice was sucked into the heat and the smoke, eaten by the riotous flames. The ash was the only silent thing about the fire. As it fell softly on his hair, his arms, his bare feet, he thought of moths. And each moth represented a part of their house, their old life: there was a floral wallpaper moth, an eiderdown moth, a dinner-set moth, a sofa moth.

He would have liked to stay and watch, but neighbours began pulling at his sleeves, telling him and his parents to come away, not to upset themselves.

'Come and we'll make you a nice cup of tea,' said one.

'I've got a drop of Scotch if you're after something stronger,' said another. 'You look like you could do with something stronger.' 'Fruitcake,' pronounced a third. 'Freshly made this morning.'

Suddenly the Mercers were in demand, the whole street thronging around them like buyers at an auction. It was Mrs Morrin who triumphed, grabbing Patrick's arm and manoeuvring him towards her driveway, her reading glasses wobbling against her chest.

'I think the Mercers would like to be left in peace for a bit. Come along Graham, Doreen,' she said, and Patrick was surprised to see his parents follow her without a word.

'My homework was in there,' he whispered. 'What will Mr Ross say?'

'You should be ashamed of yourself, young man,' said Mrs Morrin. 'At a time like this. Can't you see your mother's in shock?' She clamped a meaty arm around his mother's shoulder and said, 'Don't you worry, Doreen, we'll soon get you in front of the fire with a nice cup of tea.'

And so they went and sat in Mrs Morrin's house, where black-framed photographs of her husband clustered on the wall like blowflies, and she asked how a thing like that could happen, meaning the fire, not her husband, and just as Patrick's mother was saying that she didn't know, his father said that it must have been because someone was playing on the porch with a magnifying glass.

When Patrick woke in the morning, a few embers were still glowing in the grate. He'd slept all night with the fire in his room, he realised. He felt rejuvenated. He thought of a hint from his eight hundred-year-old manuscript, which was now locked in Faye's china cabinet. *If it should happen through negligence that your ink be not black enough, take a fragment of iron the thickness of a finger, and putting it into the fire, allow it to glow, and throw it directly into the ink.* He was, he told Faye at breakfast, getting his strength back.

Colette couldn't sleep on the flight. When the cabin attendants lowered the blinds to enforce night, she couldn't pretend. Outside the windows, she knew, the rising sun was following the plane, and she remained awake.

She didn't let herself sleep on the train from London, either. She wanted to witness every bit of the landscape on the way to Patrick's home town. Once she'd checked into the bed and breakfast, she told herself, she could rest, refresh herself for her hospital visit. She'd been careful to pack clothes that were both flattering and wrinkle-proof, and she'd bought a bottle of her favourite perfume at the duty-free shop. Trésor rose from her wrists and throat; even the soft pulse-points behind her ears were scented.

When she'd found her way to the bed and breakfast, she unpacked and arranged her things as if at home. Then she climbed into bed, her map folded open to the right place and her route for the next day marked in red ink.

Saint Luke's hospital was on the outskirts of the city. Colette got off the bus a few stops early and walked, taking in the flavour of the place, the feel of Patrick's immediate surroundings. Odd, she thought, that it was autumn in New Zealand and spring here, and both climates felt the same. She checked her reflection in a shop window, straightened her collar, smoothed her hair.

At the hospital she had to wait while the receptionist explained to a new father that Saint Luke's did not have the facilities for him to stay overnight.

'Are we living in the Dark Ages?' said the man. 'Fathers deserve to be involved too, you know. It's healthy for the child,' he shouted, and stalked away down the corridor.

'Can I help you, dear?' the receptionist said.

'Yes,' said Colette, 'I was wanting to visit Patrick Mercer. I'm not sure which ward he's in.'

'Mercer,' said the woman, tapping the name into a computer. Colette could hear the new father muttering to himself in the distance. 'He checked out on Monday, love. Maybe you can visit him at home.'

There were only two Mercers in the phone book, and one was a D. Colette scribbled down the address for P. Mercer and rehearsed silently on the way there: *Hello, I don't know if you recognise me, your friends have been sending me letters, I think we must have met before, I'm not sure if you know who I am, I'm not sure if I know you.* The afternoon was growing cool by the time she found the house, and she rubbed her hands together as she waited on the front porch. There was still no answer after she'd knocked four times.

As she walked round to the back she noticed that the carport was empty, the lawn overgrown. All the windows were shut and most of the curtains drawn. She retrieved the last Friends of Patrick letter from her bag. The address on the back was residential and, according to her map, not too far away.

It was a beautiful old place, set amongst trees and clematis vines and beds of lavender. On one side was a glass conservatory, so delicately constructed it could have been made of ice. Colette's hand shook as she rang the bell. Through the frosted pane she could see someone approaching and she cleared her throat, smoothed her hair again.

'Yes?' said the woman. She was small and slim, and although she must have been in her sixties, her skin was still smooth.

'I'm trying to find a Patrick Mercer. I'm Colette Hawkins, I was sent letters about him from this address.'

'You're Colette?' The woman frowned. 'You can't be.'

'I—I have my passport here somewhere,' Colette fumbled in her bag. 'The letters said he wanted visitors. I've come such a long way—' The words caught in her throat.

'Look,' said the woman, reaching outside and drawing Colette towards the threshold, 'why don't you come in.'

At the end of the hallway was a big, warm room overlooking the garden. An old man sat beside the window, a small red book open on his lap.

'Patrick,' said the woman, 'we have a visitor from New Zealand. She says her name's Colette Hawkins.'

The man in the chair started, looked up. 'You're not Colette.'

'I told her she wasn't.'

'But I got letters from you,' said Colette. 'Addressed to me, telling me how Patrick—' she glanced at the old man '—how Patrick was progressing.' She stopped. 'I thought he was my age,' she said in a small voice.

As she spoke the man watched her, his eyes shifting across her face. 'You've come all the way from New Zealand?' he said.

She nodded.

'Come here. Come along, I won't bite.' And he took her face in hands soft as water and turned it towards the window. 'Faye,' he said, 'would you make us some tea?'

A long time ago, when he was newly married, a museum curator was sent on a trip. As he hadn't done much travelling, he decided to combine business with pleasure. He needed to see the world as well as read about it, he told his wife, who tired easily. When she heard all the places he wanted to visit, she told him she would stay behind, and secretly the curator was glad.

He went on a journey that began at home and moved south and, to begin with, the further away from home he travelled the hotter it became. He heard two bronze giants striking the hour in Venice; he saw dragons' heads adorning Cretan sabres. He visited Malta's Ta Pinu basilica, where a peasant woman had heard the voice of God, and he saw the Step Pyramid at Saqqarah, from which the dead Pharaoh had boarded a sacred boat to carry him with the sun across the heavens. When the museum curator crossed the equator he saw an Indonesian puppet show made of shadows, an island made of coral, the dry heart of Australia. And it grew colder, and the water drained clockwise from the bath, and even the crescent moon seemed backwards. As is the case when travelling, the curator collected addresses from strangers, most of whom he would never see again. When he reached the south of New Zealand and could go no further without hitting ice, he met a beautiful young woman, much younger than himself, who told him her name was Colette. They saw each other every day, and he ignored the scenery, the mountains and the waterfalls and the lush green bush. *Am having a marvellous time*, he wrote to his wife. *Here is a picture of a mountain.* The young woman whose name was Colette added herself to his address book, but told him he must never contact her, not unless things changed. And he didn't write to her, not at first, not until eight years later, when he thought things might indeed have changed. They had and they hadn't: she was still married, but now she had two young children. She didn't want any complications. And so the curator stayed married too, for a few more years, and buried himself in books.

'That must have been why Dad left,' said Colette. 'He must have found out.' She gathered her bag and her passport, refolded her street map. 'I should go now.'

Patrick started to speak and stopped again. He reached inside his mouth and removed something very small. 'Excuse me,' he said. 'Glass.' He displayed the shard on his palm. 'It keeps turning up.'

Colette continued buttoning her jacket.

'I'm sorry if I made things complicated for your mother. I didn't know she was married too, not at the start. I never would have become involved if I'd known.'

'My mother's name is Anne, did you know that? Colette was obviously an invention. She lied to you. She never intended to stay in touch.'

Patrick examined the piece of glass, nudging it across his open book with a forefinger. 'She never mentioned me?' he said quietly.

'I asked her once why she called me Colette. She said there was no special reason, she just liked the name.'

'I see.' Patrick stared at his book. 'I don't know why I thought— it was just a few days, after all. Really just a holiday romance.' He pushed the shard right to the edge of the page.

'Here we are,' said Faye. 'Who's for tea? Patrick, you haven't had more glass have you?' She plucked the tiny fragment from the book and inspected it. 'He's already had six pieces. This is the seventh.' She placed it on the mantelpiece, where the others were arranged in a semi-circle, like baby teeth. 'We were very alarmed when the first one appeared, weren't we? But it's quite normal, apparently. It could go on for years.'

'I'm afraid I do need to get going,' said Colette.

'Nonsense.' Faye began pouring the tea, motioning for her to sit down. 'Patrick's had a lot of visitors from round here, but none from Australia. We had such a marvellous response to our letters. He didn't know he had so many friends, did you love?'

'New Zealand,' said Patrick. 'Colette is from New Zealand.'

'How lovely. What's it like there this time of year?'

Colette smiled in spite of herself. 'Cool in the mornings and evenings, but warm during the day.'

'It sounds the same as here,' said Faye. Without moving her eyes from the stream of hot tea, she said, 'And have you sorted out who the other Colette is?'

'I think so,' said Patrick. 'I think we have, yes.'

And so Colette unbuttoned her jacket and sat down again and drank tea with them, and ate two of Faye's apricot biscuits, which were delicious, and then Faye showed her the garden and told her Patrick used to watch for fireflies there in summer, which wasn't far away.

Going home took a very long time. On the plane Colette stared out the window at the miles and miles of ocean and wondered if she would ever pass over land.

The last time she took so long to return home was when she left Justin in London. It was the middle of winter, weeks after Paris, and her period was overdue. She was so cold she bought herself a woollen scarf and wrapped it around her throat and mouth. There had been bomb threats, and rubbish bins throughout the inner city had been removed. In the photos of Justin at Westminster Abbey, herself at Trafalgar Square, Justin at Piccadilly Circus, there were newspapers and McDonald's bags cluttering the foreground. Once, outside a church she couldn't remember, Justin pulled her scarf away and kissed her, and there was a stab of electricity between their lips. He laughed and said, 'It's just from the wool rubbing your mouth,' but Colette was too cold to laugh, and besides, it had hurt.

Her period didn't arrive until she was booking her ticket home. She was sitting at the travel agent's counter, trying to get on the flight via Hong Kong rather than Los Angeles so she wouldn't have to spend an extra night with Justin. The travel agent was saying, 'No, I think it's full,' and Colette was saying, 'Oh dear, really?' when she felt a twisting deep inside.

'I'm afraid I don't feel well,' she said. 'May I use your toilet, do you think?'

In the cubicle there were brochures about Hawaii, Turkey, Greece. Smiling couples walked hand in hand on white beaches, tropical fish shimmered and shone and the sky went on forever. Colette caught her breath at a tug of pain. She could feel herself clotting. She bent forward, dropping the beach, the fish, the blue sky.

'Are you all right in there, dear?' called the travel agent.

'Yes thank you. I won't be a moment. Thank you.'

'I've managed to get you on the Hong Kong flight.'

'Lovely. Thank you.'

Expecting her legs to give way, she stood. And there it was, the tug she'd felt, the size of a walnut, perhaps, or her thumbnail. Too small to resemble much at all. She wiped herself clean with fistfuls of paper, ignoring the roughness. Gradually the thing the size of a walnut or a thumbnail was covered over, and she flushed it away and went and paid for her ticket.

'Excuse me,' the flight attendant was saying. 'Ma'am? Would you mind shutting the blind now?'

Colette covered the window, pulled the complimentary mask over her eyes and tried to sleep. Sleeping made the time pass more quickly. She would be home soon.

'Did you have a good time?' said Nathan. 'Is your friend all right?'

'He's fine,' said Colette.

'He must have been pleased to see you.'

Colette rummaged in her bag. 'I got you some whisky,' she said, 'duty free.'

She scanned every page of the newspaper, even sections she normally never bothered with. She'd heard nothing about New Zealand in the three weeks she'd been away; it was as if home had ceased to exist. Now, to keep herself awake until bedtime, she read about tax cuts, bickering politicians, public transport, car crashes, burglaries, weather, the complications surrounding an All Black's knee injury. There were few reports of violent crime. She should be glad, she told herself, to have returned to such a place.

She telephoned the Pearses to let them know she was home.

'Daniel will be pleased,' said Ruth. 'He's been quite unsettled. He hates being farmed out to friends after school.'

'No more incidents with keys, then?'

'With keys? What keys?'

'Oh,' said Colette. 'It was when you were away. Nothing to worry about, forget I mentioned it.' She yawned. 'You'll have to excuse me, I'm afraid. I'll see you tomorrow, okay?'

When she finished reading she folded the newspaper neatly in half and placed it on the bench for Nathan. It looked almost unread. She couldn't help being neat, she thought, couldn't resist tidying things away, putting them in order. She pictured her mother's house with its piles of washing, its dusty magazines, its shoes and bags and loose change and dead flowers. She wanted to ask her about Patrick, to pick at the tangle, tweak things into line. Bedtime was still hours away. She took a sheet of writing paper and a pen from her desk. *Dear Mum,* she wrote, *how is everything?*

She thought of Patrick and Faye in the big, warm house on the other side of the world. She thought of how comfortable they seemed together, how Faye brought him glasses of lemon barley water, dishes of walnuts and almonds. Once or twice Colette had compared his features to Dominic's and to her own, but had to admit that there was no likeness. And the timing was all wrong, anyway. She and Dominic took after their father, and their father was in Australia, and had been for years and years.

Patrick had talked about his work at the museum, and had shown her a manuscript he owned, something he usually kept locked away. He thought she might be interested in it, as a student of history, an admirer of antiques. It wasn't richly decorated, but it was an important record of medieval book production. Colette could hold it if she liked.

She couldn't make out the Latin text, but Patrick translated passages for her. It was a manual for writing, he said, a sort of recipe book. A book of spells. It was probably written by a monk, probably in northern Germany and probably at the end of the twelfth century. It was difficult to be one hundred per cent sure. He read her passages describing how to prepare parchment with powdered bone, how to compose colours with the juice of vegetables and flowers, how to make glue from the bladder of a sturgeon, how to burnish gold with stones and teeth, how to make ink from thorns. When he retired, said Patrick, he was thinking of donating the manuscript to the museum, with the proviso that it never be sold. He didn't see this as a good deed so much as a way of safeguarding the manuscript. It was important to preserve such things.

Colette put away the letter to her mother. She was finding it difficult to keep her eyes open. One day, she thought, she would like to write about Laura. She would like to write her life. She already had the photocopies from the library, the bones of the story, its animal shape. It would not be sensationalist; any colourful speculation would be tempered with facts, cool statistics. Colette would keep things balanced. There would be a spread of light and shadow, a little vitriol. She wouldn't rush into it. She would allow the story to thicken, to form its own skin. And then she would make Laura shine.

Malcolm and Ruth would have to collaborate, of course. They would have to provide anecdotes, photographs. There was a thesis in Laura Pearse, maybe even a book. It would probably sell very well.

'Don't overdo it,' said Faye, 'you still need to take it easy.'

'I can come and give you a hand if you like,' said Rosemary. 'I haven't got any lectures today.'

But Patrick insisted he'd be fine on his own. 'It won't take long,' he said. 'I've got a fairly good idea of what's there.'

And in fact, the house didn't take long. It was scrupulously clean; there were no smears on the glass, no scatterings of mould in the bathroom, no spider-web garlands. His mother had kept most things packed away, to keep them safe, and so that they could be retrieved easily in an emergency. A lot of her possessions were brand new. Patrick found unopened boxes of cutlery, complete sets of glasses, clothes which still sprouted cardboard labels from their sleeves and collars. There were boxed sheets, two new toasters cocooned in polystyrene. There were unread books, unused handkerchiefs, chairs in plastic wrapping. His mother, he realised, had tried to fill her rooms with things common to most households, but although she'd bought so much, few of her possessions described a real person. If strangers looked at these objects, Patrick thought, would they be able to say what she'd been like? Would they be able to give even an approximate summary of her? The china and linen, the rolled-up rugs, the boxed gadgets could have been anyone's; they retained no traces of scent, no patina of daily handling. They were without fingerprints. He thought about saints' lives, how they were constructions of many different lives. A vision here, a miracle there. Chinese whispers written down. Relics were just as untrustworthy. The multiple finger bones, the fragments of tibia, the many locks of hair would form monsters if assembled. Patrick leaned the third of four identical ironing boards against the hall stand and thought about Saint Hilla, about how impossible it was to tell whether the dialogues were her original words, or whether they contained pieces of other saints, embellishments added by various scribes for the sake of telling a story. He opened an unopened kettle and closed it again. His mother wasn't here.

He didn't want to keep many of her things. He had no need for them, not even for the sleek green fountain pen he found at the back of a drawer. The only thing he might have liked was his father's Meccano collection, but that was nowhere to be seen. Perhaps, he thought, Doreen had sold it after all. So she could buy more ironing boards.

The house was stifling in the early summer heat, and Patrick threw open all the windows. From the sitting room he could see the shed, right at the end of the garden, past the plum tree and out of harm's way. When he'd finished sorting and packing every room in the place, he let himself out the back door and followed the curling brick pathway.

Patrick pushed the iron handle down. It was warm from the sun and rough, and flakes of rust came away on his palm like dry blood. He felt the hinges give but the door wouldn't open, and when he prised the edges with his fingers the chalky paint deposited itself on him too. Where it had flaked away he could see layers of colour: green, white, buttercup yellow. Here and there the wood itself was exposed, grey and grainy like a blurred photograph.

Wood remembered, Patrick knew. It warped in bad weather, stiffened like an old man's bones. It swelled and twisted, attempted to recall the curve of a trunk, the tilt and crook of branches. Old wood could crack with longing for the touch of leaves, for small cool hands that felt for the sky, collected light. And this wood was nearly fifty years old. Patrick's father had built the shed himself right after they shifted into the new house.

'Why are you building it out of wood?' Patrick's mother had asked. 'Why not brick?'

He tugged the handle once more, and the door swung open and he was inside. In the gloom he could make out strange, angular shapes towering against the walls. He pulled at the old venetian blind blocking the window, easing the knotted cords this way and that. It wouldn't move up at all, but he managed to open the slats and they lined the glass like a page, as if a message could be scribbled across the dry garden, the wide blue sky. Then he turned around.

The ship filled the shed, its masts aligned with the sloping rafters, its prow nosing the wooden wall. It was an impossible thing, fragile and skeletal and vast. There was no room for anything else. The shelves where twine and bulbs and packets of seeds and sacks of blood and bone had once stood were bare. The workbench was empty of tools; the hooks which had supported shovels and rakes jutted from the walls like bony fingers. Just enough space had been left for someone small to squeeze around each side of the ship. Someone Doreen's size. It was a wonder Patrick hadn't knocked the thing over when he reached for the window. He extended his fingers, and as soon as he touched it he realised. It had been constructed entirely of Meccano pieces.

They gleamed in the dim light, thousands of them, he estimated, each bolt tightened just enough, the red and green enamel in no place damaged by inferior spanner-work, the brass teeth new and unscratched. Here and there he saw valuable blue and gold pieces, taken from 1930s sets. He traced a hand over the hull, the fist-sized portholes, the wheel. There was an anchor made of Meccano, a crow's nest, a row of lifeboats. Looking through the broken blind and into the garden was a Meccano figurehead, her green hair bolted into spirals and curls. Even the sails had been made from Meccano, hundreds and hundreds of pieces arranged to mimic billowing cloth. Many standard parts had been used to build the ship—the common strips and girders that came in every box—but as Patrick looked more closely he picked out all sorts of complex, advanced components. The sort contained in his father's most prized sets. There were pulley wheels and crank handles, propeller blades and sprocket chains, compression springs, tension springs, hinges, grilles. There were lamp holders, wiper arms, pawls, trunnions. There were bell cranks and pinions, wire hooks and flywheels and worm wheels and healds. No instructions had been followed. It was a ship made of smaller ships, of motor cars, carousels, aeroplanes, clocks, cranes, looms, ferris wheels, searchlights, swing saws, windmills, bridges, lighthouses. It was made of everything Patrick had once wanted.

It was unseaworthy, of course; it was full of holes, like a loose piece of knitting. He opened the workbench drawer and dipped his fingers inside the dark recess, feeling for the torch his father had kept there for emergencies. He could sense the weight of the ship behind him, its shadow from the window enormous on his back, too big for the shed. There was no torch in the drawer. Instead, Patrick withdrew a neat bundle of cardboard. He undid the tissue paper and ribbon that had been tied gift-like around it and let it flutter to the ground. Some of the tissue still smelled faintly of soap. On the top piece of card was a picture of a boy dwarfed by a crane. In the background was the ocean, held at bay, and, in the border, the Eiffel Tower. He flicked through the pile: two boys framed a realistic Tower Bridge; another in a neat school blazer assembled a Giant Blocksetting Crane; another worked on a Walking Dragline. And he realised he wasn't holding pieces of card, but dismantled boxes. Opened boxes, emptied of their contents and folded flat.

He thought he heard a sound coming from the garden, a light footfall perhaps, and he flicked the blinds shut. Crouching on the ground, so close to the floor of the shed he could smell the earth underneath, he listened. Now and then above him a Meccano bolt studded the darkness like a star.

He moved the blind to one side and peeped through the crack. There was the garden, as wild as before, and the bright sky. He thought he caught a movement out of the corner of his eye, but when he looked it was only a blackbird, almost indistinguishable in the shadow of the plum tree. Perhaps it had been there all along, perhaps that was what he'd heard moving outside the thin wooden walls. All the same, he left the blind closed, let the shed keep its secrets. He eased himself out the door and pushed it shut behind him, the swollen wood groaning, the rusty handle marking his palm. Walking back to his mother's house, he rubbed his hands together, sprinkling the path with traces of rust and powdery paint. The garden was absolutely still; even the blackbird had disappeared. The only sound was the brushing of Patrick's palms. It reminded him of the ocean.

As he pulled into Faye's street, the rain began. It came from nowhere and it startled him; it was a sound he hadn't heard in such a long time, not since he'd been out of hospital. It roared in his ears like an angry ocean, a million bony fingers drumming the windows, the roof, the streets, impatient and demanding attention. Beneath a tree, a blackbird drank from a puddle, bright beak piercing the water and then lifting high, its throat open, a straight line indicating the sky. And the rain poured on, filling Patrick's head until he began to wonder whether the ship really existed, whether it was possible he had made it up. Perhaps it was an effect of the accident, or the mind's way of plotting the information that his mother, like his father, was finally dead.

'Faye,' he said over dinner that night as the rain continued, 'I think I would like some help tomorrow. I've found something of my mother's that's rather cumbersome.'

Faye nodded. 'Will we be able to manage it on our own, or should I ring Rosemary?'

Patrick thought of the size of the ship, the way it took up the entire shed. It had been made, he realised, like a ship in a bottle; impossible to remove without taking it apart.

'On second thoughts,' he said, 'perhaps I'll leave it where it is.'

That night he dreamt of Doreen's Meccano ship. It was adrift on the ocean, its silhouette a net against the sky. There were two figures on the upper deck, a man and a woman. They waved and waved at him, and called to him to come with them, and although Patrick couldn't see their faces, he thought he recognised them. And then he saw that their arms and hands were made of tiny pieces of Meccano, and their bodies were Meccano too, and they weren't people at all, just segments of metal bolted together to resemble human beings.

On the bench at Colette's flat, tucked inside her newspaper, along with the exchange rates and the cartoons and the All Black's problem knee, were the latest death notices. They'd been of little interest to her; she recognised none of the names.

The death of Edna Hicks, cherished wife of the late Walter, also escaped the attention of Ruth and Malcolm. Her name held no meaning for them, and they had no reason to care about her passing. They were having enough trouble getting Daniel to settle down.

'What about a story?' Ruth was saying as he flitted around the house toppling books, ornaments, a glass of water. 'You can choose any story you like.'

'I don't know what's wrong with him,' Malcolm was saying. 'He hasn't been like this for ages.'

'It's my fault,' said Ruth. 'I shouldn't have gone away, it's been too upsetting for him.'

'No,' said Malcolm, 'he was fine when you weren't here.'

Ruth was quiet then. She tried to arrange a spray of late flowers Malcolm had brought in from the garden but they were too big for the new vase; it tilted with the weight of them, and she caught it just in time. Daniel rushed past her, a breathless blur. She severed stems, stripped away stunted buds and leaves until the flowers were small enough.

'He'll tire himself out eventually,' said Malcolm. 'What do you feel like for dinner?'

'He'll break a bone if he's not careful,' said Ruth, thinking of the time Laura had tripped on the Persian rug. She'd fallen on her right hand, extended by instinct, and broken her arm.

'Which bone was it?' the detective inspector had asked them, his pen poised. 'The ulna? The radius?'

Ruth decided to start taking calcium supplements. It was never too late to protect the bones, her holiday magazines had advised. Never too late to stop them from thinning, becoming porous and brittle, as light as honeycomb.

'Colette rang before, just to say she's home. She mentioned there was some problem with keys when I was away.'

'Ah,' said Malcolm, 'yes. I got locked out one night, by mistake. I had to break the glass in the back door. But it's all fixed now. You'd never even know, to look at it.'

'Where was Daniel?'

'In bed.'

'Couldn't he have let you in?'

'He could have,' said Malcolm, 'but he didn't.' He and Ruth listened to their son racing down the hall.

'Well,' said Ruth, 'he's a child. Perhaps he didn't understand what was going on.'

'Yes,' said Malcolm, 'perhaps.'

Daniel flew from room to room. He hardly touched the floor. He batted into windows, hit his dressing-table mirror. He darted around his bed. On the wall, the silhouette picture shook.

In the new part of the cemetery, where everything was flat and neat and easily maintained, the sexton consulted his chart.

'Edna Hicks is the last one,' he told his assistant. 'It's a double. Block eight, row C, plot fifty-four.'

The spade moved quickly; it was mindless work. The assistant enjoyed his job, didn't find it morbid at all. He got to work outdoors, there was nobody breathing down his neck and the digging kept him fit. His girlfriend liked his biceps. She liked to bite them. He was taking her out tonight, and he'd just have time to shower and change. It amused him to think that he got paid for digging holes. Not many people, he thought, made a living by creating empty space. Little by little, the earth opened.

Acknowledgements

For their encouragement and advice, I wish to thank Fergus Barrowman, Kate Camp, Pat Chidgey, Caroline Dawnay, Robert Easting, Virginia Fenton, Rachel Lawson, Bill Manhire, and Helen and Fred Mayall. Special thanks to Greg Campbell for his constant support despite ongoing criticism of his footwear.

I am grateful for the generous assistance of Peter Churchill and AMP Asset Management, John and Philip Bougen on behalf of the Doreen Bougen Trust, the Buddle Findlay Sargeson Fellowship, the NZSA/ *Reader's Digest* Fellowship, the Stout Research Centre at Victoria University, and the Todd New Writers' Bursary from Creative New Zealand.

The following books were particularly useful in researching this novel:

Bell, Rudolph M., *Holy Anorexia*, University of Chicago Press, Chicago, 1985.

Cennini, Cennino d'Andrea, *Il Libro dell' Arte*, trans. Christiana J. Herringham, Allen and Unwin, London, 1930.

De Hamel, Christopher, *A History of Illuminated Manuscripts*, Phaidon Press, Oxford, 1986.

De Hamel, Christopher, *Scribes and Illuminators*, British Museum Press, London, 1992.

Theophilus, *De Diversis Artibus*, ed. and trans. C. R. Dodwell, Thomas Nelson, London and Edinburgh, 1961.

Tymms, W. R. and Wyatt, M. D., *The Art of Illuminating*, Studio Editions, London, 1987.

Yonge, Charlotte M., *A Book of Golden Deeds*, Macmillan, London, 1864.

Various vintage Meccano magazines, kindly lent by Stewart Gardiner.

Earlier versions of parts of this novel have previously appeared in *Landfall* and the *NZ Listener*.